T0060776

JOHN BARTEL

Archway Publishing books may be ordered through booksellers or by contacting:

Archway Publishing
1663 Liberty Drive
Bloomington, IN 47403
www.archwaypublishing.com
1 (888) 242-5904

ISBN: 978-1-4808-1742-5 (sc)
ISBN: 978-1-4808-1742-5 (hc)
ISBN: 978-1-4808-1743-2 (e)

Print information available on the last page.

Archway Publishing rev. date: 8/31/2015

No shrub of the field was yet in the earth and no herb of the field had yet sprung up; for the LORD God had not caused it to rain upon the earth, and there was not a man to till the ground; but there went up a mist from the earth, and watered the whole face of the ground. Then the LORD God formed man of the dust of the ground, and breathed into his nostrils the breath of life; and man became a living soul. And the LORD God planted a garden eastward, in Eden; and there he put the man whom He had formed.

— THE TORAH. GENESIS 2.

Introduction

The following is, essentially, a true story of one family's history. Names have not been changed both in the interest of accuracy and in honor of those living and dead.

However, poetic license was employed on occasion for a variety of reasons. The primary objective was to protect those still living. An overzealous use of honesty, though it may shed light on certain aspects of an individual's personality, can also be hurtful. In addition, the author was not always present when certain events took place, although he appears to be.

A variety of sources were utilized in order to compile this narrative. Transcriptions from living family members were an invaluable source of information on incidents and as living photography plates of personality traits. In addition, actual documents, intermingled with photographs, were utilized so as to put flesh back on those who have passed on as well as to authenticate our narrative.

To recreate Jewish life in times gone by, many diverse sources of information had to be utilized. It is fitting that our story starts with the oldest historical text we have, The Torah. The first five books of the Old Testament, or The Five Books of Moses, make up The Torah. Biblical historians generally agree that The Torah was written over 3,000 years ago. In those days, texts were created on either papyrus or parchment scrolls. I am sure that my forefathers, wandering on the desert with Moses, would have as hard a time understanding my use of the internet to access family records as they did Moses striking a rock and getting water from it. My point is that the sources of information ranged from parchment scrolls to electronics. I utilized a history of the Bartels to paint a picture of medieval life in Europe. Rabbi Joseph

Teleshkin's *Jewish Wisdom* provided me with snippets of Yiddish conversation as well as Jewish mannerisms that were essential in creating personalities for those long departed. Various books on Jewish history have helped me in painting East European settings used in our story.

Since this is a story of my family, emotions come welling up inside me that must continually be squelched so as to create an evocative narration whose written words are not smeared with tears. It is far easier to write dispassionately about some characters that you just created out of thin air but never really knew, except in your mind's eye. But having known and loved the people I am writing about, I feel obligated to immortalize their lives and to depict them as close to the way they actually were as it is within my power to do.

Now, a problem presents itself to the author as regards those still alive. After all, if I depict the dead inaccurately, all that may happen is that they may haunt me in the middle of the night. The living, on the other hand, are different. If I depict specific traits too accurately, it is a certainty that the living will haunt me in the middle of the day. So it becomes necessary for the author, if he is to ever associate, again, with those he writes about, to soften their characters a bit for the sake of his own future sanity.

The desire to know from whence we came has probably always been an urge that many of us have harbored. Yes, we can easily document the fact that we were spawned from one primal human being. That's elementary. What about after that? Finding certifiable records as to your lineage is incredibly difficult. Thanks to the popularity of the book *Roots* by Alex Haley, the subject of genealogy received a shot of much needed attention twenty five years ago. Even then, one had to search laboriously through microfilm records in hopes of tracing one's family history. Records were, and still are, scattered all over the world. In the case of Jews, many vital statistic records were destroyed during World War II. Thankfully, today we have a worldwide method of transferring information called The Internet. There are databases that were not accessible as recently as ten years ago. These databases allow a person to trace the lives of long lost relatives.

Now you have the blueprint for my time machine. To take you into our family's past, I used databases, family documents, books, and scrolls.

The genre you are partaking of is, generally, called historical fiction. Why does my story fall into this category? After all, this is an actual family, and with members alive today. Part of the action took place when your author was on the scene. Other parts of the story line had to be surmised. In addition, the scenes that took place in the middle ages had to be imagined due to the fact that family scribes, during those times, seemed to be in very short supply. The fact is that I am weaving transcribed information, documents, and historical data into a plausible context.

This book is not just a family's history or spellbinding narration. It is designed to illustrate much greater concepts: ethics, love, hate, intolerance, murder, survival, adversity, triumph, tragedy, birth, death, and finally, how readers, though living in a different time and place, could easily find themselves face to face with any or all of these concepts.

Though this introduction is being written prior to the author having to call on all the help he will need, some preliminary thanks are in order. There are individuals, without whose help, the author would not have been able to create his story. I want to thank Irving and Peggy Bartel, my parents, who brought forth an author. Jim and Sylvia Bartel deserve special mention because their memories of events past provided much of the factual fabric of my tale. My lovely aunt Ethel Nagel gifted important pictures and narrative. In addition, I owe her so much more, but that's grist for another tale. There will be those who help me recreate events; their names are deserving of mention however they are unknown at this time. I sincerely hope to give all credit due so that my accounts will not be in arrears.

CHAPTER 1
IN THE BEGINNING

• • •

Was Adam the first Jew? After all, he answered to only one God; so he was, in fact, a monotheist. He worshiped no idols. According to The Torah, he spoke directly to God. He needed neither priests nor prophets nor intermediaries of any kind in order to communicate with his creator.

Thus begins the story of the Bartel family. Its first recorded member is Adam, from which all of us were conceived.

The Torah's account of Adam's creation places the event near the intersection of the Tigris and the Euphrates Rivers, a fertile valley that lies just north of the Persian Gulf, in the windswept Arabian Desert. Many biblical accounts portray Adam residing in a lush garden cooled by the shade of date and other fruit trees. In fact, his skin must have been baked by the searing sun. His days passed with furnace-like winds screaming in his ears, sand blasting his eyes and flesh like burning needles. Thirst, an ever-present companion, tugged at his tongue.

Of course Adam was not alone, or this history would not have been written. According to The Torah, *And the rib, which the LORD God had taken from the man, made He a woman, and brought her unto the man. And the man said: "This is now bone of my bones, and flesh of my flesh."* So Eve was created to be Adam's helpmate.

Eventually, as humans have done from the dawn of history on, they made a mistake and sinned. Fruitful Garden of Eden, along with the tree of life, was replaced by death, sickness, and the sweat of their brows; thus we find my family's progenitors gathering morsels from wherever they could be found. Eve endures the screaming pangs of birth. Cane murders Abel. Meanwhile, desert winds howl a mournful tune, the prelude to my family's history.

A musky odor from the river delta drifted over Adam's sweat-streaked face as he gazed outside of Eden, sand as far as the eye could see. As waves of heat rose in thin rivulets, splotches of blood stained the desert floor—blood of millions yet to come.

In the same area where Adam and Eve's footprints were covered by the ever shifting desert sands, Abraham, his wife Sarah, and his nephew Lot—our family's direct ancestors—left the city of Ur about 4,000 years ago. Lot separated and settled on the plains of Jordan. Abraham set out into the blinding heat of the desert sun. Hot air ruffled his robes while the smell of damp Euphrates earth cooled his nostrils. Along with Sarah, Abraham traveled north following the Euphrates River, then south through Damascus, and eventually arrived in Egypt. They finally pitched their tents in Beth El, south of present-day Jerusalem. Abraham, as did Adam, had a special relationship with the Lord in that they could speak with him directly.

Sarah, at ninety years of age, shivered in the cold desert night. She would gaze up while billions of little diamonds bedazzled the black blanket of night. Small rivers of tears would fan out on her wrinkled cheeks. Her lips trembled as she uttered the word *how*. How could a woman, long in years, possibly conceive a son? Because the Lord told her she could.

Abraham is considered the Hebrew peoples' first patriarch; his son, Isaac, the second; Isaac's son, Jacob, the third. Now Jacob had twelve sons. This was where the twelve tribes of Israel came from. These tribes are my family's direct ancestors.

Centuries flew by, millennia passed. Moses led the children of Israel out of Egypt and through the Wilderness of Shur. Dark, puffy clouds descended on Mt. Sinai. The earth trembled while flaming arrows of lightning lit up the mountaintop. There Moses received from the Lord the precepts that we live by. Joshua fought the battle of Jericho while trumpet blasts brought the walls down. Eons came and went.

About 3,000 years ago, the Age of Kings was ushered in, starting with the brooding Saul; then David slew Goliath. David ultimately reigned as King of both Israel and Judea. As would be the case with most of our history, blood mixed with sobs filled the land. Philistines, the tribes of Moab, Edom, Ammon, Aram were all put to the sword. When a city was overrun, the men were first to be slain; then, innocent women's high-pitched cries mixed with those of their little ones as all clutched the steel through their bellies. But the sword returned to David in the form of his favorite son, Absalom. His rebellious son was shot through the chest by an arrow while he hung by his long hair from a tree. David's anguish, when told the news, echoes that of parents through the ages, *O my son Absalom, my son, my son Absalom! Would I have died for thee, O Absalom, my son, my son.*

Then came Solomon and his wisdom, along with the great Temple in Jerusalem.

Mighty civilizations rose and collapsed, never to be heard from again. The Israelites were subjugated by one empire after another, yet they endured. Millions of babies cried their final breaths on the point of a sword. Millions more skeletons bleached white in the desert sun.

So from the following tribes sprang the Bartels: Reuben, Simon, Levi, Judah, Zebulun, Issachar, Dan, Gad, Asher, Naphtali, Joseph, and Benjamin.

Like dust in the wind, they spread out over Africa and Europe to escape persecution. North they trudged. Hot desert winds pushed them forward, ever north along the Mediterranean's rocky shores. Gradually, stinging sands gave way to freezing hoar frost as these early Semites pushed onward. Through Asia Minor, they forged with the Black Sea on their right and the Mediterranean on their left. Mountains squeezed Semite lungs. Steep rocks gobbled up the unfortunate. Freezing blizzards seeped through thin robes. Babies turned blue in their mothers' arms. Yet forward they trudged. Forward to

Eastern Europe. There they joined the Teutons and the Slavs. Dark skin gradually turned white.

Meanwhile, persecution never abated. Bleached Jewish bones in the Middle East were replaced by rotting corpses in Europe. Jews brought with them from Babylonia the Talmud, which was a dissertation on Jewish law and dates to around 500 CE. Unfortunately, the Road of Martyrs was paved with Jewish bodies. During the Middle Ages, these people were a convenient source for blame by feudal kings, barons, and by the church. Just as the Romans were diverted from the misery of their daily lives by hatred of Christians, so too were the Christians able to place their ills at the feet of the Jews. When the Black Death brought night down upon Europe, the chattering teeth of the dying called for revenge against Jews. Men, women, and children were (according to a contemporary chronicler) thrown into deep water, burnt until they sizzled, tied to a wheel while their joints were broken and screaming to God all the while, choked until the saliva ran down their chests, buried while gasping their last taste of air, and prodded with red-hot pokers with hot blood hissing on their jerking limbs.

CHAPTER 2
SIR JOSHUA

• • •

The horse was brown. His armored faceplate had a black background outlined in yellow. Cologne, Germany in 1348 A.D. Streets oozed mud mixed with pus. The Dark Ages hung over Europe like a death shroud. Night shrieked into endless day. Meanwhile, The Black Death claimed its corpses in thousands, tens of thousands, millions. Rats scurried under deathbeds licking up the slime of dying skeletons. Cries and moans floated out windows to be carried on the vapid winds, but there were few left to lend a hand.

Who brought this plague to Germany? There were many theories but no real answers. Was it poisoned wells? Perhaps the sewage strewn waters of the Rhine and Danube rivers were the cause. Rumors ran rampant.

A gathering hubbub could be heard on a narrow street in Cologne. Distant shouts and clanging chains pierced the morning air, which was otherwise punctuated with a shriek here and a moan there. Putrid odors hung in the mist. A pungent mix of raw feces and overripe corpse smell rose up from the street.

A young woman's ear pricked up. Esther Spatz had no sooner placed the log amidst a shower of sparks when she heard the tumult. The baby let out a cry from her crib. Saul and Jacov were squirming into their pants. *Shhish,* Esther whispered so as to calm the baby and to better form a picture of what her ears were hearing. Maybe her thoughts were muddled. These were dangerous times. What was being carried over the stench? Possibly it was just more carts hauling her dead neighbors away. But wait a minute. As the sound grew louder, a distinct metallic clang could be heard. It was an unusual mixture of chains clanking and of swords pounding against shields. All the while, there was a steady thump, thush of boots in the slush. And those unintelligible words now becoming more clear, *Juden, Juden.*

A mixture of sounds filled the morning mist. Faint thumps of clubs could be heard against Jewish bodies. A shout here, a guttural cry there; all the while, boots got closer and closer to Esther's cottage. Chain maces clinked. Bones cracked. Hard, studded metal balls connected with ribs of men and women. Blood ran out of victims' mouths before even a cry could force its way from their dead throats.

Esther's baby began to cry again. Her boys huddled up against her skirt. Black hair cascaded down Esther's back as fear-filled brown eyes opened into giant prisms. Her face was small and gorgeous as a young woman's face can be. Esther's husband was far off into the forest to gather more wood for the stone fireplace. Her lips quivered instinctively as she sensed danger in the air.

Only a hundred yards away stood this frenzied mob. A Christian finger pointed the way to Esther's thatched cottage. His bony earth-stained digit resembled a wind vane blown by the gust of a mob's hot breath. As the mob approached, what looked like a moving bundle of small tree trunks emerged from a stench-laden mist to reveal its individual parts. Here, a pair of ankle-length suede boots kicked up a volcano of dust. There, a set of dark, calf-length boots squashed in a pool of pus mud. One man, dressed in a knee-length green tunic, had a long tailed hood to protect him from morning's chilly bite. A scar on his right cheek resembled a smiling mouth. He carried in his right hand a double ball flail, an instrument once used for threshing grain. It turned out to be a most effective weapon. This particular flail had two steel balls with spikes attached to chains and a hefty wooden shaft.

A young man in his twenties, who seemed to enjoy the sport, wore a brown Landsknecht Jerkin over his puffy purple sleeves. His Grosse Messer knife glinted red as it caught snatches of morning light. This piece of death was used for sweeping slices using either one or two hands and was housed in a leather scabbard on the waist.

In front of this peasant horde walked a man taller than the rest. Like a white swan in a dark forest, he stood out due, not just to his height, but to his white Crusader surcoat. Covering a doublet and headdress of chain mail was a long smock of white on which a blood-red cross was emblazoned. On the right side of his waist lay a leather scabbard housing a sword whose flat blade was thirty-three inches long. It could deliver a shearing blow that would cut mail. Its grip was sweat-stained wood. Its crescent-shaped cross guard was designed to ward off hostile sword blows. The steel pommel had a cross engraved on its face and was surrounded by brass rivets.

Inside Esther's cottage, little Saul's lips trembled. *What acht zat?*

Saul's younger brother, Jacov, was still enmeshed in the folds of Esther's floor-length dress. Her white shoulders were framed by a strip of black ruffle. This and a black sash, which was worn high about the waist, framed red and gold print fabric as it cascaded to the dirt floor.

Christian murderers, she said earnestly while clutching the baby to her bosom. *Get thee by my side! Kiddash ha-Shem. We diest as martyrs.*

Tight skin on her cheeks betrayed furrows of worry. Small beads of perspiration rolled down Esther's smooth forehead. Baby in arm, she gazed at an approaching centipede of peasants, all led by a tall, white figure with a red cross emblazoned on his breast. In the morning's cool air, Esther's bare shoulders stood ready to receive a sword's hard bite. Or maybe they'd just bash her pretty skull with one of those steel balls, and that's when final night would close her eyes forever.

As Esther watched the mob approach, Saul clutched her right hem and Jacob her left. A particular noise seemed to be getting closer and closer to the cottage. It sounded like the pop of hooves on stones.

A horse! Oh Lord, you hidest not your face.

She knew her plight. Alone she stood—just her and her faith. Three little ones—the ones *Lailah,* angel of conception brought into the world—and nary a soul to save them. How ironic is the old Yiddish proverb, *One person wants to live but can't, another can but doesn't want to.*

Esther's words burst out, *yetzer ha-ra,* the evil inclination.

Small streams of steam floated out of fifty angry mouths to mingle with the brisk morning air. A singular sound of horse's hooves quickly placed itself, strategically, in front of Esther's last bastion of hope. A brown steed with its armored faceplate stood regally facing a hostile mob of jeering peasantry. By this time, over 10,000 Jewish men, women, and children were speared, hacked to death, burned, hanged, strangled, and tortured.

Astride this warhorse sat a young man in full armor. His steed wore a blanket of black and gold checks to match his faceplate. The man was not tall but stocky. A red tassel sprouted from the top of his helmet and matched the outlines on the horse's faceplate and checkered blanket. From underneath the knight's visor bristled a short black beard. Around his waist, he wore a belt that was one foot wide; and attached to this belt was a matching brown scabbard with seven metal buttons along its length. Within this scabbard sat a falchion (blade, twenty-eight inches; weight, three pounds). It had a single-edged, wide-cutting blade, which was quite effective against mail. The point could penetrate mail with a sharp thrust. A blood groove ran along the blade's top so that a knight could more easily remove the sword from a skewered body.

Emblazoned on the shield was a coat of arms. It consisted of a gold, flesh-colored savage with ivy around his head and waist, facing front to the right of a green tree which he is grasping with his right hand below the foliage. All stand on a green ground. Above this crest is a helmet and a cascading wreath. A black background served to highlight the BARTEL family crest.

Holding his shield across his left forearm, the knight gripped an eight-foot-long tapered lance in his right gauntlet.

Stoutly facing his adversaries sat Sir Joshua Bartel. Resting on the pommel was a four-foot-long, three-foot-wide battle shield on which prominently displayed the BARTEL colors. Whispers passed around the King's court—something about saving the life of a young prince who was marked for murder. So the whispers had it that Sir Joshua, a Jew, received his family crest. In addition, the King was so grateful that he bestowed an estate with a castle, grounds, and vassals. Sir Joshua braved the lances and swords of well-known knights, in lists, all over Europe. Many had fallen to his lance. In addition, it was said that many a lady's garland had graced his shield. Yet on various occasions, he had fought alongside of his Christian brethren when the King's call came.

Sir Joshua was on his way to a baron's bidding when, passing down a narrow street in Cologne, he heard the din. Screams mixed with clanging of chain links carried over the pungent mist to horse and rider. He had seen these pogroms before. His mind brought up the picture of his mother, Deborah, her brown braids cascading down the arches of her shoulder blades. He could see understanding brown eyes proudly gazing at him. But the eyes were vacant. Her throat had a red line on it. Her head was bathed in a puddle of red. *Why? Why? Why?* Those were the only words his father could say about the Christian bastards that caught Sir Joshua's mother on the way back from town square.

That was why the BARTEL motto *The Savage Issuing, Holding The Uprooted Tree On His Shoulder* fit him like his armor. In battle, Sir Joshua was a savage. His strength was renowned throughout Germany. It was said that his sword once cut through a man's chain mail. As a witness described it, the cutting edge hewed the body in two. The man's teeth were still chattering as the top half of him lay on the ground. His legs, like severed tree trunks, still stood upright as spurts of blood cascaded down his pants. Finally, legs overcame gravity and toppled over to join chattering teeth on the ground.

Fear smothered Esther's cottage like some kind of formless blanket that couldn't be seen but could be felt in the baby's cries and in her children's shaking bodies. Fear slipped through the cracks underneath the door and made its presence known inside her home as though an unwelcome guest pushed his way in. Fear had a smell of hot sweat.

Meanwhile, an entire crowd was looking for another victim to entertain themselves with. Out of Europe's primordial past, a thing that looked like one of those apelike humans that dwelled in a cave made his way toward Esther's door. Its or his hair was hard to tell from his clothes due to the fact that his beard reached down to his beltline. A wild mane of brown straw-like hair cascaded down his back. This thing's suede smock was caked with mud and blood and was about the same color as its hair. Man or primordial ape?

Whichever, his stocky form clutched a Maciejowski war club in his right hand. This piece was over a yard long; made of hardwood, it had brass studs all along the head. Its blows could batter shields, break bones, or batter down doors, which was just what the ape had in mind. He held the war club above his head and, with a guttural shout, rushed toward Esther's wooden door.

No sooner had the weapon come down to eye level—handle grasped in two hands—than Sir Joshua's lance top pierced his belly. Riding on a river of soft intestines, it emerged red from the ape's back, lifting his legs up off the mud. A guttural scream pierced the air. Blood mixed with saliva as both bubbled out of its mouth. The rest of the mob looked astonishingly as a spiral of steam made its way to the ground while the man's mouth let out its death groans. Sir Joshua lurched the corpse's dead weight off the end of his bloody lance as he wheeled his steed around to face more onrushing Christians.

Nowhere in the Gospels did Jesus ever mention killing innocents in his name. But here were righteous gathered to interpret the word. Six foot two and two hundred thirty pounds came to do what an ape couldn't. Hairy legs like moss-covered tree stumps hung out of the bottom of a blue Everyman's tunic like moss-covered tree stumps. The tall one's beard was short, blonde, and bushy. His blue eyes gazed with rage. This mounted man before him was the only obstacle to more Jewish vermin for him to eradicate. Raised above his left shoulder was a Crusader's Ax. It had a two-foot-long hardwood handle with a crescent-shaped blade. This tool was used to hack limbs off trees and men. Among the din, his voice rose above the others. *Forsooth, murderous dog. Ye slayest our boon companion. O that his life was worth a hundred such Jew vermin as are inside that cottage. Get thee gone, Sir Knight, or thy blood joinest our friend's in making the flowers grow.*

Sir Joshua's warhorse instinctively backpedaled as he swiveled around so the lance's point faced chest level with the knight's latest adversary. Joshua knew that, with the number of foes facing him, he would be sorely pressed. A salty odor of blood hung in the cool morning air. Ravenous human dogs stood in the background barking for vengeance while ghosts of long gone Jewish warriors rose out of the sodden earth to give Joshua the strength he would need to overcome this latest travail. What difference did it make to ghosts as to who was trying to annihilate Jews? It may have been bare-chested Egyptians, fierce Edomites, or relentless Philistines with their champion, the gigantic Goliath. Spirits don't keep count of dead comrades and loved ones. They rise up as occasion warrants to protect those who come after them.

Meanwhile, a dwarf, dressed in a brown Monk's robe, snuck around to the back of Esther's cottage. The dwarf, with a hood covering his head, looked like a three-foot mushroom with fabric arms. A broad flounce covered his shoulders, and in his waist cord, he carried a dagger with a foot-long blade that was sharpened on both sides. Its handle was brown wood, and its pommel and guard were brass-tarnished by perspiration. The dwarf's miniature face was reddish from his exertion in keeping up with the rest of the Christian mob. Nonetheless, his mind pictured a baby spitted on his dagger's sharp tip.

Sir Joshua's adversary lumbered forward. His long legs carried him toward the knight at great speed. His boots made quick crunching steps toward the warhorse. Evading the lance and quick as a blur, the man and his ax lay a sad stroke upon Joshua's shield. The blade hit the coat of arms right between savage and tree. A clang resonated off the metal shield. The tall man's stale breath folded itself over the horse's nose. The Christian's upper lip drooped into a sneer as Joshua's arm collapsed against his chest due to the ax's buffet on the shield. *Ya voldt. Well struck,* yelled the sturdy knight. He then nudged his knees into the horse's flanks in a special way that caused it to double step backward. Cheers and clamoring could be heard all around them. Joshua's lance was now facing the Christian chest level. A slight kick with both heels sent the horse forward at a gallop. A sharp shriek subsided into a rattle as the lance went in through the rib cage and emerged out the giant's back. His eyes looked blankly at his comrades while his lifeless legs left the dirt, carried by the momentum of lance and horse. Upon Sir Joshua yanking the lance out, a river of red gore and white entrails leaked down the front of the man's blouse.

In the back of Esther's cottage, the dwarf was busy at his murderous work. His dagger was slowly digging and gouging a crack large enough for the little man's miniature body to crawl through. Esther was so preoccupied with the baby, her sons, and the battle taking place in front that she, at first, didn't even notice the sharp scraping sound coming from the back. Her head turned only to see the shiny steel blade cutting a hole larger and larger. In the space between the two timbers, the puffing of a little chest could be heard. Suddenly, the pug nose of a tiny face—its mouth twisted by hate and determination—emerged. Already, sweat was turning ice-cold on Esther's skin. Could the dwarf smell the baby? Could it sense fear? Could it, like a wolf, scent out its prey?

Leaning against the fireplace like a tree that's been battered by the wind lay the Spatz's last line of defense, her husband's Spiked Flail. Normally it was used to separate grain. This one was a smaller version to fit Esther's petite hands. Its hardwood handle was almost a yard long. At the end was a ring attached to a short chain, and to this chain, a two-pound steel ball with spikes going in all directions, much like a metal hedgehog, was attached. The scraping sound of the dwarf's dagger grew more urgent. A giant rat was scraping its way in to eat Esther, her little boys, and the baby. *Vat dat, Ma?* cried little Saul in terror. The words *not to worry, little one* no sooner floated out of her thin lips than a cracking sound and popping splinters of wood embedded themselves on Esther's conscience.

The dwarf, like a brown rat clawing into the hen's nest, made his way through a crevice he created with his dagger. As he pulled himself to his feet, rivulets of sweat rolled down his red pug-nosed face. His miniature mouth curled upward in a smirk. The dagger was about to pierce some tender Jewish flesh. Esther gently laid the baby into its tiny crib as she slowly edged toward the fireplace. Her movements were quick and protective. One arm pushed the boys into a safe corner while her right arm grasped the hardwood handle of Abram's spiked flail. *If I die, I want my last breath to be with my babies,* she thought maternally. Her lips, trembling, uttered the words, *Ain kei 'loheinu. There is none like our God. Oh God, give me the strength.* A scream came out of Esther's mouth as she swung the flail with all the strength she could summon in her thin arm.

Just as the dwarf's brown robed arm arched its way toward her breast, the spiked ball of the flail connected with the shiny blade of his dagger sending it end over end across the room, a shimmering shooting star arcing toward the dirt floor. After he let out a banshee cry of surprise, the dwarf looked down to see what was once his right hand. At arm's end was a blood-spattered piece of meat with bone poking out here and there. A cacophony of sound arose inside the cottage—dwarf yelling out his painful rage, baby bawling at violent sounds of struggle, and young boys crying in fear while cowering in a corner.

Quickly turning his head like a cornered animal, the dwarf looked for a means of escape; then he decided to lunge for the young woman's right arm. As the dwarf grabbed for the flail with his good hand, his fingernails ripped through the cloth of Esther's dress and cut three trenches into her soft skin. She let out a scream while grabbing her wrist. Drops of blood drizzled onto the floor. Her arm came free, and as it did, it made an arc back across her chest bringing the steel ball and its spikes flat against the side of the dwarf's head. A muffled *thump* was heard as metal struck brown hood then skull. A moan of resignation hissed out of the dwarf's bloody lips as his body collapsed into a pile of brown wool surge. Surrounding this small pile of flesh and cloth were little red pieces of skull. Arm trembling, she dropped the flail to the floor, walked on wobbly legs to the baby, and picked her up.

She then slowly brought herself over to her little sons and wrapped her arm around them, little dabbles of blood soaking through her sleeve. *It's all well. Momma has slain him,* she reassured the boys. Saul asked inquiringly, his little cherub face looking up at his mother, *He want to kill us, Mama?*

Yes, but the Lord of our fathers was with us.

Momma's hurt.

Tears slowly rolled down the little boy's red cheeks as his eyes took in the sight of blood on his mother's dress.

I fairest well, Son. That strong knight outside will savest us. Your papa will soon be back. Worry not.

If she could only know how sorely pressed Sir Joshua was looking. The clanking of assorted weapons grew louder as more and more Christians dared approach the knight and his armored horse. The *whiz* sound of an angry bee, which was actually a hunting arrow, clattered off Joshua's metal helmet. His senses were heightened. He could smell something but couldn't see what it was that his nostrils detected. This wasn't the stench of sewage and dead bodies that wafted through Cologne's narrow streets. This was a different odor—the smell of danger near at hand. Joshua was looking at the group to his right when, all of sudden, the full weight of a Maciejowski war club glanced off his shield; and the club's spikes drove into his forearm. Luckily, the shield diverted some of the force. Nonetheless, his arm went limp; and the weight of his shield rested on his saddle. He felt a sharp pain. Hopefully, bones weren't broken. The club was as long as a baseball bat, and its handle was wrapped with a spiral leather cord. Its head was covered with brass studs which could batter shields and break bones. The man who swung the club with both hands was slight of build with a full red beard that hung over his shoulder after the blow was administered. Fortunately—though not for him—because his build was slight, he only sprained the knight's wrist and opened flesh near the hand.

An arrow caught Joshua's horse in the rear flank, where a small trickle of red began to drip down its side. Quick as the man could raise his club for another strike, Joshua's sword bit through the club's handle sending splinters flying in every direction. As the sword's tempered blade severed the man's shoulder blade, he screeched twice while the sound of splintered bone filled the air around him; then he sank into a sleep none awake from.

Sir Joshua's horse, weakened by his arrow wound, lowered his back-end sending the hapless knight abruptly to the ground. Surrounding him were the dead of his doing and the living who wanted to kill him. Finally, the six-foot-two, two-hundred-and-thirty-pound leader approached. White clenched teeth, like angry piano keys, protruded behind his bushy blonde beard. The crimson cross on his chest was in stark contrast to Sir Joshua's own blood that oozed out of his wrist wound. *So now ye feet touch the ground just like mine. Soon the rest of thy body will do the same. Every poisoning Jew must die,* pronounced the Christian. Sir Joshua was much shorter than this rugged-looking warrior. In addition, he wasn't sure his shield arm would hold up after the wound he had previously sustained. Nonetheless, his spirit was much bigger than his body. *Go home! Have not enough of thy brothers fallen this day? The Jewish people have done thee and thine no wrong. Rumors. That's all ye are slaying and spilling thy blood for. Go to thy families, and leave these families be,* implored the steadfast knight. Just as most mobs are cowards beneath their brashness, so was this one as well. They sent out their larger champion to fight the smaller knight so that they could continue to slaughter helpless innocents.

A clanking of armor crackled in the morning air as Sir Joshua slid off the back of his horse and hit the ground soundly. Though there were dangerous people around him, he realized that if he could subdue the leader, everyone else would scuttle like crabs back from whence they came. Just as Joshua was trying to sort out different thoughts relating to his wounded horse, him on foot, and lastly this tall apparition in front of him, a sad stroke from the giant's Crusader Ax sent the shield flying to earth with a thud. With his left arm now useless, the knight twisted out of the way just in time to avoid a blow that would have sent his brains spilling into his helmet. Since the giant's legs were bare, Joshua managed a one-handed sword stroke that nicked the thigh of his adversary enough to stop foreword progress momentarily. The Christian's eyes looked down in surprise as rivulets of crimson rolled down his leg; then the pain and a sharp cry of disbelief followed. In his angered state, the man charged like a wounded bull. His ax blade once again found its mark as it clanged against the knight's right leg. Down Joshua tumbled. Like a turtle on its back, he lay with his sword still in his right hand and all his armor's weight to raise in order to get back on his feet. Meanwhile, the Christian's red cross drew closer, and with his ax raised to cleave the knight asunder, he never saw the sword tip enter his belly.

It was a delayed reaction. At first nothing but a slight pressure to the midsection was felt. Initially, there was a dull cutting sound of tempered steel against soft flesh; then a collective sigh rose. The mob realized what had happened. Soon the man with a red cross realized as well. As the long blade emerged from his back, the leader let out a groan that came from deep within his bowls. His eyes glazed over as he toppled to the earth with the sword's hilt protruding from his belly. As Sir Joshua used his one good arm to push himself off the ground, a mumbling could be heard coming from the crowd then shouts of panic as they pushed each other aside in order to disperse.

Gingerly, the knight walked over to where his adversary lay and, with a quick tug, removed his sword from the belly. The space once occupied by the sword now became a small, rapidly expanding, pool of blood and food. With the sword still dripping its contents, Sir Joshua carried his weapon in one hand and slowly approached his wounded steed. He jammed the blade into the ground; then, with a deft pull, he removed the arrow from the flanks of his trusty warhorse. After applying a secret salve used by his forbearers, the flowing stream of red subsided to just a trickle. His horse was, once again, able to support itself on its previously wounded rear flank. *God speed thee,* yelled the Jewish knight to the red-crossed Christian, *to hell.*

At last the knight spotted his horse's tormentor still standing on the outskirts with a bow in hand. After his sword cleaved an arrow in two that was meant for his faceplate, Sir Joshua placed his sword gently on the ground and, at the same time picking up in his right hand, the lance that lay near to where his horse now stood. With all the strength that could be mustered in his battered body, he sent the lance on a course straight and true. A *ping* and a *hiss* was heard as another arrow let loose. But its path took it harmlessly up into the morning sky. This sound was quickly followed by a *thump*. As the lance impaled the archer against a pine tree, it quivered back and forth. The archer tried to walk forward, but his feet would take him nowhere. In mortal agony, the archer mixed the words *Jesu Mari* with bubbles of red saliva. Finally, the body sagged limp against the pine tree.

A salty smell of blood rose to greet the senses. Looking at their fallen comrades, the Christian mob quickly lost heart and ran willy-nilly through thickets and trees. Bodies lay scattered to serve as a main course for famished wolves and buzzards. The exhausted knight picked up his shield. Unscathed, the Bartel coat of arms—*The Savage Issuing. Holding The Uprooted Tree On His Shoulder*—glistened in the morning sun.

Sir Joshua gently arranged his shield on his saddle's side. He wiped the bloody blade of his sword on the sleeve of a dead Christian and placed the sword back in its scabbard. Not to waste a good lance, he pulled it out of the archer's body and carried the weapon back to his horse as the lifeless archer, who now fired his arrows in perdition, slumped to the earth.

Seeing the mob flee, Esther opened her door to aid her wounded benefactor. Her young face with its fragile features greeted the handsome knight, who had lifted his visor. Both young people were gory but alive. Saul and Jacob came scampering up to the knight with twinkling little moon faces. *Get to the closet and bring me some cloth,* Esther ordered. *Sir Knight, rest thyself on our bed. Let me help thee remove this heavy armor. I'll cleanse thy wounds.* After his body was relieved of the armor's heavy weight, the knight lay down on the bed. Esther gave him a potion to drink and proceeded to apply an old Jewish salve to his arm wound. This was the same salve that she used to soothe her own injuries. Sir Joshua first glanced at the dead dwarf's body lying on the floor. He then stared up at the thatched ceiling. Something was strange. Beams and thatch circled round and round. Spinning, spinning. As his eyelids became heavier, darkness picked him up in her warm blanket and carried him into a deep sleep. *Gut gamacht, good work,* Esther whispered in the knight's sleeping ear. *If someone comes to killest ye, smite him down first as ye didest.* As she kissed Sir Joshua on the forehead tenderly, she whispered, *thou hast a varm Yiddish hartz, a warm Jewish heart. May God bless and keep thee.*

Her little cherubs, Saul and Jacov (the next generation), scampered over to get a closer look at the sleeping warrior. Esther dragged the dwarf's lifeless but bloody body out into the street to join its comrades. She then brought some oats to Sir Joshua's horse, who was pawing the ground with his hoof in anticipation. Esther slumped down, leaning her back against an oak tree. She buried her lovely face into the folds of her dress, and tears rolled their river paths down her smudged cheeks. She sobbed for her life as well as those of her precious children. There was sadness for the ones who had to die. Esther's tears, like those of millions in future generations, watered the soil of Europe.

Time flies on wings of a hawk, soaring on thermals caused by the rapid passing of centuries. Six hundred years later, the Spatz and Bartel families were destined to meet again.

Most German surnames are derived from occupations, colors, or locations. Up until the early nineteenth century, most Jewish names came from either lineage or location. Many families were able to pay officials so as to choose their own surnames, generally a name describing something beautiful. Those that could not afford to pay were assigned names that were offensive. Due to the fact that many European Jews were limited as to their occupations, few surnames are occupational in origin. Those that held the Bartel name make up a small percentage of individuals that could, today, be called relatives. There are most likely a large number of direct relatives using one of the Bartel name variations.

In almost all cases, surnames were first used by nobility and wealthy landowners. The practice then was adopted by merchants and commoners.

The name Bartel is probably patronymic in origin. What that means is that the name was a family name that was handed down. In German, the name Beutel means bottle. From this came the name of my grandfather, Puderbeutel, which means powder bottle. I surmise that the Puderbeutel name originally came from the name Beutel or Bartel due to the fact that it appears that the Bartel name is older.

Like a hand of cards dealt out to humanity, time unfolded the centuries to land my family in a small Polish town. The year was 1881.

Sir Joshua Bartel

CHAPTER 3

POLISH ROOTS

• • •

Wrapped in the protective foothills of the Carpathian Mountains in southeastern Poland lies a shtetl (small Jewish town) called Kanczuga. Just north of the town is the old Cracow-Lemberg Road. As one approaches from the main road, one can immediately spot an imposing Catholic church and cemetery that dominates the center of town. As most towns have main squares, Kanczuga is no different. It contains a monument depicting a mountain with an eagle perched atop the summit. This is meant to symbolize all the regimes throughout history that had control over this little piece of dirt.

Eighty percent of the town's population was Jewish in the year 1881. The town square was lined with trees and blanketed with a thick carpet of green grass. On a dark side street, facing each other like father and son stood the old and new Jewish synagogues. Inside the new synagogue, a Jewish school was housed.

The town of Kanczuga had been in existence for centuries. After fleeing Spain and other hostile countries during the Inquisition of the late fifteenth century, Jews found a safe haven in the kingdom of Poland where they built thriving communities such as the one in Kanczuga.

During the late nineteenth century, Poland was divided into three parts controlled by Russia, Prussia, and Austria.

In the year of 1881, the eastern part of Poland was part of the Austro-Hungarian Empire. In this area of Poland, Poles were allowed to keep some autonomy; however, this was not true in other Polish partitions. Russia wished to eradicate Polish culture by making Russian the official language in its section. Germany did the same in the part ruled by Prussia.

A warm sun glistened off dewdrops that sparkled like diamonds on Kanczuga's town square. This day was September 13. A midwife hurriedly shuffled down a dirt street on the way to a Jewish hardware merchant's home. In a small wooden cottage with sloped shingle roof lived Shmuel and Rivka Puderbeutel. At eighteen years of age, Rivka was in labor. Her cries of agony could be heard along the dusty street and through the windows of neighboring cottages. She was a strong, severe-looking young woman with a lantern jaw. Her black hair was worn in a short bun. She had a face seldom wrinkled by a smile. As tiny clouds of dust were kicked up by the midwife's shoes, Rivka's labor agonies increased. At last, the midwife's knock echoed off the front door. Shmuel anxiously welcomed her into a living area that was growing warmer by the minute. The sun's hot rays rained down on the cottage's wood shake roof. They bounced off ceiling beams and ricocheted off wall surfaces only to land on Rivka's furrowed brow, where beads of sweat cascaded down as though they were tiny creeks.

Shmuel offered a large pot containing cold water. He then tucked an armload of towels under his chin and ran at full speed to deliver them to the midwife after which he stood over in the corner watching in wonder. His brow furrowed with worry for both his wife and their child. A saying from the Babylonian Talmud came to mind, *May it be … that my loving qualities override my strict traits; that I treat my children with the quality of mercy.* Then, in a whisper (so as not to disturb the sanctity of new life's creation), Shmuel pleaded the prayer that Moses pleaded for his sister, Miriam, thousands of years ago. *El na, refah na lah (Please, God, make her well).*

Finally, after hours of labor and perspiration, Rivka's furrowed brow became smooth. Her cries ebbed into the room's sultry heat. A new sound carried out into a dusty Kanczuga street, the bawling of a baby boy—Simon Puderbeutel. For the first time in hours, Rivka's grim face relaxed while her mouth curved upward in a smile. Shmuel's shirt was soaked with sweat. One would have thought that he was the one having a baby. He, too, used muscles seldom exercised and smiled. He even laughed with an abandon that one displays after having just narrowly escaped some potentially horrendous situation.

And so the couple celebrated the birth of their new son, a ship coming in. Shmuel and Rivka set up a *kisei eliyahu,* chair of Elija for the circumcision ceremony.

Jim Bartel (about his grandfather). *Shmuel didn't want to work, but he had to.*

Ethel Nagel (about her grandfather). *He was very frugal. It might be where some of the Puderbeutel frugality came in. He would not participate in the raising of the children. It was only grandma (Rivka). He was busy every minute of the day. The children didn't have much to say to him. He was in the hardware business.*

Irving, one of Shmuel's grandchildren, told the story about how Shmuel would buy rusted barbed wire at a low price then make his children sandpaper the rust off so he could sell it at a profit.

It was also said that Shmuel and Rivka went to bed in separate rooms. Perhaps all these idiosyncrasies were reasons why she was seldom seen smiling.

Be it as it may, God, blessed be his name, watched over the young Simon and allowed him to grow into a vigorous man. Due to his religious training in the town of Kanczuga, he grew up with a love for the Torah. Simon was not a very tall man—perhaps 5'8" or so—but he was physically quite strong. At a young age—about twenty years old—he was driven to escape the stifling blanket of his father, Shmuel's strictness. So he decided to get married. In the Jewish community during that time, there existed women who were called *Yentas* or matchmakers.

About fifty miles north of Kanczuga along the San River lay another shtetl called Lezajsk. This little town lay on the left bank of the river along a sandy and flat area. Surrounding the town were green pine forests on every side. The city had existed from time immemorial, which is to say that it was a city with a Catholic church in the year 1397. This was a town with a history of violence. From 1498 to 1519, it had been repeatedly overrun and destroyed by the Tartars—those hordes originally spawned by Ghengis Khan and who swarmed over Asia and Europe from out of Mongolia. Like human scythes, they cut down everything in their path. In 1656, the Swedes ruled the city. In 1672, Lezajsk was again destroyed. Its ashes swirled within the winds of disaster. Between 1834 and 1873, the town was plagued by fires and again sent its ashes aloft. Like the legendary Phoenix, the town sprang forth from its ashes again and again quite possibly due to its superb location.

It lay in the valley of Sandomir about four miles from the San River and twenty-five miles northeast of Rzeszow near the railroad. One of the main businesses in the town of Lezajsk was the liquor factory. In the middle of the city square stood the city council building along with stores and stands (for market day). In this city, the Jews lived around the city square in one-story stone buildings with stores attached to them. Jews also dwelt on side streets, which radiated like spokes of a wheel and whose hub was the market square.

The Jewish community built a gorgeous synagogue named Beis Medrash. This edifice was built in the old style. It was twenty-four feet high. There were benches along the walls which, in all, contained 250 seats. Nothing stood in the center. The Holy Ark was engraved with artwork and was quite high. Small steps with iron banisters led up to it. The walls were adorned with artwork illustrating chapters of Psalms and the scene depicting the binding of Isaac by Abraham. There were ten brass candelabra hung from the dark ceiling beams, each one containing eighteen candles. In those days, there was no electricity. Shammas would clean the glass and fill each candle with kerosene. Men and women were separated, so the women's chamber was made up of three rooms. One thing did, however, stand in the center: the Torah reader's podium. There was a tall brass candelabrum in the center of the podium. The women's chambers also served for religious school. The street of the Beis Medrash was located to the left of the marketplace. It was unpaved and had a sidewalk only on the right side. This street contained two synagogues: the Shul and the large Beis Medrash. Also, along this street were Torah schools where Jewish children could study Hebrew and the holy works. Boznica Street was its name. The Shul was known for its impressive dome and for its beautiful wall paintings.

At the end of the nineteenth century, Lezajsk's mayor created a mile-long boulevard that was lined with trees, which provided cool shade to those who strolled its sensuous walkways.

One of the more prominent spots in the town was the Karkut (cemetery), which was created at the end of the seventeenth century. Overlooking a valley, the cemetery wore an inviting coat of green grass so as to invite the living to visit the dead. Trees shaded visitors as though to comfort them as they visited their beloved.

One of the cemetery's most famous residents was Rabbi Elimelech, who was of holy blessed memory. Upon his arrival in the town of Lezajsk, its golden age began. He lived during the late eighteenth century. This rabbi was a poor man—perhaps materially—but with a richness of spirit that knew no bounds. Jews from all over the world flocked to Lezajsk to seek the redemption or the healing of their afflictions at the hands of this rabbi whose fame spread well beyond the confines of the tiny Polish town he inhabited. This throng of Jews to Lezajsk brought an abundance of income to local businesses and hotels. Jews struck deals with others from different countries, and the result was the development of the wine and liquor industries within the borders of this city. With the death of Rabbi Elimelech, his grave became a magnet for pilgrims from all over. They threw themselves down on his grave and prayed for various favors. Prior to his death, the rabbi said that whoever spread himself over the rabbi's grave was guaranteed to have his heart's wishes fulfilled.

All this description of Lezajsk (or, in English, Lizhensk) is necessary because it is the town that our Yenta led Simon Puderbeutel to in search of a wife. Though he was only twenty at the time and certainly unlearned in the ways of the world, he came from a good, if frugal, family. In turn, that was what he was seeking in a wife—one from a good, though hopefully less frugal, family.

To provide a backdrop of the role Jews played in Lizhensk, a census was taken of the town seventeen years prior to Simon's visit. The city comprised 4,945 residents. Of these, 2,539 were Roman Catholic, 430 Greek Catholic, 32 Akot (unknown), and 1,944 Israelite (Jewish).

As it so happened, two prominent families lived in Lizhensk: the Liebermans and the Spatzs. The richest Jew in the town was Itzak Spatz, a banker. He became rich by making interest-bearing loans in United States dollars to people within and outside of Lizhensk. Itzak had a brother by the name of Kalman, who was a supplier of gravel for road making in the district of Lancut, the district Lizhensk was part of during its Austrian occupation. The Liebermans traded in firewood and coal. More about these families later.

In this little town, Jewish families held monopolies on key products. For instance, Wolf Stolbach had a monopoly on wholesale spirits. The Hollanders held a monopoly on both the wholesale tobacco trade and the state lottery. Salt belonged to Yizrael. Hirschfeld controlled wholesale gasoline. Katz controlled produce. Greenberg, plaster. These arrangements were very similar to the trusts that flourished in America.

The union of Lieberman and Spatz families produced a daughter—Leah, who at nineteen, was one year younger than Simon. She was a tall, husky girl, not lacking flesh on her bones. Her heart could be said to be as big as she was. She wore her black hair short—cropped at the neck. Her double chin was evidence of the fact that she was not raised in the atmosphere of want. Leah's clothes were austere, which was in keeping with the Jewish fashion of the day in shtetls. As to the ways of the world, Leah was well equipped. She was quite well educated, having graduated from both Torah school and Gymnasium (Polish high school). In addition to that, her parents brought her up to be a good businesswoman.

As good fortune would have it, Leah Lieberman was the girl to whom the Yenta introduced Simon Puderbeutel as his prospective wife. In those times, one traveled from one town to another over dusty roads either by walking or by means of a horse-drawn cart, which was Simon's parting gift from Rivka, his mother. He had to leave the house when his father wasn't home because the ever-frugal Shmuel would have never willingly parted with so valuable a possession as a horse and a cart. He would have much more readily parted with a son, who ate considerably more than a horse and, worse yet, had to be clothed. In fact, a family story had it that, on the Sabbath, Shmuel would sit in his underpants so as not to wear out a pair of trousers. How true this was, one can only surmise.

So it can be said that Simon had to travel with at least two outfits: one to absorb the dust of the road from Kanczuga to Lizhensk and a dressier outfit for synagogue and for meeting his future wife. As to appearance, Simon blended into Christian society to a greater extent than most Orthodox Jews did. He cut off his traditional pigtail. He trimmed his black hair neatly to neck level; and his beard, which covered up his lantern jaw, was trimmed instead of billowing down his chest. His mustache as well was neatly trimmed. When Simon Puderbeutel turned up at the Yenta's place, he cut quite a handsome figure in his three-piece suit complete with vest and tie. On top of his short black hair, he wore a black yamucha (Jewish skull cap).

As the door opened, a peach fuzz face peered out. Jovial yet quizzical was her expression. In her sixties, the Yenta had a kindly look about her. She wore a traditional white peasant dress that draped down to the wooden floor of her home. A white bonnet that was tied under the chin served as a crown for her gray hair. The Yenta's white clothes suggested marriage and weddings.

So? Come in, my freser (eater). Hmm. A strapping lad you are though short, to be sure. But don't worry, my lad. You're presentable enough. You are Simon from Kanczuga, are you not?

I am. I came for you to find me a wife.

Find you a wife? That's a fair assignment. Come in, come in. Sit down and rest your weary feeties. Let Yenta get you some soup. You look malnourished. You have to eat, my lad, eat! Lest nobody will have you. Beef on your body is what's needed, Boy.

And so Simon sat down in his well-tailored black suit and had the obligatory meal that all who visit a Jewish home must partake of. The homeowner would as soon go hungry as have a guest leave wanting.

Now let us discuss a small matter of trifling importance—gelt (money). The fee. A small matter, I'm sure. You look like a prosperous young man, a lad with a future. How much do you feel Yenta should receive to find you the wife of all your days?

Now Simon was no stranger to forging a deal. His father, Shmuel, could squeeze a coin and make the Archduke of Austria's picture cry. So he thought to himself, *What is a wife worth?* She could be of immeasurable value if he got a good one or the bane of his existence if he ended up with a kvetch (nag); then again, he had only so much gelt to spare—that is to say he had a wife budget. Simon was not terribly experienced in matters relating to bartering for a wife. So he thought to himself, *How much would a horse cost?* It may seem farfetched to relate a horse to one's betrothed, but certain similarities did exist. Both were boon companions that, if picked properly, saw a person through thick and thin. Both had to be cared for. A good horse, in the experience of Simon's father, would cost a man fifty Polish dollars at that time. So based on that, Simon was willing to pay Yenta 100 Polish dollars for a good wife. But, that's not what he offered her.

While the odor of fresh matzo ball soup whiffed through Simon's nostrils, he replied, *May He, blessed be his name, keep you and your house. I am grateful to you for your food and for what you are about to do for me. I do not wish to dishonor you nor your house. In light of my limited means and my trust in your abilities, after all you come well-recommended; I am prepared to offer you fifty Polish dollars as a fee.*

With that, Yenta brought him a plate full of boiled chicken with carrots.

Fres (eat), my lad. Yenta can see that your brain is starved from your long journey and lack of food. Perhaps a little more sustenance will clear your head. Fifty Polish dollars, you say? Was it something I did that you should bring this insult down on my head? I bring a nice girl from a good family, and you want to pay a horse's price?

Simon had to interject for fear that she would become so agitated that the end result would be that both he and the matzo balls would wind up out in the dirt street.

My dear, dear Yenta. I meant no disrespect to you or to my future bride. I am a man of modest means. This suit you see on me; it was the last thing my parents gave me as they showed me out the door. Surely, two reasonable people such as ourselves can arrive at a bargain that even a rabbi would bless.

Tears slowly dribbled down the lady's cheeks and gathered themselves as small droplets on her peach-fuzzed jaws. Whether her emotions were genuine or not, her words and tears did have the desired effect.

Though I'll not have much more to spare, said Simon earnestly, *I know you have for me a girl that will be with me till the end of my days. Seventy-five Polish dollars a deal?*

Yenta spoke softly, at first, her elderly voice a whisper, *So my young bubalah (man of pleasure), you want a thoroughbred? Woman or horse?*

Simon interjected, *No, Ma'am, you mistake my meaning.*

Then, speaking in a more amplified tone, Yenta continued, *Oh my, my. I don't think you could acquire a thoroughbred horse for what you want to pay. Perhaps Yenta can find you a village wench—not terribly educated, not much to look at, but capable of keeping your clothes clean. Oh, what do they bring me? I thought I had a mench (gentleman).*

Simon tried to speak up in a voice resonating with confidence, but the words somehow tumbled off his tongue.

I want, yes, I want from a good family. Intelligent, educated—yes, that's what I should have. The looks, the ap … what should I say? The appearance does not have to be so … so special.

Yenta's grayish blue eyes got wider.

You want family. You want intelligence. Looks not so special, you say? Probably the Queen of Sheba. Let's reach an understanding, my young simpleton.

It's Simon, he interjected.

Simon, Levi, Reuben, and all the rest of the twelve tribes. What difference does it make what your name is if we don't have a price? No, look here, my little kibitzer (chatterer). Her lips pressed together while her eyes, like drills, bored dollar signs through his eyeballs and into his subconscious. *Such a one I have for you the likes of which in a hundred lifetimes you will never see. From two of the finest families in Lizhensk. Smart? She could teach you a thing or two, my little pisser. Her looks? Well, let's put it this way. Your mother would adore her. A hundred Polish dollars and not one dollar less. Such a gift I give you. To find one like this, anyone else would pay three hundred dollars and gladly, but for you ... recommended by a kinsman.*

Simon's emotions were getting the best of him. A good family. Well educated. Probably a good cook, as well. Appearance. Well, who can say these days? In the eye of the beholder ... Isn't that what the sages say? His serious expression started turning into a smile, which he quickly squelched. One hand grabbed the other so as to stop them from trembling. Beads of sweat started to form on his forehead, and as they slowly rolled down his face, he quickly wiped them away with the back of his suit sleeve. Simon was caught in a cross fire of emotions and thoughts. He craved the bride that Yenta had for him. On the other hand, his practical side played on his conscience. What would his father, Shmuel, do? Even if his wife, Rivka, were the merchandise, Shmuel would strike the sharpest bargain he could. Before Simon could finish his thoughts, the words came out.

Seventy-five Polish dollars or I leave a bachelor. Do we have a bargain?

The deal was struck. Leah Lieberman was betrothed to Simon Puderbeutel from Kanczuga but not before he had to go through the obligatory meeting of her family, who grilled him on his pedigree and his means of support. Now Leah was a good-sized girl, so it was apparent that Simon was going to need a great deal of industriousness to support her in the style that she had grown accustomed to. Simon acquired a sense of thrift from his father. He had saved a sufficient amount with which to start a business. The lessons he learned in his father's hardware store would stand him in good stead.

As tov (luck) would have it, Leah's relations were some of the most influential in the town of Lizhensk. Her parents were of the Lieberman and Spatz banking clans. A double bonus was the fact that she was not only well educated in a general sense, but she also had received business training—a valuable asset for an aspiring businessman. A final boon for Simon (once he was able to convince his bride's family that he was not indigent) was the fact that Leah ran a hardware store that was provided as a means of support for her by her parents. How fortuitous then that Simon, as well, had a background in the hardware trade!

As the twentieth century dawned in Poland, economic conditions were difficult for many Jews. A large number from the general area of Lizhensk immigrated to other countries of the Austro-Hungarian Empire to find work. In addition, nationalism was engulfing Europe, directed mainly against Jews. In Warsaw, some shops displayed the sign "Christian Shop" on their windows.

Nothing that swirled around them was going to stop this young couple from building a successful business. Simon and Leah bought the four-bedroom home that was attached to their hardware store. Soon, Simon took to running the everyday affairs of the store while Leah tended to caring for their home. With firewood and coal from the Lieberman side of Leah's family and financing from the Spatz side, their business soon became one of the largest in Lizhensk.

As was the custom, Jews lived in one section of town near the market square while Poles lived in the other parts of town. Each had their own rules and regulations. For instance, Jews were not allowed to plant vineyards in Maritzki Square, where holiday fairs were conducted—only Catholics could; however, one would not find a Polish store near any of the synagogues. Also, the custom was to have the store attached to the home. (It's no wonder the word "commute" is not found in the Polish lexicon.) A typical Polish street would look like one taken out of the wild west in the United States: wide, dusty, with horse dung scattered all over, and lined with (for the most part) wooden buildings of one and two stories. A pungent smell of manure would waft into the windows; it grew especially strong on warmer days.

The Puderbeutel house, however, was larger than most in that it was two stories in height. In addition, like many of the other Jewish habitations, it was built of stone though the attached store was constructed of wood. Building structures of stone became a custom that was popular after the great fire that ravaged Lizhensk during the latter part of the nineteenth century. After being burnt to the ground on what had become a regular basis, a town finally comes to the realization that their building techniques were inadequate in certain respects.

These were times of plenty for those Jews who owned businesses. Being under Austrian rule gave them a great degree of equality as compared with their Polish counterparts. For those who stayed, a poor Jew was an uncommon sight in the town of Lizhensk. Local weavers created a thick wool fabric known in Poland as Bia. Every Tuesday and Friday, Lizhensk held a market day in the square. Jew and Gentile alike came from miles around to sell, to trade, and to buy goods of every type. While in town, these people would not fail to visit the local merchants.

A story was told about Simon's father, Shmuel: It seems he had a calf that he that he wanted to sell on market day in a neighboring town of Kanczuga. When calves arrived at market, they were weighed and paid for by the pound. So what Shmuel, so the story went, did was tie the calf's penis so that the poor beast would not go to the bathroom and lose any weight; thus, he got a top price for his animal.

Soon came the children. There were five sons and three daughters. First came Abraham in 1902. On January 1, 1903, Irving was born. It was one of those frigid Polish nights where the earth draws in cold from deep space. The temperature was thirty below zero. Inside the Puderbeutel home, a warm fire was burning brightly within the large stone fireplace. An odor of burnt wood mixed with that of rubbing alcohol. All of these smells drifted into Leah's nostrils as her cries of agony carried out into the cold night sky. Though it was never said that men had a tougher role in the birth process, mental agony for those a person loves many times exceeds physical pangs. So it was tears and beads of perspiration mixed on Leah's kindly but twisted face that rolled off her double chin. Her bed creaked with the stress placed on it by this large woman. All Simon could do was pray—as his ancestors did for so many thousands of years—to He, blessed be his name, who writes the book of life. Since Simon was schooled in the Torah, he recited many verses to bring comfort both to himself and for the sake of her whose agonies he was forced to witness. At last, adult cries faded to whimpers while baby cries added their part to an endless symphony of birth. A son was born who would someday, in time of need, stand forth. A bris (circumcision ceremony) was performed, and the child was named Isaak (later Americanized to Irving).

Other additions to this growing family were Gerson, Ben, Jim, Ethel, Sarah, and Reisla (Rose).

With this large brood, things were never dull around the Puderbeutel household. Leah would keep the house spotless, tend to the children, and if that were not enough, keep the accounts at Simon's hardware store. She was a large lady with a kindly face, an educated visage, and eyes that spoke gentleness. On the other hand, Simon was short and wiry, strong in shoulder. His short beard framed his handsome facial features. Simon's coal black eyes reflected a wariness that was necessary in running a successful business.

Leah was the one all the children ran to for comfort. She always had a little treat for this one, an encouraging word for that one. No matter how busy she was, there was always enough time to go over lessons, to play, and to offer a broad bosom for a crying face. With Simon, however, it was better to steer clear if you were one of the brood. He seldom smiled which meant that, when he rarely did, it could melt a block of ice. His demeanor was strict, yet he was a man who bowed down to God. Simon was very respected in the synagogue as being a devout and learned person.

Ethel Nagel (daughter). *Dad was very strict. Mom and dad sold wood to build homes with. He made sure the children went to schools and learned not only the language that we spoke, but Hebrew as well.*

You never had to think something twice. He said it, and it had to be done the way he wanted it to be. If he wasn't obeyed, he'd get very upset, and he still gets what he wanted. So everything was done by the way my father and mother wanted. You couldn't go out with a person that wasn't picked by them. In other words, that was Jewish. So we were brought up to be good Jews and good human beings. Dad was a very learned man. He studied Torah quite a bit. He was Orthodox. There were three to four bedrooms, and the store was connected to the house. We had five brothers and three sisters. Four bedrooms? Sure, they doubled. The boys doubled in one room, the sisters had the other room, and the parents had one room.

According to Irving Bartel (son), *Dad (Simon) would tell you to do something once. If you did not obey, he would give you a clop on the back of the head. With eight children, there was no time for explanations.*

In addition to hardware and building wood, Simon's store carried guns. As was the custom in business during this time, Simon saw to it that he had a monopoly on the gun trade in his area. In fact, he secured a contract to supply, first, the Polish government with guns then the Germans, who were Polish allies in World War I.

Jim Bartel (son), *Father was very strict. Very seldom did he show any affection toward the children. He sent all the children to gymnasium, which you had to pay quarterly.*

Though Simon was not to be trifled with, he and Leah believed very deeply in a good education for their children, which was a common trait among Jews for generations. Leah, however, proved to be a safe harbor to Simon's harsh demeanor. If any of the children wanted something, it was her they appealed to. Often, things would be given without asking—a sweet treat here, a trinket there. Though tight with the coin, she was, nonetheless, loved by local merchants because of her infectious smile and due to the fact that she could not resist buying treats for her large family.

It came to pass that Simon Puderbeutel's hardware business grew to the point that Simon found himself the second wealthiest man in Lizhensk. Meanwhile, wagons pulled by horses followed the clopping hooves down the dirt road from market square and would pull up at the hardware store. One could not come to Lizhensk without loading up on some spirits from the distillery and some building materials from Puderbeutel's hardware store. In addition, if one wanted a fine shooting piece, this was the place to go. Families would also make the stop at Alter Anfang's textile shop either to buy the latest fashions or to sew their version of French couture. Anti-Semitism was still prevalent in Polish society, but if a Pole wanted what Jewish merchants had, they had best leave their feelings under their coats.

Across from the large Beis Medrash synagogue were the Cheders (Torah elementary schools), which the Puderbeutel children were obliged to attend. When Sabbath (Saturday) beckoned, Jews rushed in groups to the bathhouse and ritual bath. The odor of freshly baked bread floated through the streets in the Jewish quarter, and Kugels (noodle puddings) added their aroma, which caused little Jewish mouths to water in anticipation. Children were bathed and shampooed. Their finest clothes were on display. The sexton would knock with his hammer, *Jews, Jews, to the synagogue*. Silver and gold candlesticks would be brought out to be placed on pure white tablecloths. Men would wear their Kapotes (black Hassidic cloaks) and would wrap braided Gartels (belts) around their waists. Their heads would be covered with wide Streimels (Hassidic fur hats) with fur brims. Children would carry thick prayer books.

Through the calm and prosperity, sounds of distant thunder would be heard. War clouds were forming. Lightning could be seen in the distance. A flash, a flicker. Rumbling, rolling shock waves broke over Europe and engulfed it in darkness, a darkness from which many never awoke.

Rivka Puderbeutel
Born 1863

CHAPTER 4
EUROPE AT WAR

• • •

In 1914, Apollo and Thor (gods of war), shook hands over the continent of Europe. On June 28, 1914, the summer sun basked down on a crowd of people, who were lining the street in a little-heard-of town called Sarajevo, capital of a little-known country called Serbia. The occasion was a visit by Austrian Archduke Franz Ferdinand. He was riding in an open car so well wishers could more easily see him. He felt the sun warm his face when, all of a sudden, he felt something else—a hot pain in his chest—then blackness. A Serbian assassin had emerged out of the crowd with a pistol and pulled the trigger at point-blank range.

What emerged was a domino effect of countries sucked into conflict due to alliances they were part of. First, Austria (Poland was part of their Empire) declared war on Serbia. Russia took the side of Serbia (Part of Poland belonged to Russia); then Germany, which also held a part of Poland, declared war on Russia and France. Britain, an ally of France, proceeded to declare war on Germany. Initially, World War I consisted of the Central Powers (Germany and Austria) against the Triple Entente (Britain, France, and Russia). Other allies of either side were eventually drawn into the fray. Turkey joined the Central Powers. Italy came in on the side of the Triple Entente. Eventually, the United States was dragged into the war due to the sinking of a British passenger ship, Lusitania, which debarked from New York. More than 1,000 souls perished. Millions more would follow.

At thirteen years of age, Isaak Puderbeutel was quickly growing to the height of his father, Simon. His hair was short, black, and wavy. The first faint hairs of a mustache he was so desperately trying to grow were making their appearance above his upper lip. Nonetheless, his black eyes projected a serious, determined look. He wore glasses with thin gold frames that added to his studious demeanor. Of course, a rite of passage for all Jewish boys into manhood was the Bar Mitzvah. It was at this ceremony that a youth quoted from the Torah and was looked upon by his elders as an adult. The reward for a year of study with the rabbi was a bevy of presents provided by family, friends of parents, and business associates of Simon. A special shabbas (Sabbath) day was set aside by Simon's shul (synagogue) for the especial purpose of honoring Isaak. Dressed in a black suit, white shirt, and thin checkered black and white tie, he made his way with his proud parents down the dusty Beis Medrash street to Shul. There his father solemnly presented him with a white yarmulke, talis, and telfillin (wooden blocks for shoulders and forehead). It was all Leah could do to keep the rambunctious children under control.

The family was dressed in their Sabbath's finest. Sarah and Rose couldn't stop giggling while little Ethel kept jumping up and down in the snow. The boys—Abe, Gerson, and Jim—took a shove at each other as they walked formally behind their tall mother. Inside Shul, distinguished guests filed in including prominent family members such as the Spatzs and the Liebermans. Simon stood proudly inside and looked most dapper in his tweed suit with gold watch chain hanging in a loop from his vest pocket. He wore a black yarmulke that matched his suit. His beard had been neatly trimmed. A smile, to Simon, was a thin straight line marked at both sides by his lips. So he greeted the distinguished guests. The smell of old carpets and aged wood permeated the air while warmth radiated from the coal furnace, toasting cold faces.

Family members filled up the first four rows. Isaak stood on the podium with elders sitting on wood benches behind him. It looked like he was flanked by patriarchs of the Old Testament, their beards overlapping their prayer shawls. As the rabbi pointed to the words on the Torah scroll with his silver pointer, Isaak, who had now become a man, slowly read aloud.

Sh'ma Yisra'el Adonai Eloheinu, Adonai Ekhad. Hear Oh Israel, The Lord our God, the Lord is one. And you shall love the Lord your God, with all your heart, with all your soul and with all your might. And these words which I command thee this day, teach them to thy children, and talk about them, when you are at home, when you are away, when you liest down, and when you risest up. Bind them as a sign upon your hand, and let them be frontlets between thine eyes. Inscribe them on the doorposts of thy house and upon thy gates.

As the crescendo of his voice rose, the words uttered thousands of years ago in a land faraway rose up and reverberated off the gilded gold dome. Meanwhile, bright sunshine brought the stain glass Psalms scenes to vivid life in colors of red, blue, purple, and green.

Young Isaak glanced over and spotted his mother's wide smile of pride. He turned his head to the left, where Simon sat with the elders, just long enough to see a seldom given nod of approval. Isaak could hardly contain himself. Not only did he not stammer or stutter, but he felt deserving of presents about to be received. In fact, his mind was cluttered with memorized Hebrew letters and thoughts of the pile of presents.

With the words, *May the Lord bless thee and keep thee* echoing in their ears, the congregation filed out into the brisk winter air. Women were catching up on gossip. Men wished each other *Good Shabbos.* Isaak's family made its way toward the Puderbeutel home, where apple kugels and potato latkas waited. Sara, Rose, and Ethel skipped and crunched their shoes in the snow. Little Jim picked up a snowball but quickly put it down when he saw his father, Simon, turn in his direction. Isaak walked next to his father on the left and slightly behind—a place of honor.

In the distance, drums were beating—drums of war, drums of intolerance. One could hear them. During that silent time when clinking glasses were laid to rest, soft thunder rumbled in the distance.

Life went on in Lizhensk. Sara, Rose, Ethel, and Jim went to elementary school. Sara had long, black, wavy hair like Isaak. Her face was beautiful and thin. Her expressive brown eyes could bore through a pine tree. Rose was shorter. Her hair was brown and was trimmed to neck level. Her skin was tan and her lips more pursed. She looked like a Polish Anne Frank. Rose made sure that her mother got her the latest clothing styles for school. Little Ethel was the precocious one. She was youngest of the girls but with the most energy. One couldn't be completely sure she was actually part of the family since Ethel was the only one with blond hair and a light complexion. She liked to wear a big, white bow in her hair. When serious, she had that far-off wandering gaze. The Puderbeutel boys, except for their ages, were hard to tell from each other. All of them wore fashionable thin-rimmed glasses. They all had black, wavy hair like Isaak.

Most Jewish sons worked for their parents after graduating from elementary school but not Simon's. They would go to gymnasia and Latin school. Simon and Leah saw to it that their sons would receive a superior education. In the elementary schools, a troubling trend was starting: insulting names, put downs, and insidious remarks as to Jewish origins became a daily lot in life, dished out by both professors and by Gentile students. Sometimes after school, rocks would be thrown at Jewish children followed by taunts.

As children will, Jewish children played in the forests surrounding Lizhensk. Students of Hebrew school and of the Talmud Torah would go into the pine forests during the festival of Lag Baomer. Boys would carry homemade bows and arrows and commemorate the might of Rabbi Akiva and Bar Kochba. With his bow, each Jewish lad could stand up to the might of the Roman Legions. With bows and arrows, the lads felt secure from both Romans and modern day anti-Semites.

At the same time, a very real war was being fought in Europe. Men were being sent into thickets lined with barbed wire. They were stung to death by swarms of machine gun and rifle bullets. Vast open fields were the battle fronts. Long trenches faced each other. Whoever charged first died. And so it went. A stalemate developed. The air shrieked with artillery shells while plumes of deadly mustard gas drifted over the pockmarked landscape. Men's cries for their mothers, Jesus, God, or a medic mixed with the high-pitched whine of a new form of destruction: the biplane. As if the earth choking on blood it was forced to sop up was not enough, a new form of killing monster was introduced into the fray: a large lumbering armored machine on tracks called a tank. This thing could fire a cannon in all directions and run over anything unfortunate enough to be in its path.

One day, as the casualties lay like twisted logs on the barren battlefields, a visitor came to Puderbeutel's hardware store, a tall man with a large, handlebar mustache. He was stocky at the shoulders but thin at the waist, where his brass buckle reflected the bright outdoor light. He wore a gray uniform with the shirt buttoned up to his thick neck. On his head was a helmet with a short spike on top of it. His shoulders bore the epaulets that signified his rank—that of general in the German army.

As was his custom, Simon personally greeted all who entered his store. He was considerably shorter and more thinly built than this career military man

Mr. Puderbeutel?

Yes, Herr General? What brings you to call on me?

I represent the Kaiser and his Austrian allies. We have heard that you have supplied good quality rifles to the Galician nationals. Is that true?

Yes. My guns are known to be the best that can be had. Mausers. Perhaps you've heard of them, Herr General.

Indeed. My troops need weapons, good ones to fight the French and the Ruskies. Rifles and carbines. How many can you get?

As a patriotic Austrian citizen, I will do what I can. How many do you need?

50,000.

Quite a few. It will take a bit of time. How do I get paid?

We pay in gold. How long will it take?

Herr General, for the war effort, I will assemble them here as quickly

as possible. Let me check my sources. My guess, three weeks. How may I contact you?

You may leave word at the hotel's front desk. When the guns are assembled, I'll see to it that the gold is delivered.

Herr General, no disrespect intended. Long live the Kaiser. But, you see, I am just a hardworking Jew. The kind of money needed to purchase 50,000 guns … I do not have. You deliver the gold, and I will acquire the guns. You have my word on it. If the word of a Jew is not enough, you know where to find both me and my family.

Mr. Puderbeutel, or should I say gun merchant, you are testing my patience.

The general stood ramrod straight to make obvious the difference in his height of six feet two inches and that of the much shorter merchant. His cheeks, like little tomatoes surrounded by a large bushy mustache, turned blood red in anger. The general's right hand slowly became a clenched fist. His teeth were clamped so tightly together that they almost broke off in his mouth. Here was a large man used to those he spoke to instantaneously obeying with a crisp, *ya mein general.*

For Simon's part, he was of two minds. On the one hand, his weary attitude toward Jew haters caused him to think of the Walther automatic pistol he kept under the counter. As anger welled up inside his five-foot-eight-inch frame, all that could be detected was a slight trembling of the hands. From a different perspective, killing this German would surely bring more of them and would result in his family's execution as well as his own.

In as calm a voice as he could muster, Simon inquired, *What type of Mausers do you want?*

Model 98 rifles and both Model 98 a and b carbines. You can have them in three weeks?

Yes, Herr General. Three weeks from the date you deliver me the gold. Long live the Kaiser.

Understood, Mr. Puderbeutel. Long live the Kaiser.

And so it was that the Puderbeutel store sold guns to the German army. This was the first of several large orders. But no matter who you were or how prominent or what business you had with the German army, when the troops marched through (as they eventually did), only three things were on their mind: plunder, rape, and death.

Then came the day that dust rose up on the main road leading to Lizhensk. What is now Poland, in past times, had always been a throughway to conquest. Large armies of great nations had moved through, had occupied, and had ravaged the province for centuries. This time, it was the German army. The smell of sweaty horses pulling artillery and munitions wagons floated over the forests from miles away. A distant rumbling of wheels and tramping of heavy boots could be heard slowly but inexorably approaching the little town of Lizhensk. Stout German bodies that would later turn to bloated corpses upon the pockmarked fields of Europe confidently clomp, clomp, clomped through the little villages and towns of what is now Poland.

These men were armed. As far as Jews were concerned, killing one of them would mean as much as swatting a gnat to a German soldier. Wives and daughters were to be hidden in secret hiding places. Stories of what a Hun soldier would do to a pretty woman had traveled far and wide. Whether true or false, nobody wanted to find out.

Simon Puderbeutel had already made his bargain with the German general. He had collected his gold—one ounce per rifle or carbine—and had secured his earnings in his relative Spatz's bank vault. He had nothing to fear in that regard. Some readers may debate the politics of Puderbeutel's actions. After all, it was the Germans; half the world was their enemy. It is also true that many otherwise decent individuals turn into monsters during wartime; however, Simon's province was allied with Austria which, in turn, was allied to Germany. It was purely a business decision. For if he did not sell guns to the Germans, the outcome was better left to the imagination. What's more, they would have found someone else to sell them arms.

The large dust cloud approached Lizhensk. A stench composed of sweaty horses and their dung floated in the air. Squeaking wagon wheels were heard above thousands of tramping boots. Each foot stomp created its own little cloud of dust on the dirt road that led into town. Citizens hid themselves in fear of what was approaching. Allies, perhaps, but Germans.

As the army passed down the main street through the market square, officers would branch out with smaller units to forage at various stores. When he saw the column approaching, Simon gathered Leah, Abe, Isaak, Gerson, Jim, and the girls. He ordered all of them, except Abe and Isaak, into their cellar which was concealed below the house. Their small feet, except for Leah's made fast little pitter-patters as all of them scampered down the cellar stairs. As Leah followed the children down, the stairs groaned and squeaked with her weight. A German shepherd that was the Puderbeutels' constant companion started barking its warning as an officer and five soldiers approached the store.

Fritz! Simon ordered the dog. *Come!*

The obedient dog immediately trotted over to his master's side and sat by Simon's left leg.

As the soldiers approached, one of them said to his companion.

Fritz? Why, that's my name. The dog probably gets treated better than I do.

Silence! barked the captain, who led this small company of soldiers. One could see that he made rank at a young age. He looked to be only twenty with his blond hair and deep blue eyes though, in actuality, he was quite a bit older. His complexion was so light that he looked almost baby faced. He wore the usual peaked helmet of an officer, and on his waist was the Walther pistol favored by German officers.

As the group approached, Fritz, the loyal guard dog, first growled menacingly then lunged—as generations of his kind were bred to do—toward the captain of the soldiers.

No, Fritz! Simon yelled at his dog. But it was too late. Instinctively, the captain pulled his pistol out, aimed, and fired. Two loud pops rang out. The dog, in mid-stride, seemed to somersault head over heels then lay quivering on the dirt. Blood drooled out of its mouth into the dust. Two red holes showed up on its black chest, where the fur was caked with splotches of dark crimson. Isaak and Abe, tears streaming down their faces, ran sobbing over to their fallen comrade to comfort him. It was no use. Simon looked on in astonishment, his eyes watery.

Your dog should learn better manners, said the Captain coldly. *Your next dog, I'm sure, will learn to behave more civilly toward your allies. Now, what have you for my men?*

Simon knew he had to pull himself and his sons together and get rid of these soldiers before they found the rest of his family.

Isaak! Abe! Though food is scarce these days, I think we have some things in the kitchen that should please your men, Herr Captain.

Ah, I see you are a good man after all, Herr merchant. Actung! Men, help yourselves to this man's kitchen.

With a quick glance at the concealed trapdoor that led to the cellar, Simon could picture in his mind his wife and small children shaking with fear at the sounds of heavy German boots over their heads. With a stern look, he pointed his finger toward the kitchen.

Abe! Isaak! Show these good men some victuals! Fres (eat), gentlemen!

Obediently, the lads did as their father ordered even though, inside, they hated these German pigs for murdering their beloved dog. With cheeks still wet from tears, the boys led Herr Captain and his men into their kitchen, hoping that food was all they would take. Of course, the soldiers not only took what the boys showed them but then proceeded to ransack for every other foodstuff they could find. Fortunately for the Puderbeutels, the Captain had orders from above not to loot the homes of private citizens in allied areas. With canvas sacks full of food over their shoulders, the men tromped out of the house upon completing their task. The Captain touched the front of his helmet as a good-bye salute to Simon. He then marched to the front of his group of soldiers and led them out of town toward their fate.

Meanwhile, on some distant battlefield, a German soldier raised himself up out of a trench in preparation to charge the enemy. No sooner had his eyes taken in the bleak landscape with its fog bank of gun smoke than a brrriittt came from the direction he was staring at. Not much time to think about what the sound was. He knew but a split second later that there were three red holes in his chest. His lifeless legs collapsed sending his body, like a sack of potatoes, tumbling back into his trench. On the same battlefield, a freckled English lad huddled behind a dirt mound to escape an artillery bombardment. His uniform stunk of fear. His eyes were bloodshot. His helmet looked like a metal bowl with a wide rim on it. Shells shrieked all around him as he huddled for cover. He was somebody's son, brother, uncle, buddy; then a shell shattered the air above him—first with noise then with shards of metal. One piece entered the middle of his back, severing the spine. He lay with his face against the dirt mound feeling a dull pain but nothing else. Though he quivered, he could not move any of his limbs. Day slowly became darkness as his life dripped out of him. These were just two out of millions cut down in their prime.

While this was taking place, Simon rushed over to the trapdoor and opened it. Abe and Isaak, beside themselves with grief over the fallen pet, lay their heads on his still chest. Down in the cellar, the three girls were weeping in fear while Jim tried to keep a brave face. Leah calmed them by singing lullabies in a soft, lilting voice. After letting Abe and Isaak dig a grave for their dead dog, Simon grabbed what food was left and herded his two sons into the cellar with the rest of his family.

For three days, as Germans marched through the town looting where they could and grabbing what chance presented them with, the Puderbeutel family stayed huddled in their hiding place with virtually no food or water. Occasionally—one at a time—each had to sneak over to the outhouse to relieve themselves and then scamper back to the cellar. While the children cried over their hunger pangs, Simon and Leah calmed them with songs or stories about how hungry the Israelites were out on the desert with Moses and how finally the Lord, blessed be his name, brought them manna from heaven. Here, too, the Lord, blessed be his name, would provide manna.

Finally, the German army left the town of Lizhensk behind them as they headed toward the Balkans and death. As the dust clouds created by tramping boots subsided, residents came out of their hiding places like rabbits out of their burrows. Neighbors ran to greet each other. Though the Germans sacked what foodstuffs they could, there were provisions that had been hidden away. Jewish family helped Jewish family.

Out of the cellar crawled the Puderbeutels. After spending days cooped up in a confined space, each of them had a pungent odor.

Simon sent Isaak to his uncle Lieberman to get food. Even at an early age, Isaak was a dependable lad. He could be trusted to carry out any assignment that his father gave him. Isaak ran to his uncle's place and secured items that Leah turned into the first tasty meals the family had tasted in almost a week.

Gradually, life got back to normal. But there was something lurking that was even more frightening than the German army.

Sara, Rose, Isaak, Ethel Puderbeutel
Taken In 1921

Ethel, Rose, Sara, Abe, Leah, Gerson, Ben, Jim, Simon
Puderbeutel Taken In 1925

CHAPTER 5

WARNING SIGNS

• • •

No sooner had the *Mazel Tovs* from Isaak's Bar Mitzvah ceased than he soon found himself confronted by an insidious enemy: his fellow students and teachers of the Gymnasia. Simon, as was true with Jewish parents throughout the ages, believed that education insured good positions in society for his children. Though the cost of higher education was expensive, Simon had the means and felt that his children would lack for nothing when it came to preparation for making their way in the world. (In Poland, high school was called Gymnasia.)

Because Abe and Isaak were the oldest, they were first to enter the hallowed halls of Gymnasia. Many Jews attended Lizhensk high school. The rich ones received tutoring from Professor Yosef Depovski, who later became principal of the high school.

Gymnasia provided a special education. Latin was taught. One learned to read Caesar's *Gallic Wars* as he had originally written it. Higher mathematics was part of the required regimen. The group of students was small due to high tuition and consisted of a mixture of Jewish and Gentile students. Attendance on the Sabbath (Saturday) was required though one did not have to write on that blessed day. Isaak and his brother Abe were dressed in their best brogans with lederhosen (calf-length socks) to keep their legs warm. As they made their way to Gymnasia, they and their fellow Jewish students were greeted by catcalls and anti-Jewish slurs flung in their faces by Gentile youths. When they reached the classrooms, certain professors would separate the Jews from the rest of the class by seating them in the back. In addition, some professors laced their lectures with diatribes aimed at the Jewish portion of their class.

Jim Bartel (Simon's son), *He (dad) sent the children to the gymnasia, which you had to pay. Isaak was sent to a different town, a different gymnasia. The Jews had to sit separately. If they didn't sit where they were supposed to, they picked them up bodily and threw them out.*

Sometimes Isaak or Abe would come home from school with dirt splotches like leopard spots sprinkled all over their nice school outfits. At other times, their knuckles would be bloody; or welts would mysteriously turn up on their cheeks and foreheads.

Of course, Leah would view her children's shoddy condition with concern and a mother's love.

Isaak, you left the house spotless. Now your clothes look like your mother washed them in a mud barrel. What has happened to my lovely boy?

Nothing, Mother. I just took a little slip on the way home from gymnasia. I'm truly sorry, but it's nothing.

Look at your clothes! And your face—oh Son, the cuts on your face. Nothing, huh? A little slip. We'll see what your father has to say. I'll put something on those cuts, and you go get yourself cleaned up!

What Isaak dreaded was not the tone of his mother. Her words bore the bite of anger mixed with love. His father, however, was a different story. Simon was too busy with business to be bothered with raising eight high-spirited children; that was Leah's domain. Such was the reason he was feared. When he did have to talk with someone, the conversation was short and one-sided (sometimes, with a painful ending). So it was with foreboding that Isaak spent the rest of the afternoon until his father returned from the store.

First, supper would be served. All sat around the supper table with the head of the table occupied by Simon. A blessing was said for the food they were privileged to eat. The girls chattered with each other about their teachers or about some cute boy they saw at school. They would tease their younger brothers. Naturally, the older brothers were too grown up for foolish girl chatter. Abe would question his mother about the store and about different customers. Isaak, generally, would inquire of his father about what happened in the store during the day. Sometimes he would be quizzed by his father about Torah study, a subject Simon was well versed on as he studied at the Shul and was considered one of the learned.

This night, however, Isaak was strangely silent. He knew a serious talking to was in store and dreaded the prospect. As usual, Simon was rather quiet during supper but Isaak knew. He was aware of the words his mother would have used to relay the details of his dirty clothes and his banged-up face. But his father ate his meal while issuing the usual compliments to his wife relating to her fabulous cooking skills. He especially had praises for her boiled chicken though it didn't have an herb to its name. Leah would beam and ask everyone if they would like more. Most of the family politely declined. Simon, though, would ask for an extra drumstick just to let his wife know that her efforts were appreciated.

After dinner, Simon looked straight at Isaak and, without saying a word, pointed his index finger to that corner of the living room where serious chats took place. Rose, Sara, and Ethel looked at each other then scampered up the steps to their room. Abe, Gerson, and Jim knew better than to ask their father for anything right about that time and, in turn, slowly shuffled their feet up the stairs in hope of hearing some choice bit of conversation.

Leah hastened their departure. *Vamush, vamush (get, get), you scamps. You should be ashamed of yourselves wanting to listen in on your brother. Father has some serious business with him that is none of your concern. Now get to your room!*

Simon heard the sound of rapidly moving feet hit the wooden stairs then the slam of a door. Isaak sat in a chair facing his father and certain that he was not about to have a good time. As wood popped in the fireplace sending meteors of sparks cascading against the screen, Simon's words were slow and deliberate.

Isaak, your mother tells me that you came home with your freshly cleaned school clothes covered with dirt.

Yes, Father, it's so.

And look at your face! You've got cuts all over your cheeks.

Yes, Father.

And you told your mother that you slipped on the way home from school. Is that true?

I told her so.

Isaak had forecasted the storm correctly. Simon's face went from calm white to raging red, and fingers spasmodically turned from relaxed to clenched fists.

You wouldn't tell an untruth to your mother, would you?

Not intentionally. I wouldn't.

What do you take her for? A peasant ignoramus? A schlub (idiot)? Do you think she doesn't have eyes to see or a mind to know?

No, I do not take Mother for a schlub, but—but there was—there was a reason. Father, I couldn't tell Mother about the Gentile kids, about the fight.

Isaak, weren't you brought up to tell the truth, to not lie? Your mother has a warm heart that goes with a keen mind. She knows more in her little finger than all of you, children, combined. Who do you think I go to when I have a question? Come now! My leisure time's scarce. To the point, Son, what really happened on the way home?

Tears started rolling down Isaak's cheeks. Though he tried hard to squelch them, his thoughts turned to all the sacrifices his mother made to raise both he and his seven other siblings. In addition, smoke from the fireplace caused his eyes to water all the more.

I—I—I'm sorry, Father. I c—c—couldn't tell Mother. Abe and I were walking home from Gymnasium. We were just talking when some Gentile boys, who were standing around by the side of the road, started calling us names and saying mean things. They called us Hebrews. They said we should join our relatives, the swine. Father, we just continued walking, ignoring them. Then they started following us. They said our parents had Christian babies for Passover dinner. That's when my brother turned around and told them to shut their mouths. A taller boy with a knit cap threw a snowball that hit Abe in the chest. Father, we couldn't ignore them anymore. I turned and walked up to the boy who threw the snowball and gave him a push so that he fell back into the snow. He got up then started hitting me. Two of his friends helped. Abe joined me, and that's how I got the cuts and how our clothes became so dirty. Father, I didn't want to tell mother an untruth, but I knew how hurt she would be.

Simon's eyes began to soften, though the red color remained on his face. His jaws were tight.

Isaak, you have to set an example to your younger brothers and sisters. They look up to you. Number one. don't let me ever hear of you telling an untruth to your mother. It's the same as telling an untruth to me. She loves you and respects you. Don't make her lose that respect. Number two, when someone, Jew or Gentile, hits you once, hit him twice in return. That's all I have to say. Apologize to your mother! Good night.

Isaak couldn't leave the living room fast enough. It almost seemed as if his shoes wouldn't get out of the way of his feet. He reappeared in the kitchen, where Leah was finishing up with the dishes. Remorse radiated from Isaak's fogged glasses. The words emerged slowly from his lips—words of shame.

Mother, I'm deeply sorry for not telling you the truth. It will not happen again in the future.

He kissed her on her plump cheek and ran up the steps to his room, where his brothers greeted him like a conquering hero. After all, Isaak had emerged from their dreaded father's presence physically intact with the only wear and tear being his reddened eyes.

This was not to be the last of Isaak's or his siblings' encounters with anti-Semitic Gentiles. More facial abrasions accompanied dirty and torn clothes. Being the eldest, Isaak stood up for his brothers and sisters. Though his wire-rimmed glasses made him look like a bookworm, his appearance belied his physical strength. He was thin and wiry. His arm muscles resembled tight cords, developed from lifting heavy loads at his father's hardware store.

Jim Bartel (Simon's son), *My father went to a Yeshiva, which means strictly a Jewish school. Irving (Isaak), like I did, went to a religious school called Hoika. They will teach you also just the Jewish religion the Torah and the interpretation of the Torah. There was a Rabbi who was teaching those things. Irving said I'm not living here anymore. I'm getting out of here. That was about 1920.*

Isaac's Gymnasium Graduation Certificate read, in part, as follows: "Private Real-Gymnasium of Lezajsk having by decree of Ministrium of C.A.R. of 25 July 1916 ... Certificate ... Lieberman (mother's maiden name), Izak born on 31 December 1903 in Lezajsk, Galicja, Jewish religion ... Progress of the objects of study: religion, Polish language, German language, history, geography, natural history, drawings, gymnastics. He has missed twelve school hours unexcused."

On June 19, 1922, Isaak was issued his graduation certificate from The Municipal Real Latin School at Lezajsk. On it was stamped the seal from the Republic Of Poland. He attended this school—as well as pursued his other studies—from 1915 to 1922.

The dark of night was imperceptibly descending over Europe once again. Before the sun of human decency set behind the hills, darkness was preceded by a growing nationalist spirit in Poland and other parts of the continent. Nationalism began with an us-and-them mentality. "Us" were the Christian Poles who found a feeling of pride in reviving long dormant Polish institutions. "Them" were the others, the outsiders. Very slowly, the community proceeded to exclude Jews from civic and national institutions. Jews were, at first, segregated then economically strangled.

Isaak could see that his future boded ill simply because he was born Jewish and happened to live in Poland. His heart's desire was to be a doctor. He had the education and intelligence to achieve his dream. The only problem was that Jews were not allowed in Polish medical schools.

Ethel Nagel (Simon's daughter),

After Irving (Isaak) was finished with Gymnasium, he wanted to go to college. Unfortunately, the Poles would not let him get into the university because he was Jewish. So he decided to leave Poland.

It was a momentous decision in this young man's life and one that would not only change his life forever, but also change the lives of many others. He was a quiet, introspective young person. He talked little and listened much. At twenty years of age, Isaak could see that the opportunities were limited in his hometown. He had resoluteness and resolve to build a future for himself in America, though it had to be said he had a great deal of misgivings about leaving his parents and siblings behind. What faced him was the dark unknown. First, however, he needed to devise a plan to escape an increasingly hostile Europe. But how? Who did he know? He didn't have a lot of money, just a burning desire to make good in the world.

He went to his mother, Leah, and told her about his plans. When she broke out in tears, he almost wished he hadn't said a word to her. Maybe he would have been better off staying in Poland and working in his father's store; however, despite his mother's tears and pleadings, he convinced her that his future was to be found in America.

America. The word rang with promise and opportunity for all. It didn't matter what religion you have or nationality you were; America welcomed you with open arms and said, "I'll give you a chance." It didn't matter what family you were born to or how little money you had; If a person possessed determination and the desire to work hard, he could make it in America.

So it was that despite his mother's tears, Isaak won his parents' blessing to seek his fortune in America. Ever practical, Simon sat down with his wife and son; together they devised a plan. Isaak was sworn to secrecy. He could not, under any circumstances, discuss this subject with his brothers or sisters. If they, innocently, opened their mouths to someone, it could jeopardize Isaak's life. Though he longed to tell his brothers and sisters about his aspirations and about the land of opportunity he was going to, he had to still his tongue.

During the early 1920s, anti-Semitic nationalism was sweeping through Eastern Europe. The Nazi party was just beginning to gain power in Germany. Everywhere the question was "What to do with the minorities? We want them here for their money. We want them out because they're different from us. The perfect solution would be to have them out but for us to keep everything they have." So thought the Gentile population; thus, it was becoming quite difficult for a Jew to legally get out of many countries in Europe due to the fact that prior to departure, the Jew would be fleeced like a sheep.

For Isaak, the trip was going to be hazardous. It would take him through Nazi Berlin, where he had an uncle who would help him with the papers he needed to immigrate to America. Simon laid the plan out to Isaak in his private office at the hardware store so no one would listen in. He told Isaak about the uncle named Lieberman, on his mother's side, who lived in Cleveland, Ohio. He then told Isaak about the uncle named Thurm, who lived in San Francisco, California. Simon provided specific instructions on getting from Lizhensk to Berlin, Germany. From there, an uncle would provide him with papers that would get him out of Europe and over to New York. The plan then was to contact his uncle in Cleveland.

This perilous journey was Isaak's first step toward assuming family leadership. In a black-and-white photo taken in 1923, Isaac was thin with a resolute cleft chin. He had just a wisp of a black mustache to help hide his identity.

He called his brothers and sisters into his room and told them he was leaving to live with an uncle faraway. Of course, they pressed him for details; but he was closemouthed per his father's instructions.

I am going to reside with one of our relatives, who lives many miles from our town. My intention is to learn a trade and make a future for myself in a place my religion will not be held against me.

Surrounding him were seven teary-eyed faces.

Come now. Sarah, Rose, Gerson, the rest of you. Please don't cry. I will write. When successful, I'll return to you. Oh, little Ethela, not you too!

When his little blonde sister saw all the others crying, she too took up sobbing though she wasn't quite sure why.

Simon and Leah made plans for their son's departure though it broke their hearts. Isaak, more than they, could feel the smothering blanket of prejudice slowly covering his country. Plans were made. Due to fading memories—and perhaps a desire to protect the identity of those culpable—we shall call the uncle in Berlin Uncle X.

It was a warm spring evening in Poland when young Isaak Puderbeutel kissed his loving mother on her tear-stained cheek.

Oy Vey, Oy Vey (My God, My God) were the only words she would say. It was as though she were losing her son forever.

Isaak then put his head on her chest as she was taller than he and tried his best to comfort his mother.

Mother, I'm going for a better life, for our future. I will be back to you. I will always love you.

His father, with a face devoid of expression, beckoned his son to the wagon that would take them to the train station. Isaak lugged the heavy bag over the edge and into the wagon; then he climbed in next to his father. The departing son was dressed for his journey in a black suit so that he would look the part he was to play—a businessman.

The days were starting to get warmer. Flowers were sprouting in the fields and sending their fragrance floating on the warm evening air. Stars winked at each other. The wagon's metal wheel rims crunched against the dirt road as Isaak twisted his neck around for one last look at his home of twenty years. He lifted his glasses to wipe the tears off his face. He was a young man determined yet afraid of the unknown to come. Simon looked sternly ahead, expressionless. Yet underneath his unbending countenance lay a pained heart. He hated to lose his trusted son and worried about the hazards the young man would face on a journey through hostile territory. And what of the unknown America? Were the streets really paved with promise or was his second eldest son heading into an abyss? An unwelcome thought more and more found itself encroaching into Simon's consciousness, *What about our future?*

Horse hooves clopped a cadence in the night as they approached the railroad station. Down the Street of The Train they rode silently, each with his own thoughts. Back at the Puderbeutel house, a pall of sadness fell over Leah and the children; they had lost one of their own and had no idea if he would ever come back.

When father and son reached the train station, a slight pull on the reins brought the wagon to a halt. Slowly Simon handed Isaak the train ticket to Berlin. For the first time, as he looked his son straight in the eyes, an expression came to his face. He smiled with pride, and as he grabbed Isaak's shoulders with his powerful hands, he said,

Feel these hands, Son! With these I made my way in the world, and with yours, so will you in America. Remember, when you arrive in Berlin, only ask for Uncle X. He will take care of the next part of your journey. Be a pride to your mother and myself! May God, blessed be his name, watch over you.

Simon's face smiled proudly but his heart cried. The night air started to cool; on it, the sound of a train whistle was carried far into the distance. It sang a mournful tune, the song of loved ones leaving each other. Isaak, in his business suit, hopped down from the wagon. With his powerful arms, he swung the heavy suitcase to the ground. He then walked around to the driver's side and kissed his father on the cheek. Simon, who would not allow himself to show emotion, looked his son in the eyes and reminded him to check his papers. Did he have his ticket ready? What about his emigration papers?

Yes, Father, they are all in my left pocket. Tell Mother and the others that I'll write. I won't fail. I ...

Simon turned his head and got back up on the wagon. With a slight shake of the reins, the horse started off at a trot with a father who couldn't bear to have his son see tears rolling down his cheeks.

Meanwhile, Isaak lugged his grip up to the platform. The whistle blew louder and with more urgency as the train approached Lizhensk station. Steam whooshed out of all sides of the engine as it slowly puffed to a stop. This iron monster was one of those streamlined engines that were built in Germany.

The trip was going to take about ten hours and cover 500 miles across the heart of Poland and through the border of Germany. Isaak knew he had adequate papers for Poland. Germany? He wasn't so sure. The last thing Germany wanted was another Jew.

Dressed as he was, Isaak looked the part of a businessman and melted in with the other passengers. After the conductor took his ticket, Isaak found a car in the middle of the train. He stowed his suitcase in the luggage compartment and unobtrusively blended in. The conductor shouted out his universal *All Aboard!* A loud hissing emerged from between the engine's wheels while large puffs of smoke belched out of the smokestack. Pretty soon, all that could be heard inside the train was the clack of steel wheels on rails and staccato chattering of passengers.

Used to being alone because he was Jewish, Isaak found an empty seat and dozed off. And so the engine's Cyclops headlamp cut through the night. Towns with strange names rolled by: Tarnow, Krakow, Breslau. It was as if the syllables tumbled off one's tongue as quickly as the towns tumbled out of sight and faded back into Poland's night. Meanwhile, Isaak slept, knowing he would soon need all his wits about him.

Something jarred him awake. Possibly his mental time clock was giving him a warning. It was four o'clock in the morning. There was a passenger near the far end of the railcar who was having trouble sleeping and was reading a book. Isaak walked over.

Pardon me, Sir. Do you happen to know where we are near?

Why certainly, young man. I thought I was the only one who couldn't sleep on this cursed train. I could probably sleep better on the back of my horse, Blintzer. Oh, so sorry, but back to your question. Let me see. I'll take a look at my watch. Sush! Don't tell the Germans, but the Swiss make better timepieces. Those Germans, you know, think that they make everything better, but when it comes to timepieces, it's the Swiss. Oh yes, your question. I'm sorry, young man, you've had to stand there and listen to my gibberish. According to my watch, we've been traveling nine hours. That means we're very near Blubice on our side of the border.

Sir, I'm from a small town. Where is Blubice?

Right next to the border, young man. My, you certainly haven't traveled much.

Actually, I have, but in the eastern part of the country. This, if the truth be known, is my first international trip.

Well, you sure are well dressed. Pardon me asking. What business are you in?

Hard goods. Isaac didn't want to open his mouth and reveal too much. Better to keep the conversation sparse.

The passenger then gave Isaak the clue he was seeking.

By my watch, we should be at the German border town of Frankfurt in about fifteen minutes. Young man, where are you going?

Isaak gave the passenger a slight smile and a *thank you* as he turned upon his heels. Quickly, his mind raced as its time cogs began to turn.

Let's see. In fifteen minutes, we'll be in Germany, the riskiest part of this train trip. My papers, I don't know if they'll pass. The Germans are worse than the Poles, I've heard, when it comes to Jews. If they don't like the looks of my papers, they'll send me back to Poland. I didn't travel all this way for that. Hmm, there's risk either way. If I hide … if I don't hide … Probably five minutes from Frankfurt.

Isaak took a seat by himself at the rear of the car. He took something out of his pocket and started folding his papers; then he placed them back into his pocket. Suddenly, the engine's breath started getting longer. Puff … puff … puff … The train began to slow. Outside, little lights started to dot the side of the railroad tracks. They were coming into a town. It must be Frankfurt. The black-suited conductor walked through the cars, smiling at the passengers while the salutation, *Achtung! Frankfurt* punctuated the morning quiet. Sleepy eyes opened. Rustling of papers could be heard throughout as passengers got ready for their welcome to Germany.

The monster train came to a halt amidst screaming brakes and a hiss of steam. The doors of the first car opened to reveal four German policemen standing at the siding: three to check the papers of those departing and one whose job it was to move quickly through the train and make sure those onboard were fit to be let into Germany. Their uniforms were brown. This was a time when the Nazi party was just beginning to gain popularity. Ten years later, it would rule the country. Some said that a Jew was less welcome in Poland than in Germany. If one were Jewish, it probably didn't matter which country hated you more.

Isaak thought, *Here I am in Germany—the launching point to a better life or to a swift trip back where I came from.*

At the other end of the train, Isaak could hear a voice of authority: the German policeman was barking an order in his guttural voice, *Achtung! Staatsangeborigfeit! (Attention! Birth papers!)*

Shuffling of papers created a crackling sound throughout the train as hands reached into purses or pockets while the policeman, with a person's life in his hands, peered then stiffly walked over to the next passenger and the next and so on until he approached a young man with wire glasses.

Though sweat was soaking through the back of his suit, Isaak looked calmly up at the policeman

Yes, Officer, I have them right in my pocket. Here they are.

As the policeman, with the German Luger pistol strapped to his side, opened the papers, a small, shiny gold coin stared at him from inside the folds. It was a ten mark piece with the portrait of the Kaiser on its front. The coin was about the size of an American dime. Papers rustled as the gold coin slid from Isaak's identification papers to the policeman's right hand and from there into his pocket.

Dass Goot! (They're fine!)

With a stomping of military cadence, the policeman then marched off into the next car. Isaak felt like he was stuck to the train seat. His calm exterior soon disappeared and was replaced by wet palms and shaking hands.

An *Achtung! All Aboard* was shouted as the train huffed and puffed its way out of Frankfurt station. It soon gathered steam as Isaak's destination grew closer. Judging by the mental map he'd made of the journey, he would be in Berlin in about one hour. Isaak sat alone so as not to draw attention. Meanwhile, a bustle of activity took place all around him. People were gathering their belongings together in preparation for departure at Germany's capital city. Passengers of every description shuffled in and out of seats. Sleeping cars disgorged their mysterious strangers. Peasants sat near men in military uniforms. More and more of the latter began to be seen throughout Germany. After World War I, they didn't have jobs; but with the changing political tide, they were once again employed in their chosen vocation.

How far away I am! My home is stretching farther and farther behind me. These people look so different, so much more sophisticated than those at home.

So thought Isaak as the train's whistle blew and as the puffing of the engine slowed down. Dawn had not broken over Berlin yet. Lots of lights started showing up in the railcar window. He was approaching Germany's capital.

At the Berlin station, Isaak sat while all other passengers who were departing grabbed their luggage and stepped gingerly down the train steps. Some were chatting with each other; others lugged their burdens silently.

Berlin had a smell of sophistication. Businessmen and well-dressed women could be seen milling about. Cigarette smoke rose like burning bodies into the dark. As Isaak stepped off the train, he anxiously glanced from side to side, looking for suspicious police. There were none nearby. He was taken aback by the size of the Berlin station as compared with the small building in his hometown. This was a hub of international travel. Here was a small-town lad, dressed in a nice suit but was lost in the world. He noticed an abundance of men in crisp military uniforms going to their duties in various locations of the "new" Germany.

Over in the bowels of the depot, a pay phone beckoned. He dialed. The operator put him through.

Hello? Uncle X? This is Isaak, Leah's son.

CHAPTER 6

HUDDLED MASSES

• • •

The phone was answered by a caring but careful voice.

Isaak? Where are you now?

Berlin station, Uncle.

What do you look like?

Wavy black hair, wire-rimmed glasses. I'm about 5'8." Uncle, I am wearing a dark double-breasted suit.

Nephew, you stay near the pay phones. Understand? I'll be there within half an hour, and I'll find you. Don't go anywhere!

So Isaak stood by the pay phones watching various kinds of people drop their coins in and make contact with their connections. He tried to blend in with an air of sophistication which he, coming from Poland, did not possess. Actually, all his senses were assaulted by a grandness of scale that the city possessed. He stood and watched those that came and went, thinking that if he watched long enough, he too might become as cosmopolitan as they are. Suddenly, he was jerked out of his reverie by a tall, stout man, who looked him up and down. The man was dressed in a gray three-piece suit with a vest that had a gold chain drooping from it. A smell of tropical islands emanated off of him—a result of the imported shaving cologne he used. Before Isaak could comprehend, his uncle addressed him.

You must be Isaak, my sister's son.

The lad looked up and answered humbly. *Yes, sir, I am he.*

So you're the one I've heard so much about. A handsome young man you are, just like your father. A little short perhaps, but that runs in the Puderbeutel family. Ah, I see my sister dressed you well. She has very good taste. You look just like a business person. Such a mench you are. Oops! Better hold my tongue. This country's becoming as bad as yours as far as the Jews go. I see you have your suitcase. Guess you have everything. Is your belly empty?

Yes, Uncle. A meal would be most welcome.

You follow me!

With that, Uncle X took Isaak through the Berlin train station. Because his uncle was so tall, long strides were required to keep up. The pace was so fast that Isaak almost had to run while dragging his suitcase behind him. Finally, they reached the street with Isaak hastily gulping great quantities of air despite the good physical condition he was in. As the lad stared out into the street, he almost lost what little breath he had. Chattering past were machines that had never made an appearance in little towns like the one he was raised in. These machines carried passengers without the aid of horses in front. Furthermore, they were boxy and black and occasionally would backfire, causing those standing nearby to jump then look to see who'd been shot. These strange self-powered machines had windows like a stage coach. Their tires were made of a strange substance called rubber. Truly, Isaak had arrived in another world far more advanced than his. He wondered if he would ever be able to go back.

There, next to the curb, was Uncle X's car, clattering and chattering.

We'll put your suitcase in the trunk here. Get in, Lad!

With that, Uncle X opened a piece of metal in the back to reveal a storage area. He then opened the door facing the sidewalk while motioning his nephew inside. Entering, Isaak noted a big wheel on the side opposite from him. He couldn't figure out what that big lever sticking out from the floor was for. He saw a bunch of gauges and wondered what mysteries they revealed.

This was Berlin. Gone were the dusty, manure-strewn roads of Lizhensk. In this city, boulevards were paved and wide. Cars, like the one Isaak rode in, clattered past each other at the amazing speed of thirty-five miles an hour. People seemed like blurs in passing. Uncle X deftly pushed the clutch pedal while moving a lever on the floor to its appropriate gear position. At the same time, he moved a lever on the steering wheel that controlled their speed.

Isaak was amazed. He was sure that, at thirty-five miles per hour, his uncle would lose control and that they would end up a mangled mess, smashed against either another car or a light post. In Berlin, large buildings loomed out of hard concrete.

Finally, this monstrous machine reached Berlin's outskirts, where Isaak's uncle lived. X pulled into the driveway of a picturesque-looking dwelling. It was a large home in the French provincial style. The house seemed to be way too large for a single man. As Isaak was soon to find out, a woman had lived in this large home, which had been happy at one time.

As Uncle X brought the throttle level even with his right hand, a loud explosion burst out of the car's exhaust pipe. A sharp shudder almost bounced Isaak's head against the roof. He looked around to see if his clothes were on fire. It simply was the manner this early Mercedes used to shut down. It was hard to convince Isaak that this car was not trying to kill him.

A log was smoldering in the living room fireplace while another was giving off its smoke in a wood-paneled study. Mature trees stood majestically as they guarded a well-manicured garden. The smell of leather and burnt wood greeted Isaak's nostrils as he entered. He dragged his suitcase behind him like a ball and chain. By now, his suit was beginning to give off the pungent odor of his own sweat. X guided him to his room.

You must be tired. Take a shower, change. Helga, my housekeeper, will clean your clothes when she gets here a little later. How about a nap? We can talk later this morning. Does that meet with your approval?

Yes. Thank you, Uncle, for … everything.

Don't thank me yet. We have some work to do.

Later that morning, Isaak came to his senses. Where was he? It seemed as though he had slept for days. He changed into a pair of brown trousers that were calf-length. On his lower legs were lederhosen (calf-length socks). Over a red wool shirt stretched a pair of suspenders. This was the alpine fashion of the day. Except for a beer belly, Isaak could easily have passed for a burgermeister. Groggily, he stumbled into the study. His uncle spotted him out of the corner of his eye and shouted into the kitchen for Helga to get them some sauerkraut. He then motioned Isaak to sit down in one of the leather chairs. Before Isaak could wipe the sleepers out of his eyes, a schnapps was in his right hand so as to clear out the cobwebs. The leather made a snapping noise as it stretched to accommodate his body.

X began. *My dear nephew, son of Leah. We don't have a lot of time, yet there is much to be done. You see, documents must be obtained for you—special documents to get you out of this country and into the United States. The papers must be just so or ... Isaak, I hate to think about it. As you are well aware, this country does not like Jews, and it's getting worse. Yes, they put up with us for our money, for what we can do for them, but if most had their way—why, they'd shove us all into the ocean! Do you think getting out of this country is as easy as eating a piece of pumpernickel?*

The lad knew otherwise. He had no illusions that the trip out of Germany would be any less challenging than the trip into it.

Yes, Nephew, you were fortunate to get into the country. The political climate is changing. As you told me, a policeman turned his eye the other way. But luck is a fickle companion and may not always travel with you. As I said, the political climate in Germany is different now. That is why I live alone in this large house. My wife ... Gretchen ...

His words choked up in his mouth. X's eyes bored right through Isaak's thick glasses and into the subconscious. The young man squirmed a bit in his leather chair. As X's eyes grew bigger, they began to moisten.

I ... I ... don't know if I can bring myself—Pardon me, Isaak. She, along with some of her friends were walking from the Shul after Shabbus service and ... There was a group of youths who didn't like Jews. They had bats in their hands. It would be great sport to beat some Jews. My beloved Gretchen was such a beautiful woman. I wish you could have met her. Anyway ... Gretchen and her friends were kibitzing about this and that. They were about a block from the shul when these youths approached, laughing with their bats in the air. As one of the others, who survived, reported, Gretchen saw them and screamed. No sooner did her screams join those of her friends than the bats fell again and again. All the women were hit on the back, in the head. There was blood spattered all over the sidewalk.

Isaak gulped what was left of his schnapps to fortify himself. He had to pull his eyes away from his uncle for a moment. The man's hand gestures became more agitated. Rivulets of moisture ran down his cheeks as the words struggled out of his mouth.

None of the women were moving. As the youths walked away laughing, one of them turned around and kicked two of the women in the ribs just to make sure the job was done. Then after leaving their bloody bats lying on the sidewalk, they gaily sauntered away, each bragging to the other what he had done. As was told to me later, one of them was heard to say—"Juden shit." Isaac ... it ... it is hard. I ... I ... don't ... even know what words to use in describing to you. My beautiful, my loving Gretchen. One of the women played dead and, when these monsters left, crawled, as can best be described, over to the rest to see how badly hurt they were. She shook them, but none moved or even seemed to breathe. By now, a crowd had formed. Some others, who had left shul, came along and recognized through the blood their fellow congregants. Only one had a pulse—the woman who was left for dead. I won't horrify you with details of what the face of my Gretchen looked like. I was at home ill that day. A policeman knocked on the door. It seems there was a little disturbance near the shul. "Your wife, we think, is dead. Would you please come down to the morgue and identify her? It would be so helpful. The youths escaped down the street. It seems no one saw them or heard anything. But you can be sure that we will use our best efforts to find whoever did this."

X's hands shook. His cheeks quivered as he continued.

Isaak, it was the sorriest day in my life the day I had to go down and view Gretchen's body. I could hardly tell who it was. Her face was so swollen and covered with blood. Her beautiful dress was stained with gore. Oh … if … if it were only me there instead. I told them it was my wife then claimed that swollen semblance of what was once her. Well, Nephew, I buried her along with my happiness. As I threw clumps of dirt onto her coffin, I felt like I was throwing parts of me in there as well.

Isaak would not have been surprised if the back of his own chair burst into flames; that's how intense his uncle's stare was.

I'm a businessman. Our entire family has made its money in various business ventures. We are not, by nature, violent but certain things … certain things … have to … must be avenged. Those youths, there were four of them. They thought they had gotten away with it. After all, three Jews dead? In Germany? Who would care? The police? Are you kidding? A few marks here, a few marks there, and somehow the perpetrators disappear into the city. Nobody sees, nobody knows. Years go by. Case closed! But, unfortunately, one woman lives. She is able to supply descriptions. Isaak. I know people. I know how to grease palms with ten-mark gold pieces. These contacts of mine pointed out where I could find the bastards. "Vengeance is mine," saith the Lord. True enough but also mine as well. The first one was walking out of his house one morning, whistling a German folk song. I'll never forget his face as long as I live. His hair was blonde and down to the neck. He had blue eyes and a goatee. On his right cheek was a two-inch scar. Whether from a duel or fight, I couldn't tell. What I remember most were those thin lips, those cruel thin lips. Naturally, he didn't know me, so as I approached, he just kept on whistling his happy tune. A nine-millimeter slug doesn't make a very big hole, just large enough to kill you. The look on his face changed when he saw my Luger. It changed from nonchalance to fear. I only hope that he felt one-tenth of the fear those poor women felt. I pulled the trigger. He tried to yell, but all that came out was a grunt. Two more rounds in the head—just to be sure—and I quickly walked away, disappearing into the vast city of Berlin. The other three met similar fates at different times of the day, in different places. Just like in my wife's case, nobody saw a thing. Yes, Isaak, the police came calling.

Gun and bullets? Nothing to be found. Both lay at the bottom of the Elbe River. No evidence of gunpowder. The gloves I wore were nothing but ashes in the fireplace. They would have prosecuted me if they could. The evidence. The evidence … They couldn't find any. Sad and sordid though the whole situation was, Isaak, it's funny how the police cared a damned sight more about who killed some anti-Semite pieces of human garbage than who murdered three loving Jewish women.

The nephew's body was burning from head to belly. Could this be his uncle? This was his gentle mother's brother? Why, she didn't have a hateful bone in her. Who was Isaak to judge? What would he have done in similar circumstances?

That is why, Isaak, you and the rest of the family are to refer to me as X. I keep a low profile, do not stir up any interest in myself by others. The authorities are content to let matters rest. Now that you have heard, my distinguished-looking young nephew, we heat up that cold plate of sauerkraut for you. I know you must be hungry.

If the truth were told, Isaak was famished, except for the fact that his body was so shocked by his uncle's story that, hungry though he was, he didn't feel like eating. The two of them repaired to the dining table, where the housekeeper brought them some lunch. Isaak politely put a few forkfuls into his mouth and chatted about his family until his uncle finished eating. When X mentioned the mound of sauerkraut still remaining on Isaak's plate, his nephew remarked that he was saving his appetite for later.

Well then, we must get to work, X asserted. *You don't have long until you must leave Berlin for America. There are plans to be made, papers to be gotten. Do you have money?*

Yes, Uncle.

How much?

Five hundred United States dollars sent to me by my Uncle Abe in Cleveland. I will work for him to pay the sum back.

Abe? Abe who? inquired X.

It's Uncle Abe Lieberman.

Ah yes, I should have guessed. Another branch of the family. His generosity should have led me to know he was from our side. Helga! More schnapps!

Uncle, at the rate you're filling me with schnapps, I'll be a shicker (drunk) in no time.

Nonsense. A little alcohol steadies the brain and warms the heart. Besides, you'll need a steady brain to make sure you get out of this country in one piece. You've got a good plan, Isaak. Now let's go about executing it.

An intense month was spent by Isaak at X's home. Contacts were made, papers were acquired, boat passage was secured. For Isaak, it was a delightful interlude. He drove with his uncle all around Berlin, seeing the sights while studying various characters involved in his emigration to America. Some of those characters may be described as less than savory but necessary nonetheless. Finally, Isaak received his German passport—that coveted document with an Imperial Eagle stamped on the lower left-hand corner. It said all the right things in German. It was stamped in all the right places. The printing at the top was crossed out and replaced by just the right words that made Isaak a citizen fit to get the hell out of Germany. Below the photograph of a well-dressed but serious young man with wire-rimmed glasses was Isaac's scrawled signature and the date, June 23, 1923.

It was time to say farewell to a hard but generous man, who Isaak would be forever indebted to. X had taken the youth in, provided for him, and finally sent him forth.

So Isaak took his final car ride in Germany. He said his thank you and good-bye to the trusty housekeeper, Helga. Destination now: the port of Hamburg.

Waiting to take Isaak to America was the SS Thuringia. She was brand new—built in 1923 by Howaldswerke. Her length was an immense 473 feet. Her cruise speed was a brisk thirteen knots. The Thuringia was built for the Hamburg-American Line. The ship was painted all black with a white trim near the top. A single smokestack stuck out of her middle while fifty-foot radio towers sprouted from both the bow and stern decks. Radio wires radiated from these towers and were attached to the deck.

The sight of this immense steamship waiting at the Hamburg port overwhelmed the passenger from Poland. He had seen riverboats plying their wares up and down the Sun River but nothing that even came close to the size of this immense vessel. Capacity was 830 passengers in first class, 150 passengers in second class, and 680 in third class. The latter occupied the bowels of the ship in close proximity to the boiler room. Isaak was to be in second class—not at the top—but at least he would not roast at the bottom either.

X's car delivered its cargo right up to portside. X then got out to check Isaak's papers one last time. A little moisture showed itself in X's right eye as he hugged his nephew then kissed him on both cheeks. Isaak couldn't bear to look at his uncle. He was leaving everything familiar and heading into the unknown. He turned his head away while lugging his suitcase up the ramp. His voice was choked as he yelled,

God bless you, Uncle. I will never forget you.

Isaak, dressed in his double-breasted suit, then melted into a group of uniformed men checking luggage, tickets, and papers. A little while later, he made his way to the railing facing the shore. He looked vainly for his uncle's car, but both it and its owner were gone.

The trip would take slightly over two weeks to complete. The passenger record read as follows: Name—Puderbeutel, Isaak. Ethnicity—Poland, Hebrew. Place of Residence—Berlin, Germany. Here was a person who had never seen the ocean in his life now surrounded by saltwater. As Isaak soaked in the sun and the ambiance on the top deck, who should he spot but his longtime friend from Poland, Otto Huebner! After feeling alone in the world, despite being surrounded by an ocean of humanity, Isaak could not believe that of all the people in the world, Otto would turn up on the same ship headed to America. Smiling, Isaak rushed over to hug his friend. He could remember the countless hours they spent listening to the rabbis chant and sway in Shul when the boys would rather be out playing in the forest. Both of them had fathers who ran successful businesses. The salt air lightened Isaak's head.

So, Otto, my friend. Where have you been? What have you been doing? Married? Yes? Well, congratulations! Who is the lucky girl?

Rebecca? Ah! I remember her. She's a smart one and from a good family too. Otto, you've done well. Are you leaving the continent for good or just taking a trip?

Isaak found out that Otto had searched everywhere in their hometown to provide a livelihood for himself and his bride, but at every turn, he was thwarted by the Polish government because he was a Hebrew. Otto had reached the same conclusion as Isaak that there was no future for a Jew in Poland, and like Isaak—through family connections—he was able to acquire the necessary papers to spirit both himself and his wife out of Poland and ultimately out of Germany as well. Otto's wife had family in New York. They were in what was referred to in Yiddish as, the shmata (ready to wear) business.

As the days onboard ship passed by, Isaak reveled in the warm sun that bathed his body. Though he slept on the second deck, he was dressed so well that he was able to mix and mingle with those of society's upper crust who inhabited the top deck. Those of lesser means, who Isaak was actually more akin to, slept in the hot depths of the lowest deck. They could, however, frequently be seen looking out over the vast Atlantic Ocean while breathing the invigorating air of freedom and promise. Though it was unseemly for first class passengers to be seen in the company of those bilge rats from down below, Isaak found that each émigré had a compelling story to tell. Though their clothes were plain, there was knowledge to be had if one but opened his ears. Isaak spent much time visiting his friend Otto and his wife. All three had much in common. They would chat about their past and what opportunities lay ahead in their futures. One day, Isaak confided in his friend. They were getting close to New York. A warm sun tanned the young men's bodies as they lounged on the top deck. Trade winds carried smoke from the ship's stack west to New York as an advanced ambassador of a thousand new citizens. Water lapped at her sides as SS Thuringia made headway to her destination. Smelling the clean salt air made Isaak euphoric but also cautious.

Otto, my friend, we are getting close to our new home. Many years have we known each other. Otto, I can only trust in you right now. There are those onboard who will steal. Four hundred dollars is all I have. Keep two hundred of it in safekeeping. You will return it to me after we pass through immigration.

Itch, you are a true friend. Being trusted with two pictures of Ben Franklin is a grave responsibility. I will have my wife hide them away with her private things. I tell you she can keep things better than a bank vault. Itch, when she gets hold of a gold piece, it disappears to the point that not even her purse knows where it is. I once bought a bottle of 100-year-old Napoleon Brandy. When I went looking for it for, you know, a little sip, it was gone. Everywhere I searched. When I asked her if she had seen it, she said it was in a safe place. I said, "A safe place for whom? Me or it?" She told me that it would serve well for a special occasion. Two years later, Itch, it surfaced at her parents' silver wedding anniversary. I'm lucky the fumes didn't leak out in the meantime. Ha, ha, ha.

Finally, through the haze, land was spotted. A loud bellowing erupted from the ship's steam whistle. Passengers from all decks gathered by the top deck railing and gazed to see what their future home looked like. Of course, all they could see initially was a thin black line. As the outline of tall buildings grew clearer, passengers rustled to fetch their luggage (if not so rich) or to summon help (if better heeled).

Look, look!

Words of wonder wafted through the summer air. The date was July 25, 1923. It was just turning hot while humidity fell over everyone like a warm, wet blanket. The scene looked like a black-and-white photo. The steam ship was black and white. Its steam was black. The passengers' clothes were black and white. Even Jewish beards were a mixture of salt and pepper. New York's tall buildings were black, white, with an occasional brown one mixed in.

A sight greeted these two-week voyagers that brought New York Harbor back into real-life prospective—Ellis Island in living color. This was the passageway through which all who entered the east coast of the United States would pass. An expanse of blue ocean outlined a large, castle-like building that was surrounded by cool green lawns and by mature trees. This building had four delicate Islamic-type spires and one large building wing on each side of the main hall. This castle-like edifice was made of brick and plaster. Just west of Ellis Island stood the Statue of Liberty, welcomer of huddled masses.

As the SS Thuringia approached the shore, the crush of humanity on deck was almost suffocating. Those who were hoping to emigrate looked with wonder at their home-to-be. Those just traveling for pleasure could not help but to be impressed by what they saw.

As the ship approached Ellis Island, its whistle bellowed a challenge. *Booo! Booo! Welcome these strangers into your midst for they may be better men than you.*

On that hot July day, over 1,600 souls watched Ellis Island's spires reach out from the Atlantic's deep blue waters. Finally, the gangplank was rolled out to accept a crush of humanity encompassing every segment of social strata. Men, women, and children pressed against each other as they lined up to be processed. Ellis Island Immigration Hall looked like a huge train terminal accepting incoming passengers while jettisoning the outgoing into ferries that took the new arrivals past the majestic Statue of Liberty and onto the Port of New York. First, arrivals would pass through a long archway that led to the front door framed by an arched window thirty feet high. There were two equally large arched windows on either side of the door. Inside waited immigration officials ready to check papers and luggage. In addition, each person or family who wished to become a resident had to have a sponsor—someone who would guarantee that the immigrant would not become a ward of the state.

Isaak looked for his friend Otto but was unable to locate him. Otto and his wife would wait until Isaak processed through. Of that, he was sure; then his two hundred dollars could be recovered. Though Isaak could speak little English, his papers passed muster; and he presented a document showing that his Uncle Abraham Lieberman would sponsor him. Isaak cut a trim figure in his suit. He was quickly processed through while other more shabbily dressed souls were detained for further questioning. As Isaak passed out the rear of the Ellis Island

Terminal, he was sure he would spot his friend Otto waiting for him. To his horror, his so-called friend was nowhere to be found.

So as Isaac waited for a ferryboat to take him to the Port of New York, he learned his first lesson in the new world: trust few. Warm air blew over Isaak's face as he was crowded along the edge of the ferry's deck. His right hand held a viselike grip on his only possession: a suitcase. Finally, the crowd rumbled off the ferry speaking enough languages to confuse the Tower of Babel. Along with the rest, the ferry also spit out Isaak. With only two hundred dollars left in his pocket, he was in no position to build up a wardrobe. In all his days, he had never seen such tall buildings. How did they keep from tipping over? Practicality prevailed over circumstance. Isaak found a Yiddish-speaking cabbie who took him to a ten-dollar-a-night hotel. From there he contacted his Uncle Abe Lieberman in Cleveland. Isaak told his uncle about his boat trip, his supposed friend, and his present finances.

Uncle Abe wired him a sorely needed $500. With that, Isaak secured some American casual clothes and a train ticket to Cleveland. This young stranger to the home of the free held a train ticket and a piece of paper which had on it, *Abraham Lieberman, 10100 Olivet Avenue, Cleveland, Ohio.* Of course, Isaak wasn't really sure where Ohio was, much less, Cleveland. Distances were so large in this new country that he would leave it up to the train to find the place for him.

This trip would probably take as long as the one from Lizhensk, Poland to Berlin, Germany or about ten hours. Never in his life had Isaak seen so many people crammed into a city so huge. All ethnicities of the globe were represented here: Irish, German, Russian, Jew, Hispanic, Black, and who knew what else? There were streets of grandeur and of slovenliness.

A taxi, driven by a Negro, dropped Isaak, who now sported a short-sleeved shirt and khaki trousers, off at the Manhattan train terminal. Fare was fifty cents; so Isaak, not accustomed to tipping, handed the driver the fare, took his suitcase out of the man's hand, and headed for the terminal entrance. He couldn't understand this black man's angry utterings because, first of all, he didn't speak very good English, and secondly, he paid the man. So why was he angry? *Sonofabitch foreigners* made no impression on one of New York's new arrivals.

Highlights of Abraham Lieberman's Affidavit of Support for Isaak read as follows: Where were you born? Posdklostov, Austria. When were you born? April 2, 1882. When did you arrive in the United States? November 10, 1904. How many dependents have you now? Wife and three children. What is the approximate value of your real estate? Ten thousand. What is your occupation? Huckster.

Once again, Isaak found himself aboard a steam train huffing and clacking to strange places. On this train, however, Isaak could relax in the knowledge that there were no anti-Semitic conductors or police to kick him off. With his wire glasses, he looked like an intellectual and quite blended in with his surroundings, except for his accent and limited English. Once again, the clicking of metal wheels over steel trails beat out a cadence of hope in Isaak's subconscious. Here was a country of unsurpassed marvels: primitive forests that stretched for miles, then industrial factories belching jobs up into the stratosphere. Isaak had trouble making out what his neighboring passengers were saying. They spoke a language foreign to him: English. Some words could be made out such as *car, factory, dance the Charleston, stock market.* He had no idea what these words meant. Yes, that would be a challenge. Learn this strange language. He could do it. Many English root words came from Latin. That was a language he knew well. If there were only any Romans left to talk to! Oh well, there would be many challenges for sure, not the least of which was the debt he owed his Uncle Abe. It was well known in his family that nothing was free. If money was borrowed, it had to be repaid; if money was given, it was to be returned.

Isaak knew that to begin with, he would, in effect, be an indentured servant until his debts were paid off; only then could he forge his future. Through Pennsylvania and over the Appalachian Mountains, the locomotive chugged while the warm night air wrapped its arms around the young immigrant. America was hugging Isaak to its bosom and saying to him,

You don't have to speak English. All languages are mine. Just have a desire to better yourself, and I will provide.

He fell asleep amidst the hypnotic swaying of the train. Eight hours later, when his eyes opened, he thought it was a mirage he was viewing outside the windows. What he saw was Pittsburgh, a huge example of America's industrial might. This was a steel town that blasted heat from out of the mouth of hell. Isaak had never seen such tall smokestacks in all his life. Maybe they were just some leftover from a dream. The smoke and hiss, however, were very real. The train sped on, stopping off in Akron after crossing the western border of Pennsylvania.

Smokestacks filled the warm air with the choking odor of warm rubber. Unbeknownst to Isaak, he was passing through the tire-making capital of the United States. What other passengers on the train took for granted flabbergasted this young man from Poland.

Finally, the locomotive's rapid puffing turned into a cough. They were approaching Cleveland. The hot summer air started to cool down; its temperature lowered by the presence of Lake Erie. Isaak found himself in the midst of another huge city. But this city was different. It sat on the edge of a lake that was as large as an ocean. Each clack of the steel wheels took longer and longer until finally this metal caterpillar shuddered to a stop amidst a giant plume of steam. The conductor, dressed in his black uniform, went through picking up tickets.

All aboard for Cleveland. Make way for those getting off!

Isaak could understand only one word: Cleveland. He knew he was at his new home, so he lugged his suitcase down the metal steps and walked into the crowded terminal. He now stood at one of his newly adopted country's commercial crossroads—a city bounded on one side by the east, on the other side by the Midwest, and on the north, Lake Erie. Isaak had much in the way of intelligence and business acumen, yet he also had little. He was lacking in financial resources, knew nothing of his new country's customs, and was unable to even understand what these Americans were talking about. Yes, this young man had lots to learn.

His education started the minute he picked up the telephone to call his Uncle Abe. In Poland, there were very few telephones. In fact, his family was one of the first to have a phone. Initially, as is the case with many new innovations, only the wealthy had them. This phone was made out of two pieces, one of them attached by a long cord. Each piece looked like a black ice cream cone. Isaak clicked the receiver ten times, got the operator, and heard an unfamiliar voice with a European accent on the other end of the line. It was his aunt. She sounded kind but rushed. With three children to raise, a husband to care for, and an immigrant she was about to provide shelter to, this was understandable. Abe Lieberman, on his Application of Support for Isaak, put his occupation as Huckster. That was not entirely true. He was a Fruit Merchant. At four thirty in the morning, he would go down to the produce market, buy his goods, then stock his fruit stand in downtown Cleveland. It was harsh work, but it paid the freight for a wife and three children. With great excitement, Isaak's aunt told him she would fetch his Uncle Abe, and he would pick Isaak up at the terminal entrance.

July heat pounded the sidewalk in oppressive waves. Isaak stood at the front of the Cleveland Terminal waiting for his "rich" uncle to arrive when up to the curb pulled this clickety clacking contraption, the likes of which Isaak had never laid eyes on. It was black and looked like a buckboard wagon with an engine attached to the front. In actuality, this was an early pickup truck. It was a Model A Ford with a truck bed in the back to carry fruit. Isaac's "rich" Uncle Abe was wearing denim overalls with suspenders to keep them attached to his body. He resembled a Jewish Santa Claus, except he was not fat but tall and had a brown beard instead of a white one. His arms were large and his shoulders broad from hauling fruit. A smile creased the whiskers of his face. He hugged Isaak and just about cracked his nephew's shoulder blades. The hot summer air brought forth various fragrances of the fruit that stained Abe's overalls. Sweat streamed off his forehead.

Isaak got into the front seat, not sure if he was about to ruin his new clothes by sitting on a peach, a tomato, or, heaven forbid, a plum.

So, you young mench, how was the journey?

The Ford's four-cylinder engine clickety clacked down the street. Each gear made a grinding sound as Abe moved the shift lever. Beads of perspiration started to drip off Isaak's face as heat welled up from inside the truck. Odors of innumerable fruit loads made themselves available to Isaak's nose. So this was his "rich" uncle?

As he wiped sweat off his face, Isaak answered his uncle.

Enlightening but exhausting, Uncle. I started in my hometown then went by train to Berlin. Luckily my papers worked. There Uncle X took me in, got me the needed passport papers, and sent me by ship here. This country is so big. Everything's so big. I can't believe it! The different people, strange machines ... It's so much to take in.

As the sweat dripped down the back of his neck, Isaak continued though he almost had to shout to make himself heard above the clattering truck engine.

Uncle Abe, I want to work for you, pay your money back. Then I will study at night to learn a profession.

Isaak, you don't have to worry about the money.

Yes, Uncle, I do. It was a kindness you extended me but a kindness that must be paid back.

This was the pledge that began Isaak's sojourn in Cleveland. Summer turned to fall. Soon icy winds of winter blew in off Lake Erie. These were cold northern winds from Canada. The cold was similar to European cold—a kind that could chill a man to the bone and leave him sick or dead if he did not respect it.

And so it was that young Isaak shared Abe Lieberman's home. True, the house was a crowded place; but room was found for the newcomer, a garret up in the attic area. The quarters were cramped but warm in winter from heat that rose from downstairs. It became very hot in summer for the same reasons. None of this mattered to the ambitious young man who occupied this garret. He was up at four in the morning to help his uncle fetch fruit from the produce market. He would then sell fruit at the stand during the day. When evening fell, he attended school toward an end of learning a profession. It was not an easy life. During winter, cold northern winds swept into Cleveland. It was as though Lake Erie wrapped the city in her Arctic glove and squeezed the life out of it. Isaak would bundle himself up and join his Uncle Abe in their chattering truck as it slipped and slid down to the produce mart. It was dark and cold. Oftentimes, snow flurries were so blinding that one could only see five feet in front of the truck. Abe would pray in Hebrew that he didn't hit anybody or damage his only means for earning a living. Isaak prayed that he would reach a year older in age.

Meanwhile, Lake Erie's freeze tried to chill the life out of Isaak; but his shoulders were strong from hauling hardware and fruit, his arms hard as tree limbs. Sometimes in the morning, tears of tiredness from studying late the night before would actually freeze to his cheeks. He didn't let it faze him. He was going to become a pharmacist. He was going to do what the government of Poland wouldn't allow him to do. They'd not allowed him to be a doctor because he was a *Hebrew.* But this was America. If a person had desire and stamina, they could become whatever they wanted. No one cared if you were Jewish, Catholic, or Pagan.

It came to pass that after spending one year in Cleveland, Isaak received his Certificate of Preliminary Education from the Ohio State Board of Pharmacy. At this point, Isaak was becoming Americanized. His fashions were those of an urban swell. He still wore his trademark wire glasses. In addition, when not selling fruit, he would sometimes go out on the town wearing a white shirt buttoned at the neck, a black bow tie, a sport coat, and a leather cabbie hat. By day, Isaak plied his trade as a Huckster (Fruit Vendor). By night, he was either learning to socialize with American girls, who found his broken English cute; or he was studying to become a pharmacist. Everything was going according to plan, or so he thought.

The Thuringia

ADD TO YOUR ELLIS ISLAND FILE

Associated Passenger	Date of Arrival	Port of Departure
Puderbeutel, Isaak	July 25, 1923	Hamburg

Built by Howaldtswerke, Kiel, German
11,343 gross tons; 473 (bp) feet long.
wide. Steam turbine engines, triple
screw. Service speed 13 knots. 830
(150 second class, 680 third class).

Built for Hamburg-American Line, Ger
1923 and named **Havelland**. Rename
Deben in 1945. Scrapped in 1949.

Photo: Arnold Kludas Collection

SS Thuringia

SS Thuringia

LIBERTY ELLIS ISLAND

192.168.4.70 ▸PASSENGER SEARCH ▸GIFT SHOP ▸FAMILY SCRAPBOOKS ▸YOUR ELLIS ISLAND FILE ▸IMMIGRANT EX

- Passenger Record
- Original Ship Manifest
- Ship
- View Annotations
- Create an Annotation
- Back to Search Results

PASSENGER RECORD

Here is the record for the passenger. Click the links on the left to see more information about this passenger.

ADD TO YOUR ELLIS ISLAND FILE | VIEW ORIGINAL SHIP MANIFEST | VIEW SHIP

SAVE AND PURCHASE DOCUMENTS

View both the original image of the ship on which this passengertravelled by clicking on the blue buttons above this Passenger Record.

Name	Puderbeutel, Isaak
Ethnicity	Poland, Hebrew
Place of Residence	Berlin, Germ.
Date of Arrival	July 25, 1923
Age on Arrival	19y
Gender	M
Marital Status	S
Ship of Travel	Thuringia
Port of Departure	Hamburg, Germany

Passenger Manifest for Isaak Puderbeutel

Ellis Island

CHAPTER 7
GO WEST

• • •

Just when Isaak's world was totally organized and in order, a telegram arrived addressed to Irving Bartel. In line with his adoption of a new country, new ways of dressing, a new language, and a new profession, Isaak decided it was high time to Americanize his name. Isaak was too Old Testament. Puderbeutel was awkward and hard to pronounce. With a little coaching from his Uncle Abe in Cleveland, Isaak had changed his name.

Irving had another Uncle Abe. This one was his father's brother who went by the name of Abe Thurm. The reason his last name was Thurm, according to Jim Bartel (Simon's son),

He had to take the mother's maiden name. The reason was they were not married. They were married according to the Jewish religion, not according to the law. That is why he was named Thurm. That was my great-grandmother's maiden name.

Abe Thurm lived in San Francisco, California. He was a spitting image of Irving but an older version. He had the wavy black hair and dark features and wore glasses, except for the fact that his were a thicker black-rimmed variety. Abe had a women's ready-to-wear clothing store on Market Street. In Jewish vernacular, he was in the schmata business. Most of the people in it were Jewish. The telegram, to Irving, read as follows:

March 25, 1925. Irving Bartel. My advice is come to San Francisco. Business prospects and living conditions much better. Preparations

unnecessary. Do not go to any expense other than railroad fare. Give up the idea of going to New York. Consider your future first. Wire when leaving. A. Thurm, Twelve Seventy-Five Bay Street.

Irving thought long and hard. What road to take? He had a new name. Why not a new career? What were his odds of becoming a pharmacist in New York with his limited English skills? Not only that, but getting up at four in the morning to sell fruit on a street corner was not what he wanted his future to be. His Uncle Abe Thurm could introduce him to those who would teach him how to sell women's coats and suits. He could, at the same time, hone his English.

Once again, Irving was fortunate enough to find a relative that would include him in a crowded house. Abe Thurm had a wife Fanny, a three-year-old son Gerson, a two-year-old son David, and a seven-year-old daughter Hilda. His women's coat and suit store was named after his wife and was called Fannette's. It sat on the south side of Market Street, between Third Street and Fourth Street, and about half a block away from a well-known department store called The Emporium.

One day after work, Irving told his Uncle Abe Lieberman of his decision to seek his fortune in San Francisco. His uncle was sad to see him leave because Irving had become part of the family, so to speak.

Irv, it's probably for the best. You'll find the California climate much more to your liking and won't have to freeze your tuchas off like we do here. Of course, it saddens me to see you go. You were like a son to us. A mench, you've become. So very Americanized though we still have to get that Yiddish out of you. Whether your future is in the schmata business or the pharmacy, only he who made us knows. Your aunt and I send you off not only with our best wishes, but with a little street knowledge as well. Now our little ones can have their garret back to play in. Irving, your memory will always dwell there. God be with you.

For Irving, it was once again the moist eyes. Once again a loved one he must leave. A wayward voyager, leaving one port only to land in another. Though he was leaving Cleveland, never to return, the memory of his experiences stayed with him all of his days. He was proud of what he learned in the freezing darkness of predawn. His merchandising, haggling, and sales skills were to serve him well in later years. Strangely enough, the smell of fruit never completely left Irving's consciousness.

For the last time, Irving sat in Abe's Ford pickup truck as it clattered down the street, back to the Cleveland train terminal. Ironically, it was summertime again. Heat sent its shimmering waves up from the asphalt. As the truck's engine clattered, Irving reflected back on where he was and where he was going. Were they tears or just sweat that he quickly wiped away with his hand? The young man with wire-rimmed glasses had arrived in the United States as Isaak Puderbeutel and was now heading west as Irving Bartel. Again, weeping relatives were wished farewell. Irving had salted away enough to pay his Uncle Abe Lieberman not only the five hundred dollars loaned to him, but also a little more for the kindness tendered. In addition, he had sufficient for train fare to San Francisco.

The pickup truck clattered up to the entrance of the Cleveland train terminal. One year before, the truck had picked up Isaak. This time it was depositing Irving. Whenever Irving would start to think he was better than he was, he would recall his days selling fruit on the street corner. Those thoughts would invariably bring him down to size. Uncle Abe deposited his pupil, along with the ever-present suitcase. Uncle gave nephew a hug that would have squeezed the breath out of most; then Abe pinched Irving's cheek the way he would have pinched a peach to make sure it was ripe—gently but firmly. Irving hid his wince behind a broad smile.

Uncle, I can never pay you and Auntie back. No matter how much success I achieve, there will never be enough I can do to repay your generosity. I learned much. What I have learned, I will wisely use. Many thanks to you and your entire family from the bottom of my heart. If you or yours ever call on me, consider me your servant in whatever you may seek. Irving's eyes looked up into his smiling uncle's bearded face. It was time to move on.

A cool breeze blew off Lake Erie, caressing Irving's hair and drying the beads of sweat on his forehead. A train was once again waiting to carry him into his future. This trip was to take him two days, 2,200 miles, and nine states.

The engine stood at the head of a long string of cars. Like a dog eager for a walk, it panted and puffed. Irving got onboard, stored his battered suitcase, and settled into a plush velour seat. No more hauling fruit for him. He was going to be a merchant—a clothes merchant. Before his trip was through, Irving would pass through Ohio, Indiana, Illinois, Missouri, Kansas, Colorado, Utah, Nevada, and finally the golden state of California. The train huffed, and it creaked, and after that, it squeaked. Finally it got its running breath. The odor of Lake Erie was still in the air as Cleveland receded into the distance. This train of opportunity quickly made its way toward the business cross-road of America—Chicago—where it would disgorge some passengers and take on others who were heading west. That was where the new America was. Gold and silver had long since been wrenched from the ground. Now there was a different kind of gold; it was in the form of growing businesses and in real estate. Ironic. In the previous century, a piece of land was valued by what was in it. Now it was valued by what could be put on it. As this centipede of dreams sped along, Irving's thoughts floated out over the Great Lakes. Some thoughts were pleasant like puffy white clouds. Others were dark and troublesome like the black thunderheads that brought winter storms tearing out of the north.

Away from Chicago chugged Irving's train. The damp smell of the Great Lakes gave way to a dry odor of wheat as puffs of steam floated into the clear, hot skies of Kansas.

CHAPTER 8

A FAMILY GROWS TO PROMINENCE

• • •

Meanwhile, back in Lizhensk, Poland, Simon Puderbeutel was building his family name into one of the most prominent in Lizhensk. His hardware store was flourishing despite the fact that Germany was defeated in World War I. Instead of military rifles, he supplied fine hunting pieces to those with means to purchase them. In addition, hardware items never went out of style. Jew and Gentile alike found their way to his place of business—though the latter, grudgingly. Irving's sisters Sarah and Rose were beginning to blossom into attractive young ladies. Bespeaking their social position, they generally dressed well though conservatively. Rose had the delicate attractive look of her father with her black hair short and parted in the middle. Sarah, on the other hand, had her mother's stocky features along with the kind smile. Sarah's hair was even shorter than her sister's but worn more stylishly with black bangs hanging over her forehead. Though a relatively young man, Simon's short beard was gray, which added to his reputation as a wise man—someone who's opinion was sought after by many. Simon was seldom seen in public casually or shabbily dressed. Generally, he wore wool slacks, a sport coat, a tie, and a Homburg hat—unless, of course, he was in temple. There he would wear the required skull cap. The Puderbeutel brothers were beginning to grow up as well. Abe took over Irving's role as caretaker for his sisters and younger brothers. Increasingly, Jews were being segregated in public schools and excluded from attending institutions of higher learning. Simon and Leah insisted on education as a cornerstone to their children's upbringing.

Ethel attended primary school. Her sisters and brothers were of high school age excepting little Ben. Simon's solution was to see that they all attended private Jewish schools and gymnasia. By doing so, he removed his children from a lot of the prejudice that was prevalent in Poland. In Jewish schools, there were other affluent children for the youngsters to forge friendships with. As for gymnasia, it was mostly affluent Jewish parents who could afford this form of advanced education. While little Ben and Ethel were in their early school years, they were still exposed to the stricter educational standards of Jewish rabbis.

Leah kept the books while Simon courted customers for their hardware store. Letters dutifully arrived from their son who had voyaged to foreign shores. Irving would usually address his letters to Leah because he knew how worried she was for him. He would then relate interesting business tidbits to his father. Naturally, he would inform Leah about her brother Abe Lieberman and tell her all about how Auntie Lieberman was and what the kids were doing. Whenever Leah would read these letters, she made sure her children were gathered about. Irving knew this; as a result, he would be sure to include some fact of interest for both his brothers as well as his sisters. Due to the fact that he wrote once a week, a running commentary was maintained. Irving's brothers thought he was making up stories to keep them entertained. In Lizhensk, there was no electricity or telephones until the late twenties. Among the first, in town, to own a telephone were the Puderbeutels. Only the financially elite could possess one of these marvels. Imagine being able to talk to someone across town or across the ocean through a thin wire attached to the wall! Such was the stuff magic books were made of. Naturally, laughter would break out when Leah read Irving's accounts of telephones in train stations that everybody could use. Abe would punch Gerson in the shoulder.

He, in turn, would hit Jim. The girls were too mature for roughhousing. They would just face each other and laugh; then Irving would mention all kinds of cars. Car? What was that? A wagon with no horse in front? What did Irving take them for, ignoramuses? Then when his letters mentioned city streets with electric wires running down them and large conveyances that carried fifty people, his siblings were sure Irving had made up these stories just to spark their imaginations.

The vast distances prevalent in America were vividly described by Irving. In addition, he told his family about the city of New York, where there were as many people as there were in all of Europe. Sarah and Rose's eyes would open wide. Little Ethel could barely comprehend the things her older brother was describing. To her, it was as though this place called America was a land found in fairy tales. Abe, Gerson, and Jim loved hearing about what kind of lives their cousins lived. They could scarcely believe that there was this conveyance that you loaded your goods in the back of, and it chugged down the street at thirty miles an hour. Either their brother had a wondrous imagination or America's streets were truly paved with gold. The girls giggled to no end when Irving described young American women wearing sleeveless dresses. Though Irving still was not very proficient in English, he found the term "flapper" awfully funny. So, too, did his siblings in a little Polish town; then Leah would read out loud,

You would not be able to grasp the immensity of a city like Chicago. It sits on a lake as large as an ocean. As far as you can see, there are buildings as tall as the Alps. Beyond that are the great manufacturing facilities. Then, there are huge rail yards for shipping grain and all types of merchandise. The buildings are so large that a person can walk in the shade a good part of the day because the sun never reaches the ground. Black cars are everywhere and are owned by common people. Everything is run by electricity. You don't light oil lamps for light. You simply turn on a switch! People use wood fireplaces for entertainment. They heat their homes with coal furnaces.

Little Ethel's blond hair silhouetted her wide eyes.

Mother? What's a switch? What is that word elec ... Oh, I can't pronounce it.

Jim laughed a hearty laugh at his little sister.

Silly sister. The word is electricity. Not that I've seen any. But some customers in father's store have talked about lamps that don't have to be lit and about machines that don't require steam to run. It's hard to believe. These customers say they saw things like this in big cities such as Vienna.

Leah, of course, had a few choice words for her ill-traveled son.

Jim, my loving nudnik, you should know better than to talk that way to your sister. Have you traveled so far and so wide as to know for sure that what you have read about exists or not? Until you positively see, it would do you well to be more patient with those younger than you.

Yes, Mother.

Jim, though he got some laughs from his brothers at the expense of his sister, was sorry he opened his mouth.

CHAPTER 9
AMBER FIELDS

• • •

The train carrying Irving, raced across the wheat fields and the prairies of Kansas. Smoke pushed its way out the stack at a fast staccato pace as though the engine was about to have a heart attack. Brown flatland, as far as the eye could see, greeted the young man's eyes.

By my father's talis, there's enough wheat here to feed the world.

And he was right.

It was a good time to take a nap. All there was to look at was miles of featureless flatland. A slight nudge would wake him when it was time for another delicious meal. In all his travels, Irving had never eaten such scrumptious dishes. He still kept pretty much to himself since his English was halting and since Yiddish speakers were hard to come by in the vast stretches of Midwest America. Soon the terrain changed, and there were more mountains to be seen. The train was passing through Mormon Utah. This state threw up a challenge to those wanting to pass through, whether they were aboard a covered wagon or riding in a steam-powered passenger train. Mormons had forged a trail of blood and sweat so that trains could glide on shining steel all the way to Provo and beyond. There were peaks, mesas, and mostly flat, desolate land fit for buzzards. Humans had settled in Provo and Salt Lake City, where the train stopped. As usual, some passengers got on while others got off. Little inkling did Irving have that his future wife came from Salt Lake City. She would be from a family that composed part of Salt Lake's small Jewish community. Not only were they tolerated, they flourished. At the time Irving was passing through Salt Lake, his future wife was but a little child.

Irving's train sped through the barren landscape of Utah and into the much more interesting topography of Colorado. It was a state of unsurpassed beauty. This region still bore vestiges of the Wild West. Denver next greeted the train. It welcomed visitors from all parts of the country with its golden capitol dome. Its homes were built of brick to insulate their residents from the cold snows of winter and from the heat of summer. Irving heaved his chest to suck in more of the thin air that permeated these high altitudes. He relished the cool breezes that swept down from the Rockies as though they were ambassadors of the west, greeting those who had enough pluck to brave mountain ranges called Rockies and Sierra Nevada. Those with stalwart hearts could, if the mountains would let them, find their fortune in San Francisco.

It seemed to Irving that gold nuggets lay on the sidewalks of Denver for citizens to pick up as they passed by. Of course, in his heart, he knew that the gold in this town was not everywhere. Yet somehow, he could feel that it was there; he could smell it. Out of Denver, the train chugged and grunted as it wound its way through the snow-laden gorges of the Rockies. Everything, it seemed, was bigger in America. Irving was familiar with the Austrian Alps though not through actual experience. But these peaks had to be much higher. His train barely made thirty miles an hour as it huffed and hissed its way over one tall peak after another. Surely these mountains had no end and would, ultimately, dump him and his fellow passengers into the Pacific Ocean.

The train's character changed. Those aboard were not just ordinary passengers, for the most part. These were fortune seekers, men who were going to California to wrest her wealth out of her by dint of brains, determination, and sometimes by blind luck. Irving observed all that took place around him. Those heading to San Francisco seemed to have a sense of style. They were more fashionably dressed than those he saw in the Midwest or even in Denver. Irving listened. He heard words like: *building contractor, real estate, orange orchards.*

Strange words to a Hebrew from Poland. What was a building contractor anyway? So while panoramic mountain vistas rose up to greet his eyes, new words were entering his consciousness—words that he was going to have to master.

The puffing picked up cadence. No longer was the engine struggling against high mountains. Instead, it was headed across the flatland deserts of Nevada. Irving caught his breath again. Gradually, cool breezes gave way to stifling heat. Temperatures hovered in the low hundreds while nary a tree could be seen. Everything radiated heat: the ground, the windows, even the engine itself as it struggled to breathe at sixty miles an hour. Nevada took all and gave little. Shimmering air sapped the body of whatever life it had while Nevada's ground sucked the souls dry of those who tried to wrench long-gone silver out of her dry dust. Only one thing welcomed hapless travelers in this barren state: a town with the sign that read, *Biggest Little City in the World,* the town of Reno. Here Irving saw the gateway to the Sierras. Their snow-capped peaks called out to those brave enough to climb them, *Welcome to California. First, however, you must conquer us.*

Reno provided this tired train some badly needed coal and water. Ahead of the towering Sierras lay California's agricultural flatland. After stretching his legs and seeing, for the first time, slot machines in the train station, Irving wondered to himself about these mysterious devices. Never had he heard of machines that gave you money. Of course, he was in no position to gamble; nor did he realize that these machines were not there to give money away.

Finally, this train that had seen so many miles puffed itself up over Donner's Summit and, after pausing for a majestic view of crystal blue Lake Tahoe, headed downhill at breakneck speed, toward the city by the bay—San Francisco. It was a summertime contrast of temperatures—the moderate temperature of the Sierras and, once again, the blast furnace heat of Sacramento's Delta area. As far as he could see, Irving gazed at immense orchards of every type. Cotton and alfalfa poked out of the rich black loam. In addition, huge dairies could be spotted with their contented cows mooing at the speeding train. Irving thought, *This is just one state. How many people can this country feed? Maybe the whole world with food left over.*

Into Sacramento came this train full of gold seekers. These people were surely on the right path. For three quarters of a century, men and women had followed this same path to fortune—some leaving with bags of gold, some with broken dreams, others not leaving at all. Here was Sacramento, capitol of the Golden State. It looked the part with its domed capitol building springing out of nowhere. Destiny was decided here: who would get water, who would thirst. But to an immigrant from Poland, destiny was to be decided a hundred miles west. Irving had no interest in water rights or anything else political. He was going to be a merchant; that was all he knew.

As the engine steamed toward Oakland, where it made its final westward stop, the burning air began to show some mercy. A coolness drifted through the train cars. Passengers finally stopped wiping their brows with napkins, sleeves, and any other item of cloth they had at hand. Wisps of fog could be seen. At first, Irving looked to see what was burning. Nothing was burning—just gentle, cool fog to refresh those seared by the inland valley's smothering heat. Irving's shirt was alternately stuck to the seat and then frozen there by a chilling fog. It only seemed that way because his blood was thinned out after being barbecued in Nevada and then pan fried in California's Sacramento Valley.

CHAPTER 10

SAN FRANCISCO OPENS ITS GOLDEN GATE

• • •

A large body of water that was San Francisco Bay came into view. Since it was in the afternoon, the bay was covered by white, wispy fingers of fog. Irving felt a strange sensation of cool wind blowing in the railcar's windows, a wind that resulted from the meeting of cold fog and warm inland air. He smelled a familiar scent. Saltwater. As the train stopped at the Oakland Train Depot, steam hissed out everywhere: from the wheels, from the stack, and even from the engine's metal skin. After the passengers made their way through a train-generated wall of steam, they found themselves gazing up at a natural white sky that was the Bay Area's afternoon fog cover. Those that were lightly dressed quickly put on some kind of coat to ward off the unexpected summer chill, a reminder of the winter that was summer in San Francisco.

Oakland was a large commercial city and San Francisco's little sister. It had large buildings downtown. It even had a port. What it lacked was San Francisco's size and panache. It was like everyone's little sister, who tries to keep up but whose efforts are in vain. Nonetheless, it did have one of the west coast's largest train depots and was the stop off point if one were heading to that part of the world. At that time, there were no bridges crossing San Francisco Bay; so one had to take the ferryboat.

Irving had become quite adept at dragging his suitcase to a public telephone and making the call to a helpful relative.

Aunt Fanny? I just got off the ferry. It brought me over here from Oakland. Where am I? The streets, I'm not so familiar with. I'm at this ferry dock, and next to it is this tall, thin building with a clock on it. How is Uncle? Oh yes, and my cousins? It is so good to hear your voice. You're the first person in about 2,000 miles that I can really talk to. Unfortunately, nobody understands me. Aunt Fanny, I'm standing here with all my worldly possessions. What do I do now?

Worry not, my wonderful nephew. You'll have no cause to kretz (complain). Your Uncle Abe will leave the store right away and bring you home. By the way, you are on the corner of Market and The Embarcadero. The building you are in is called the Ferry Building. Just stand out in front of it, and your uncle will spot you. Can you follow those directions?

Yes, Aunt Fanny. They are perfectly clear. I look forward to meeting you in person. By the way, Uncle Abe Lieberman and the family send their love. In addition, Father and Mother send theirs as well. I will see you shortly.

Irving clicked the phone receiver down on its handle. He then walked out into the gray of the afternoon. The cold air seemed to weave its way through his coat. A short time before, he had been baking in ninety-five-degree Sacramento heat. Now it was forty degrees cooler, and his body had not yet adjusted. Since Abe's store was only a mile away from Market Street, Irving did not have to shiver very long. A black Model A Ford pulled up to the curb. It was easy to tell that the smiling face inside was that of his uncle because Irving was looking at a mirror image of himself, except an older version. This man was about Irving's height—five foot nine. He was very nattily dressed: charcoal Brooks Brothers suit, white shirt, black-and-white striped tie. Instead of wire-rimmed glasses like Irving wore, Abe's were a thicker black-framed variety. Instead of his other Uncle Abe's warm, outgoing personality, this Abe had a more subdued, distanced type of approach. Yes, he smiled a welcome to his newly met nephew; but like his brother Simon, he was not a hugger. He would give out his affection at a distance. Abe opened the trunk of his Ford, lifted Irving's suitcase in, and proceeded to wind his way down The Embarcadero. Stretched out to the east was the vast expanse of San Francisco Bay with just Yerba Buena Island as a dot in the middle and Oakland's downtown skyline as a backdrop. The bay was choppy and gray to match the sky and gulls swooped like living kites down by the piers that formed large spokes of wood on San Francisco's waterfront. The fog blew its icy breath through the car window, sending a shudder through Irving.

Just like Irving's father, Abe asked about things rather than people. In addition, his attention to detail as regards a person's wardrobe could be quite unnerving.

So, young man, aren't you a bit cold in that short sleeve shirt and thin jacket? You know, I've seen others catch pneumonia dressed like that in this city. What did you see on your journey out? How was life with your Uncle Abe in Cleveland? Did they treat you well? What do you think of The City?

And so the questions came. Abe was more curious about other places and things. He cared about others in the context of how they behaved; thus, he was able to glean insights into human nature. By the answers to his questions, Abe could read character traits of his new visitor. Abe enjoyed pointing out relevant facts. As the Ford chattered around the curve near Fisherman's Wharf, he motioned to his left.

See that mound of green weeds? That's Telegraph Hill. There's this wealthy lady here in town. Her name is Lilly Coit. She's raising money to build a tower up there. It's going to be a monument to honor San Francisco firemen. It's said about town that she is an honorary fireman. This is from something she did with the fire department during the great earthquake.

Sorry, Uncle, but what earthquake?

What? You never heard of the great 1906 earthquake in San Francisco? What do they teach you in school—how to talk with Julius Caesar? In Jewish school, don't they teach you anything that happened after Solomon built the second temple? Son, let me tell you about the rest of the world. In 1906, a horrible earthquake hit San Francisco. The city almost burnt to the ground due to a furious fire that resulted. Many who could not escape died. As you will soon be able to see, San Francisco is even now rebuilding from that disaster.

Uncle, I did not know.

There's a lot you don't know. But don't worry, my boy, you'll learn. See? Off to the right by the bay?

Yes, I see the area you are pointing to.

That's Fisherman's Wharf.

What's Fisherman's Wharf?

Irving, have you read nothing about San Francisco?

No, Uncle. I've read about Jerusalem and about Rome. Even about the major cities of Europe.

Well, it's time for you to learn about San Francisco. As far as you're concerned, this is your Jerusalem.

You're right, Uncle.

As the car headed up Bay Street toward Abe's house, Irving looked out his window to the right and asked,

Uncle? What are those large stucco buildings and that big lawn for?

Irving, that's Fort Mason. It's an old artillery post that dates back almost 200 years. And that lawn ... That was for drilling the troops. OK, we're home.

The Ford rattled its way into the driveway of a two-story house, which stood across the street from scenic Fort Mason. Beyond the grassy area lay stone-colored San Francisco Bay with its wind-whipped whitecaps. In their excitement to greet their newly arrived relative, Fanny and the kids seemed to tumble down the stairs in their haste to see who could hug Irving first. Though kindhearted, Fanny Thurm was used to winning; and after kissing her husband on the cheek, she immediately swept Irving into her arms and gave him a big bear hug. Right behind came the kids, yelping and laughing. Since Hilda's mop head only reached to her older cousin's armpits, she gave him a big grin along with an even bigger hug around his waist. Her blond-haired little brothers, Gerson and David, completed the welcoming committee with each one grabbing him by the leg and pulling him toward their front door. When he got upstairs, he gazed out at a breathtaking view of San Francisco Bay. To his right was an island with a beacon on it—Alcatraz. Suddenly, he heard a sound he had never, in his life, experienced. It was a deep, bellowing sound as though there was a gigantic bull who lived out in the bay. So he gazed to his left, where the sound seemed to come from, and saw a domed building that was sort of pinkish in color—the Palace of Fine Arts. Beyond that, all he could see was billowing clouds of white entering the bay from the Pacific Ocean. From within those floating clouds of fog came warning sounds of foghorns letting ships know to beware.

But Irving had little chance to gaze at the spectacular setting that greeted his eyes. A hubbub of welcoming activity was taking place around him. Little cousins vied for his attention. Fanny put her hostess qualities on display. Meanwhile, Abe took it all in rather taciturnly. He saw no reason to celebrate until his nephew actually accomplished something. Everyday pleasantries of life often passed him by. Like his brother, Abe cared about money and business. Most other things were a distraction. The Thurms, however, were not going to allow their patriarch to be a party pooper. They were thrilled to receive their newfound relation from Poland. What's more, they were going to welcome him with San Francisco hospitality.

Finally, the children's energy ran its course; and they were packed off to bed. Fanny showed Irving to his new room; thus, he settled down to his new life in America.

Part of his new life revolved around his helping Fanny with her house chores—a role he was most familiar with from his days at home in Poland. In addition, he helped her care for the children—another task his siblings had given him plenty of experience in. Irving was an inquisitive young man. Never did his questions cease.

Uncle? What is Fisherman's Wharf?

It's that area I pointed out to you, where the boats are, at the foot of Columbus Street. That area's called North Beach or Italian town. Where those boats are is where fishermen bring their catch and sell it, some to commercial buyers and some to the public directly.

Uncle? What is that domed building over there near the entrance to the ocean?

Irving. That's called the Palace of Fine Arts. It was built as part of a fair we had here in 1915 called the Panama Pacific Exposition.

Uncle, what is that island over there toward the end of Van Ness Avenue?

That's Alcatraz. It is a historic fort that guarded the bay.

Uncle?

My God, how many questions do you have in your head? I swear, if I knew half the things you have questions about, I'd be the wisest man on earth. Look, Irving, save your questions up until the end of the week. That way, we can take them to temple with us so that if I don't know the answer, we can give them to God and maybe he'll know. Now, let's talk about your future.

Irving was familiar with this scenario. How many times had he sat with his father, Simon? How many times with his Uncle Abe from Cleveland? As lights of the Marina District twinkled like stars through the Thurm's living room window, Irving and Abe sat down to talk. Occasionally, a moving light could be seen on San Francisco Bay. Ships passed to and fro in front of Alcatraz. This young man from Poland was in a strange setting indeed. It was midsummer, yet the cold fog kept struggling to break in.

The kids were put to bed against their will, of course. Fanny and Abe sat on their velour couch while Irving sank into an overstuffed, matching easy chair. Abe began,

Irving, you are now settled in all right?

The room is very comfortable, Uncle. Thank you and Fanny for your hospitality.

It is your future we're here to discuss.

Irving was holding a Scotch on the rocks. His hands must have grown hot at the words of his uncle as what was said lay on Irving's shoulders like a shirt of lead. All at once, Irving became aware of ice popping in his Scotch glass. At first, he was in a daze and staring out at the ships which, like his life, moved slowly through the haze. The pop of ice jerked him back into the present.

Firstly, your wardrobe needs upgrading. We will go to Brooks Brothers and get you some suits. You're a Puderbeutel and will look like one. After that, we'll go to The Emporium so you have some regular clothes. Not only will you be ready for fall but might even survive a San Francisco summer.

Fanny interjected.

Irving, my mench of a nephew, your uncle is right. We'll have you looking like a society swain in no time at all.

Aunt? What's a swain?

Oh my, oh my. How many years will it take to teach him? May God give me enough time! Irving, a swain is a young man who captures young ladies' affections. Not a bad thing to be. You and your uncle are birds of a similar feather.

Abe brought a sense of seriousness back into the conversation. As Irving tensed up, the ice cubes in his glass continued to crack as though they were little glaciers.

Now that your aunt has addressed the clothes issue—

But Uncle, I thought the clothes I have are very American.

Abe did not like to be interrupted, especially by someone who knew less than he did.

Being that you interjected your thoughts, your clothes are American ... from that part of the country that is not known for its style ... from the Bowery most likely. Listen, San Franciscans are known all over the world to be better dressed and to have better manners than almost anyone else in America, including New York though New Yorkers will always deny it. All right, back to your future. What are you going to do with yourself now?

I want to work in your store, learn your business.

Hmm. Learn my business? Admirable goal, don't you think, Fanny? Let me be straight with you, Irving. I didn't bring you out here to fail. Now let's be realistic. You don't know any aspect of the clothing business.

You can't sell clothes. Your command of the English language is not good, and that would be an understatement.

But, Uncle—

But, Uncle nothing. If you want to go into my business, here's a course of action you must take. One, go to night school and improve your English. Two, learn how to sell women's clothes. I'll have Mr. Zukerman at Zukor's train you in how to sell coats and suits. Then, when you have improved your English and have learned something of the clothing business, come talk with me!

Ok, Uncle—a deal. I'll do those things. By next July, I want to talk with you about going into your business.

You do the things I told you then we talk. In the meantime, your aunt will teach you how to be a well-dressed man about town. Tomorrow, we get you clothed then you come to the store. You'll learn a little about the ready-to-wear business.

And so Irving's apprenticeship began. His Uncle Abe and Aunt Fanny instilled in him knowledge of San Francisco social graces and of how a successful store was run. At night, Irving would attend Washington High School to improve his English skills. By day, he would work in Zukors as a shipping clerk for Mr. Zukor. Gradually, he acclimated to San Francisco's climate. Irving would bask in the morning Marina District sun. He delighted in looking out the living room window and observing voyagers from all over the world float through the Golden Gate. What parts of the earth did they come from? What stories could they tell? Irving gradually made himself acquainted with various San Francisco landmarks. He enjoyed watching ducks and swans glide across the Palace of Fine Arts lagoon at the end of Baker Street. He would take Hilda, David, and Gerson down to the vast lawns of Marina Green next to the bay, where they would watch their kites soar, carried up by Pacific breezes. On weekends, he would wander down to Muni Pier and watch old salts catch cod, halibut, crabs, and sand sharks. He reveled in the salt air while his nostrils breathed in the scent of dying fish. With his improved English, he was able to talk to these grizzled fishermen about fish, weather, and, yes, about life in general. He learned that you don't have to be rich to know something about life; you just have to be living.

Abe took his nephew into his business after the lad obtained his education in both English and in the field of selling women's coats. Abe's store, Fannette's, was located on Market Street between Third and Fourth Streets, one of the city's best retail locations. The Emporium was half a block away, and the exclusive Union Square was just around the corner. Irving learned all aspects of the retail business. He worked in the basement, marking goods and carrying them upstairs to the sales floor. He also filled in as a salesperson when needed.

Meanwhile, changes were taking place in the Thurm household. To make room for their new arrival, the family moved to a larger home on Jackson Street in the prestigious Presidio Heights neighborhood. Their home had a stately white facade and stood on the south side of Jackson Street. San Francisco's Jewish merchant elite were their neighbors: the Zuckermans, the Magnins, and the Levis.

Hilda was turning into a preteen princess and dressed as such. On special occasions, her parents would let her wear a wool coat that had a fox collar and fox-trimmed sleeves. She would tuck her curly locks under a matching wool beret—the epitome of upper crust girlhood. David and Gerson Thurm had turned into rambunctious young boys who would trail Irving anywhere he would take them.

Irving began to look like a younger version of his Uncle Abe. He got rid of his wire-rimmed glasses in favor of the thicker-rimmed ones his uncle wore. He took on his uncle's mannerisms, one of which was dressing like him. At the store, he could always be seen with a dapper striped tie. Meanwhile, prohibition laid its heavy hand on the land. San Francisco's Barbary Coast on Broadway Street always had a reputation for wide openness. There, speakeasies were found in abundance as well as whatever else a man had in mind. In San Francisco, the world knew that liquor flowed and good times rolled. On weekends, Irving put on a sport coat and tie, bid his aunt and uncle a good evening, and took off to enjoy some the city's nightlife. Exclusive nightspots such as the Fairmont Hotel's Gold Room and top of the Mark, with its panoramic view, were known to have both expensive women and liquid refreshments for those on the prowl. Regulars they were called. Irving made friends with other up-and-coming young men such as Arthur Grey and Norman Wolfe. The latter was in medical school at the time. Since those in Irving's circle of acquaintances were Jewish, that's where his friends came from. The guys would dress up, split a taxi fare, and, on the weekends, go out on the town—maybe to Broadway to catch a girlie show or maybe take a date to the top of the Mark, where you could go dancing with the Anson Weeks orchestra.

During the week, however, it was all business. San Francisco's streets didn't just seem like they were paved with gold; they were. These were the roaring twenties, and a person just had to know where to look. In Irving's case, gold was found inside a women's coat and suit store. His Uncle Abe taught him everything about running a store. He would take his nephew with him to Lilli Ann, where they would buy highly styled suits for discriminating women. He learned to run a service-oriented business, where the owner was not above delivering a coat to a customer's house after a long day of work. Abe taught young Irving how to balance a cash drawer so that the day's proceeds were accounted for.

Meanwhile, back in the town of Lizhensk Poland, Irving's sister Sarah got married at the age of twenty-two. She gave birth to a full-faced daughter, who looked much like her mother. Both had black hair, which Puderbeutels were noted for. Sarah's face bore a radiance that only giving life can provide. Her hair was cut in a stylish flapper look. Both she and her daughter had bangs that drooped over their foreheads.

Abe and Fanny Thurm decided that they would take a trip to Europe and visit his family. Irving, by now, knew enough that he could run the store by himself.

Jim Bartel (Simon's son). *When the Thurms came to visit, they stayed with us. Abe wanted to visit his father, Shmuel, in Kanczuga (Poland). It was about seventy miles from Lizhensk. After he (Abe) left Kanczuga, about a week later, Shmuel comes to our town. How does he get there? He walks. The reason he came? He felt his son (Abe) didn't leave him enough money.* Those were the happenings in the old country.

In San Francisco, Fannette's at 771 Market Street was flourishing. When Abe was away on buying trips, Irving managed the store. Profits never missed a beat. Abe taught his nephew that a store owner should be able to do any job within the store. He was able to sell, be a cashier, trim the windows (i.e. create a pleasing window display), take inventory, buy goods, and deliver merchandise when needed. Finally, in 1929, that long-awaited day arrived. Irving Bartel earned his United States citizenship certificate. He gave his address as 771 Market Street. He might as well have; he just about lived at the store. There certainly was reason to celebrate.

It was March, a month where cold winds howled through the canyons of Montgomery Street. Abe and Fanny bundled everybody into their Ford; and off they went to Jacks, a restaurant that had been in existence since the 1860s. Since March winds could leave a person's teeth chattering, Fanny made sure the men were protected by wool top coats while the women put on their fur-trimmed coats. Even David and Gerson were included though they kept punching each other in the back seat until Irving gave one of them such an elbow that the cousin thought he was paralyzed. This joyful group finally piled out at the restaurant. A fabulous time was had by all. The story goes that the upstairs area was used by gentlemen for discreet rendezvous with ladies who they had no intention of introducing to Mother. The aroma of Jack's New York cut steaks soaked into the hardwood floors and whet the appetite. The Thurms sat at their "regular" table. Everyone had a "regular" table at Jack's, depending on your social position and on how much you put into the maître d's hand when you shook it.

And so it went. Irving mastered every aspect of the women's ready-to-wear business. He wrote home, telling his proud father and mother about his experiences in San Francisco. Of course, the ones still at home—Ethel, Rose, Abe, Gerson, Jim, and little Ben—would eagerly gather around Leah to find out what life in America was like and what people there wore. They wanted to know what their cousins

Hilda, Gerson, and David were like. Irving gave them all a running commentary.

In Baghdad by the Bay—as Herb Cain, the well-known columnist called it (San Francisco)—the good times and the fog rolled; and the money, just like the liquor, flowed. Everyone was in the stock market. It could go only one way—up; then, on October 29, 1929, it all came crashing down. Black Tuesday, they called it. As things turned out, economic laws were no more inviolable than those of physics. What goes up, indeed, can come down and did. On that one day, New York Stock Exchange issues lost their investors nine billion dollars and sixteen billion dollars for the month of October in 1929. In Kansas City, Missouri, John Schwitzgebel (an insurance salesman) put two bullets in his chest and, unfortunately, lived. In Rhode Island, a man dropped dead while watching the stock tape. Others threw themselves off buildings or under trains. People's savings were wiped out. All they held were some worthless pieces of paper that said they owned part of a company that couldn't pay its bills. A great chill fell over the industrial machine that was America; its gears began to freeze.

The Great Depression was about to begin. Swells, as Irving and his friends Arthur Grey and Norman Wolfe were called, continued to people local watering holes. But these were young men on the way up. During the day, they worked long hours at their assorted occupations. Others were not so fortunate. President Hoover appropriated $116 million to put those that were jobless back to work on emergency construction projects. Elsewhere—in New York—400,000 depositors tried to withdraw their money only to find the banks' doors locked. At the same time, an ecological tragedy was unfolding in the form of a Midwest drought.

In San Francisco, cool breezes blew through the Golden Gate. But it wasn't cool inside Abe Thurm's store. He adapted to the slowing economy. Reluctantly, he had to let some of his seasoned salespeople go. He cut his window trimmer's hours. His merchandise orders were diminished. As always, Abe made sure he got the ten percent discount for paying cash by the tenth of the month. Instead of going to New

York twice a year to buy merchandise from his buyer, Jack Bronstein, he would only go in June. Where personnel were lacking, Irving picked up the slack. He'd fill in on the sales floor. His English was so improved that ladies loved his accent and persuasiveness. He would make up for the missing window trimmer by creating attractive displays himself. As business dropped, Irving would spot his uncle as cashier.

At times, he would be sent to Lilli Ann to pick out and bring back hot-selling coats or suits. This is where he developed a friendship with another rising star in the merchandising field, Lilli Ann's owner, Adolph Schuman. Here was a man similar to Irving in many ways. His roots lay in Europe. He had arrived in San Francisco by way of New York. His business was built on toughness. He was so handsome that his black hair and blue eyes could charm a lady out of her clothes (though dressing ladies in highly styled clothes was what he built his fortune on). Adolph would go to France, pick first-run designs from the high fashion houses of Paris, then copy them at his San Francisco factory. He cared about making money, attractive women, and the finer things that the first could acquire. Schuman was ruthless in obtaining what he wanted. He treated most like garbage unless he needed something—in which case, he would turn on his charm. A more volatile temper could not be found on the globe called Earth. Irving admired the man because he possessed traits Irving would, in time, make his own and because he helped hone Irving's taste in the better things life offered. That was later, however. In the early thirties, both were in the early stages of developing their business reflexes.

The year 1932 was eventful for many reasons. Firstly, it was the year that "Lucky" Lindy's kidnapped baby was found dead. Next, Hoover funded $500 million to save failing banks and railroads, which was one of his final acts as president. As a relief to a floundering country, Roosevelt took office promising a "New Deal." Here was a man who promised to pump prime the economy in order to get the little guy back to work. Amelia Earhart became the first woman to fly solo across the Atlantic. People were succeeding and failing in spectacular ways.

As hard times stalked the streets of America, Abe Thurm and his nephew Irving learned to thrive amidst misery and want. They made do with less and still prospered; then it happened.

1923 Isaak Puderbeutel

THE CITIZENS' BUREAU

OLD COUNTY COURT HOUSE — WEST THIRD STREET ENTRANCE

CLEVELAND, OHIO

STATE OF OHIO
COUNTY OF CUYAHOGA, } ss. AFFIDAVIT OF SUPPORT

BEFORE ME, a Notary Public, in and for said State and County, on this day personally appeared Abraham Lieberman residing at 10100 Olivet Ave., Cleveland, Ohio who under oath says that the answers given to the following questions and all the facts and allegations herein set forth are true to the best of his knowledge and belief.

1. What is your name? Abraham Lieberman
2. When were you born? April (Month) 2nd (Day) 1882 (Year)
3. Where were you born? Posdklostov (Village or City) (County) (State) Austria (Country)
4. When did you arrive in the United States? November (Month) 10 (Day) 1904 (Year)
5. Where did you arrive in the United States? New York, N.Y. (Port of entry)
6. Have you taken out your first papers? Yes, April 15, 1918, in the Common Pleas, Court of Cleveland, Ohio.# 32940 (When and where)
7. Have you taken out your full citizenship papers? Yes., U. S. District Court, of Cleveland, Ohio, on November 12, 1920, certificate # 1506827 (When and where)
8. What is your occupation? Huckster Average weekly earnings? $ 60.00
9. What is the approximate value of your property? Real Estate $ 10,000.00 Personal $
10. How many dependents have you now? Wife and 3 children
11. What are the names and addresses of arriving immigrants? Ages? Relationship to undersigned?
Isaak Puderbeutel, Lesajsk, Poland, 19 years old, Nephew.
12. Are any of the above named married? No.

1923 AFFIDAVIT OF SUPPORT ABE LIEBERMAN FOR ISAAC

1923 Affidavit of Support Abe Lieberman for Isaak

1926 Rose Puderbeutel

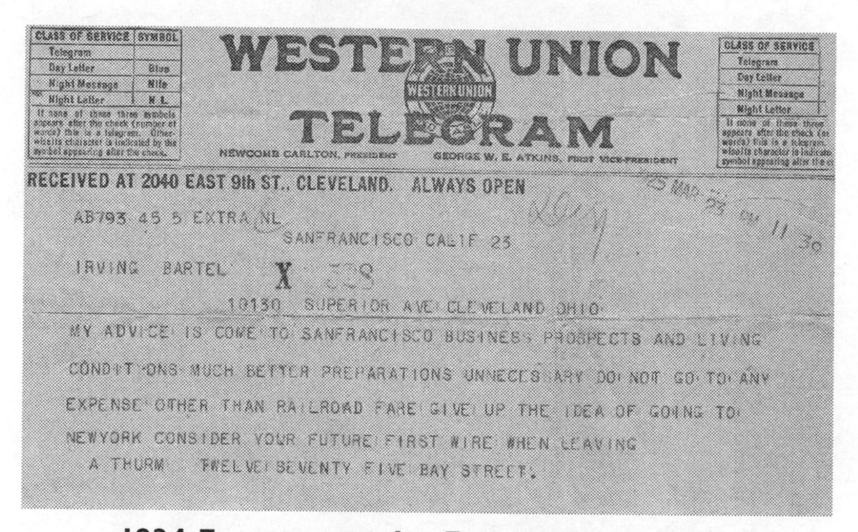

WESTERN UNION TELEGRAM

NEWCOMB CARLTON, PRESIDENT GEORGE W. E. ATKINS, FIRST VICE-PRESIDENT

CLASS OF SERVICE	SYMBOL
Telegram	
Day Letter	Blue
Night Message	Nite
Night Letter	N L

If none of these three symbols appears after the check (number of words) this is a telegram. Otherwise its character is indicated by the symbol appearing after the check.

RECEIVED AT 2040 EAST 9th ST., CLEVELAND. ALWAYS OPEN

AB793 45 5 EXTRA NL

SANFRANCISCO CALIF 23

IRVING BARTEL

10130 SUPERIOR AVE CLEVELAND OHIO

MY ADVICE IS COME TO SANFRANCISCO BUSINESS PROSPECTS AND LIVING CONDITIONS MUCH BETTER PREPARATIONS UNNECESSARY DO NOT GO TO ANY EXPENSE OTHER THAN RAILROAD FARE GIVE UP THE IDEA OF GOING TO NEWYORK CONSIDER YOUR FUTURE FIRST WIRE WHEN LEAVING

A THURM TWELVE SEVENTY FIVE BAY STREET.

1924 Telegram from Abe Thurm to Irving Bartel

1927 The Thurms and Irving Bartel

1928 Sara Puderbeutel and Daughter

CHAPTER 11

A HOARFROST GRIPS THE LAND

• • •

Irving was helping a customer with her coat selection. As it often happened, when a customer couldn't make up her mind, the saleslady would call Irving over for his opinion. Any lady was flattered that he would pay attention to her wants and needs. After all, he cut a handsome figure with his trim physique and colorful striped tie set off by a white shirt. Not only that, he was decisive. He could tell what size a lady took just by looking at her. He would never embarrass by asking someone their size. Large or small, he would just pick a coat off the rack that he knew the store had either too many of or an item that had a high markup; then the customer would be told to look in the mirror and see how beautiful she looked. Irving was so handsome and so persuasive that most fell under his spell.

He had just placed a size twelve camel coat on a woman who swore she took a size eight.

This is the coat you should have. Notice how ...

His words were interrupted by a quick patter of feet along the store's gray carpet. It was one of the salesladies.

Mr. Bartel, there's an urgent phone call for you.

Irving excused himself from his customer and turned her over to the saleslady who brought him the message—but not without first telling the customer that this coat, that looked so good on her, was mislabeled size twelve and, fortunately, turned out to be just her size, an eight.

Irving launched himself up the back stairs, skipping every other stair, and in no time was up to his uncle's third-floor executive office, where he took important calls.

It was early April, spring in San Francisco when flowers were starting to bloom in Golden Gate Park. Warm rays of the sun began to chase away the winter chill. This was an in-between time prior to summer fogs wrapping the city in their chilly throes. San Francisco radiated promise even though the rest of America was caught in an icy grip of The Great Depression.

As he picked up the phone, his Aunt Fanny's frantic voice, like some kind of verbal bullet, drove into his brain.

Irving, you must come quickly!

What's wrong, Auntie?

Irving. Irrv! Oh, my God, my God! It's your uncle. He's ...

He'd never heard his aunt sound like this. The note of urgency caused his skin to prickle. He tried to stop his hand from shaking uncontrollably.

...not breathing. Abe was just getting ready to leave for the store. He put his coat on, looked in the mirror, and fell over. I heard a thump and found him lying in the bedroom. His color is white. Irving! DO SOMETHING!

Auntie, it's all right. Stay calm. I'll be right there. Call an ambulance! Make sure you reach Dr. Goldman! Aunt Fanny, I'm on my way.

How ironic. Irving was sitting in Abe Thurm's office, on Abe's chair; yet one life was ebbing while another was cresting. All of a sudden, his movements were double-time while things in the world around him slowed to a clearly focused crawl.

Irving bounded down the stairs at a horrid pace. Upon his arrival on the main floor, his hair was disheveled, his eyes teary, and his collar soaked with perspiration. There was an emergency. No, his uncle would not be in.

That coat is you, Irving breathlessly told a customer who was proudly carrying her new coat out the door in its distinctive blue Fannette's box. He then resumed his run out the front door. Sunlight radiated off everything on Market Street: white terrazzo buildings, black granite monoliths, silent green and white electric trolley buses, and rumbling street cars. He, however, was not going to utilize any of them. Waiting for him by the curb was a yellow box on wheels called a taxi. This was the new and improved Model A Ford. It clattered more quietly than the previous model.

Ye look in a hurry, remarked a ruddy-faced Irishman, who opened the passenger door for his sweaty faced fare.

What would make you think that? asked Irving.

Why ye be dripping like ye be a sieve.

So I am. Look! I've got an emergency. Get me to Jackson and Presidio in a hurry, if you know what I mean.

Aye. By St. Christopher, who protects such as we, I get ye there so fast that ye'll be there before your tie arrives.

Cabbie! Use some caution. I'm not ready to meet St. Christopher in person just yet.

As the taxi raced down Post Street, Irving had his own thoughts to keep him company. What was he going to do when he arrived home? How would he react to the tragedy that was unfolding in front of him? North on Van Ness Avenue, the cab raced with the Irishman flogging his machine to the breakneck speed of forty miles per hour. He weaved from lane to lane while pedestrians jumped to save their skins.

Aye. Ye be to your emergency as quick as a lass can wink.

Irving liked this man's style but was hesitant to tell him so lest the cabbie speed up more and kill half of San Francisco in the process. It seemed like just a couple of minutes when the taxi's thin tires squealed around the corner of Van Ness and Jackson Street. After that, frightened drivers pulled to the curb and cursed as this crazy man in a yellow car sped on his way into the exclusive neighborhood of Presidio Heights. As the taxi screeched to a stop near the corner of Jackson and Presidio, Irving had to brace his hands on the back of the front seat lest he be tossed in the air and land on his cabbie's lap.

That be fast enough for ye?

Irving, as he got out, fished for words that were diplomatic enough to tell the Irishman that he was glad to be alive. But with the diplomacy he had learned from his mother, a *thank you* along with a $5 gold piece passed hands.

Keep the change!

A prince ye be! A prince among Philistines! May St. Mary bless thee!

Thank you, Cabbie. I can use all the blessings that are available.

With that, the two parted. A clank of first gear and down Jackson Street clattered the cab. Irving brushed his disheveled hair across his head and bounded up the stairs to the Thurm house. Parked by the curb was an ambulance with its red lights blinking on and off like his uncle's life. As Irving opened the front door, he saw himself lying there. But it wasn't himself; it was someone who looked like him—his uncle. On her knees by the barely breathing body was his beloved aunt, the one who had taken him in and cared for him like one of her own children. She was racked with sobs, hardly noticing him through her cascade of grief. Irving had to remain calm though everything was falling apart. He asked the medics.

What's it look like?

He won't make it.

Just then, fresh primordial wails came from his Aunt Fanny's throat. These sounds hadn't changed in 4,000 years. They were the same sounds heard by Abraham, Isaac, and Jacob in biblical times.

Oh, my dear God. What caused this? Abe's wife inquired.

A medic's emotionless prognosis was, *His skin is yellow. Looks like kidney failure. He's still breathing, but it won't be long.*

Irving bent down next to his aunt and placed his arm gently around her shoulder. His tie swung like a pendulum, now and then touching the dying man's lips. He was aware of death, but seldom witnessed it. Now, on the floor, wheezing his final breaths was the man who had done so much to make him what he was—an emerging merchant prince. Irving felt like the weight of the world had descended upon him.

Away sped the ambulance with Abe Thurm onboard; its siren wailing a death knell. Irving had to hold his aunt back because she insisted on climbing into the ambulance to be with her husband. With words that would wake him in the night for years to come, she implored,

Irving, Irving. My life is over. What's to be with myself and the kids? What can I tell Gerson, David, and poor little Hilda? Why God, can't it be me in that ambulance? Oh Irving, he was such a good provider! Barely forty years old and he's leaving us. Who will look after us now? Why the serus (trouble)? Ohhh God, why him?

Aunt Fanny, as sure as these two arms have strength in them, I'll see that you and the children are taken care of. My heart is broken. I can hardly talk. We must pull ourselves together. The children will soon be home. Then, we must go to the hospital. It's in God's hands.

One by one, the children romped up the stairs; but there was a pall in the air, invisible but perceptible. Immediately, each could sense there was something wrong. Their mother had a look on her face they had never seen before. Cousin Irving's features were strained, yet his voice was calm. To each he would say,

Sit down! Your father is at the hospital. He is very ill, and God may take him from us.

Then tears would start.

Come, come. We must be strong now. Your mother needs us. Come over and feel this back.

The children could hardly see Irving because they were sobbing and their tears temporarily blinded them, but they obeyed. Each put their hand of the upper part of Irving's back and was able to feel muscles hard as rocks.

Feel that? My back is strong enough to carry the cares of you all, including your mother.

Each one, sobs having tuned to whimpers, hugged Irving around the neck.

Now, we've got things to do. First, we must pray to God so that

he might spare your father's life. Next, we'll all go to the hospital and visit him.

Irving's words were able to bring hope to the hearts of his distraught aunt and to her children. If God willed it, Abe would return to health and to his loving family. Thanks to the lessons on driving provided by his now dying uncle, Irving was able to start the family car. Fanny and the children had composed themselves as best as they could by the time Irving pulled the Ford out to the front curb. He courteously opened the front door for Fanny and let the kids scramble into the back seat. The drive was quite short, just a couple of blocks over to Divisadero and then down to Geary. They parked the car and approached the bleak white building called Mt. Zion Hospital.

In San Francisco, every religion had its own hospital: for the Presbyterians, it was Presbyterian Hospital; for the Catholics, it was Mother Seton; and for the Jews, the hospital of choice was Mt. Zion. Of course, each hospital served all faiths; but a patient could feel confident with finding a doctor and numerous other patients of his own religious belief. The point was moot in Abe Thurm's case.

Irving led the group to the reception desk.

Abe Thurm please.

Are you a relative? The attending nurse inquired.

I'm his nephew. This is his wife and children.

The nurse picked up a clipboard with the names of all those unfortunate enough to be in that place. She looked at the last name *Thurm* then the notation behind it.

Please have a seat, she told Irving. He took his seat. Next to him, holding handkerchiefs in their hands, sat Fanny and the kids; then the attending nurse picked up the phone. *Dr. Goldman* was all Irving could hear. The rest of what the nurse said was veiled in a whisper.

Doesn't look good, Fanny exclaimed as she nudged Irving with her elbow.

I don't like this place, offered Gerson Thurm.

Me neither, agreed his brother David.

Doctors scare me, volunteered Hilda.

At that, a tall, handsome man with black hair, thin-rimmed glasses and a kind face approached. Through his glasses could be seen tired, care-worn eyes. He looked like one who was trying to save the world but could only succeed in saving part of it. His navy blue tie and white shirt could be seen beneath his light blue smock.

Although he was one of the city's most prominent surgeons, he approached Fanny like he would a personal friend, which she was.

Hello, Fanny. So glad to see you though not necessarily under these circumstances. My, the children have grown! Who is this with you?

I don't like doctors, piped up David.

Shhh, admonished Fanny as she gave him a clop on the back of his head. He then went whimpering over into the corner.

This is my nephew Irving from Austria.

People from Poland preferred to say they were from Austria because Poland was once part of the Austro-Hungarian Empire and because it sounded better.

Pleased to make your acquaintance. I hope you are finding our country a welcome place.

Yes, it is a welcome place indeed. I am living with my uncle and aunt.

I have known the Thurms for some years now. I trust you are well looked after.

Dr. Goldman ushered the family to his private office, where he motioned for them to sit while he remained standing. His face then turned grave while his voice took on a more medical and less personal tone.

Fanny, it's about Abe.

Irving turned aside just in time to see his aunt collapse off the chair. David held one arm, Gerson the other, while Hilda let her lap serve as a pillow for her mother's head. The famous surgeon then directed his conversation to Irving.

Irving, you must take care of details for your aunt and her children. Abe? There was no hope. He's gone. Kidneys. They failed. He was a young, robust man. You'd never be able to tell. But on the inside was a time bomb. He could have lived to be a hundred, or he'd be lucky to reach forty.

A low moaning sound could be heard on the floor along with children's sobs. The doctor continued.

Sometimes the kidneys fail gradually, and the family has warning. At other times, they quit all at once and death is sudden. You may be comforted by the fact that your uncle had relatively little pain. He was semiconscious when he arrived here. By the time I saw him, it was too late. It was just a matter of keeping him as comfortable as possible. Praise God, he passed on peacefully.

Irving felt sick to his stomach. Everything around him made him want to throw up: his moaning aunt and crying cousins, the surgeon's antiseptic odor, the floor's antiseptic smell, the antiseptic words. Irving's beloved uncle, the one who taught him how to run a retail store, was gone now; and his passing was being described in sterile medical terms. Ever after, Irving would have a hatred of hospitals and anything having to do with them. All he could think of now was how he was going to take care of his aunt, cousins, and the store. It was funny how things worked. First, the Thurms took care of him; now it was his turn. In addition, the employees of Fannette's depended on him for their livelihood in these precarious times.

While all these thoughts raced through Irving's head, Dr. Goldman's words brought him back to the here and now.

Oh Fanny, children, and Irving, I have no words that would be adequate enough to express my sorrow over my good friend Abe's passing, Now, there is the matter of his body.

Fanny tried saying something, but whatever words they were gagged up in her throat. Irving snapped out of his reverie.

I'll make arrangements, Doctor. He belonged to Congregation Sherith Israel. Initially, Sinai Memorial Chapel will take care of his body, then he will be put to rest at Eternal Home in Colma. Fanny, if you have any wishes otherwise, I'll adhere to them.

Irving, you take care of things.

And so he did. Irving took Fanny and the children home. He then proceeded to pick out Abe Thurm's best suit from his closet. He laid it out on the bed, along with matching shoes and tie. All these the devoted nephew delivered to Sinai Memorial Chapel. He then had the job of picking an appropriate coffin—one of rich black mahogany. The funeral service was held within forty-eight hours in keeping with Jewish tradition. Friends, business associates, and employees streamed into Sinai to pay their respects. The coffin lay up front in an alcove. Those who were Jewish would walk up to the coffin, touch their fingers to their lips, and touch that rich black container where the recently departed Abe Thurm lay. Although he was dressed in his finest, the coffin lid remained closed.

Only close friends followed Abe's body to Eternal Home Cemetery in Colma. It was a warm spring day, yet the short ride in the Thurm sedan seemed as frozen as though the car was driving to the North Pole. Hilda was dressed in her little pink suit. Gerson and David both wore suits with ties. Fanny, of course, was dressed in a black suit with a black hat. Irving, though surrounded by the black of death, decided to wear a red tie to symbolize spring and rebirth. It was too much to take. As they emerged from their car, there stood a gaping hole—a little over six feet long by four feet deep—their loved one's grave. As the coffin was lowered in, the words of the Kaddish (Jewish prayer for the dead) mingled with Fanny's sobs. First, Fanny threw a clod of dirt on the coffin, followed by Gerson, David, little Hilda, and finally Irving. As the echoes of dirt reverberated off wood, Irving felt numb inside.

The Old Testament tells us there is a time to be born, a time to die, a time to grieve, and a time to heal. It fell upon the guest, Irving, to take care of the host, the Thurms. His aunt did not know how to run a store, but he did. He needed to insure that his aunt and her children would have an adequate income to live on. In order to affect this, he made arrangements with his Aunt Fanny to buy Fannette's. He prepared a written agreement to pay her a fixed amount per month with the store to be paid off in full within five years; then, Irving would not only own the women's coat and suit store, but also the real estate it sat on. On the day following Abe's funeral, Irving was back at work. This was 1932. Times were tough. Millions were unemployed and didn't have money for anything other than necessities—which women's coats and suits weren't. That failed to deter Irving.

He bought shrewdly and priced his merchandise lower than his competitors. In addition, he set up a layaway program for those that couldn't afford to pay all at once. He would let his layaway customers pay a little each month until the garment was paid in full. People knew they could go to Fannette's and would not need to fill out a credit application. Their word was good enough. Irving trimmed his staff to a skeleton crew. He kept a seamstress and a couple of salespeople. By sharp cost cutting and clever merchandising, Irving was able to make sufficient profit to pay his expenses and to put money away for savings. Like Simon, his father, Irving believed that interest was only paid by spendthrifts. He paid cash for everything and took manufacturer discounts religiously. Every garment was priced in terms of next lowest price point. In other words, instead of a coat being marked $100, it would be priced $99.99. Irving didn't have a hundred-dollar coat in stock but plenty of $99.99 ones. Of course, during the Depression, $99.99 was a very highly priced garment—a designer sample. These samples were one of a kind and were used by French couture houses as models to mass-produce from. Most coats and suits in the early thirties sold for $24.99 to $49.99.

Irving was on the selling floor with his red pen, which he used to mark down slow-selling items. He'd draw a line through the printed price and handwrite a new price that was $10 to $20 lower; thus he was able to recover his money from slow sellers and put it back into higher profit goods.

CHAPTER 12

SWIMMING WITH BARRACUDA

• • •

A salesperson called him to the phone.

Yes?

Irving never felt the need to announce his name when he answered the phone; it was assumed you could recognize his distinctive accent.

Irv, you old son of a bitch. How are you?

It was his friend, Adolph Schuman, owner of Lilli Ann Fine Fashions in San Francisco. Both these young men were socially on the rise in The City. But times were hard and Schuman also was struggling to make ends meet.

Look, Irv. Ya gotta come down here. I got some items you must have.

Adolph, there's nothing I must have. I've got no time to go over there.

Shuman, with his black hair and piercing eyes, was not a man to take no for an answer. He was used to getting his way, and besides, he wanted to do his friend a favor. After all, Irving loaned him some money to keep his business going.

Shit, Irv, your store will still be there. Listen, I just received some Dior original samples. Not even Magnin's has items like these. Don't be stupid. I've got a bitch modeling them in an hour. Get your ass down here! You won't be sorry.

What'll they cost?

Irv, you cheap bastard. What the hell you care what they cost? You know I'll give you a good price. Just get your ass over! They're yours.

Ok, Adolph. You convinced me, but the price had better be good.

Oh, you cheap son-a-bitch. I'll see you shortly.

Irving knew full well that if he could scoop his larger competitors on these items, he could take a large markup on them. Even in tough times, the wealthy were still out there and would pay for a designer original. Irving also knew that if he passed these items up, he would be seeing them in the window of some merchant around the corner.

He left his senior salesperson in charge, walked half a block to Fourth Street then down to the garage, where his teal-green Buick was parked. The car had a brown convertible top, wide whitewall tires, and brown wooden-spoked wheels. This was one of a breed of high but functionally styled automobiles. They were moderately priced yet high on the "I've Arrived" scale. He pulled into the garage at the corner of Sixteenth and Valencia Streets in the Portrero Hill section of the city. There stood a white two-story building with black italic letters on it—"Lilli Ann." Irving walked quickly to the receptionist's desk. He was in a hurry. Anytime he was away from the store, a sale might be lost. The air was full of fabric scents. Various furs could be seen lining sleeves and collars. No doubt the souls of these animals haunted Adolph Schuman; thus, his eccentricities could be explained. As Irving would later say, *If you're rich, you're eccentric. If you're poor, you're crazy.*

The receptionist smiled and picked up the phone.

Mr. Schuman, Mr. Bartel is here.

I'll be right down, came the shout from a distant office. Down the stairs bounded a handsome man wearing a black-and-white glen plaid suit along with a solid gray tie. The tie was attached to his light blue shirt by a round piece of gold with a two-carat diamond in the middle. Though Schuman had to borrow at times, he always put on the style. When Schuman shook Irving's hand, he gave it a squeeze, belying his shorter size.

Ah, Irv! for Christ's sake, I knew you couldn't resist a bargain.

Listen, if Teller Weinman of the Emporium ever got wind I gave you these Diors, why he'd have my ass. Let's go up to the showroom, where the model bitch is strutting them now.

They walked up two flights of stairs to where the modeling room was. There, on a raised ramp, models would show special Lilli Ann goods to prospective buyers. Of course, designer originals only came in sizes a model could fit into—usually sizes eight to ten. A model would walk up the ramp then sashay toward the buyers. Her hips would wiggle first one way then the other. As she reached the end of the ramp close to covetous eyes, she would slowly turn around 360 degrees, smile, and wiggle her hips until she finally exited the ramp. It must be mentioned that the covetous eyes were, in actuality, lusting for what the model was wearing. She was just a walking mannequin on which goods that meant profit to these clothing merchants hung.

Irving could appreciate a thin waist and a well-turned ankle, but he could even more relate to a 150% markup. Schuman, on the other hand, had no patience with any of his employees. They were there to do his bidding and nothing else. From his point of view, they should have been grateful for their jobs.

A model would slowly turn around; and Schuman would jump up from his chair, point one of his blue-sleeved arms at her, and, like a German Shepherd, bark.

Stop right there! For Christ's sake, I had to bribe the House of Chanel to get this piece, and you twirl it around like it was a potato sack. Is this what I'm paying you for? Now, Vera, get your goddamned ass back down that ramp and present this suit like it deserves to be shown, like the piece of art it is. This isn't a suit you're wearing: it's a Monet.

Yes, Mr. Schuman.

Deep down, Irving felt sorry for these models. Admittedly, he would, at times, berate his own salespeople this way, just not quite to the extent of his eccentric friend. Basically, he felt uncomfortable here. He just wanted to secure the goods and get back to his store.

Ok, Adolph. I'm sold. I'll take them. All the Diors you have.

Why, Irving, you goddamned bastard! You're smarter than I

thought. Those suits'll sell like they had ten-dollar gold pieces glued to their sleeves. Girls, girls, back the hell to the dressing rooms. Irv made a wise choice.

Naturally, Irving had his misgivings. He knew what a good salesman Schuman was and was also aware that this barracuda of a showroom wasn't always looking out for the interests of anyone but himself. Nonetheless, Schuman usually picked winners. Though a clothing merchant had to be careful with his dollars in tough times like these, Irving had confidence in Schuman's ability to come up with unique items that would allow Fannette's to stand out from the competition. Irving enjoyed being around this man because his friend's will seemed to knock down anything in its path. Yet his rough edges were counter to Irving's refined nature.

Each suit hung on a wooden hanger and had a long paper bag protecting it. Irving clutched five of them at a time in a sort of lover's hug and carried the samples to his car. Driving down Mission Street was almost a relief from the tenseness of being around Schuman.

Irving's instincts were right. He made a fifty-dollar profit on each of the Lilli Ann suits. In the Jewish community, a friend was good; but if you could also make a profit from your friend, even better.

Being the only man in a women's ready-to-wear store made Irving feel like a cock in the henhouse. Not only were all his employees women, but so were his customers. Truth be told, he did enjoy lording it over his sales help. It was even more rewarding to convince a customer that his taste was superior to hers and could be trusted to make her look better when she walked out the door than when she entered. As circumstances would have it, attractive women who were unattached would find their way to Fannette's. Being that Irving also had a fondness for attractive young women, his social life was never found wanting. His taste was impeccable. When taking a date out, or even visiting local nightspots with his cronies, he would only frequent the finest establishments; however, deep down inside, he was frugal.

When the night fogs embraced the streets of San Francisco in their dampness, Irving would just as soon find himself at his date's house, eating a home-cooked meal as opposed to spending money at an expensive restaurant. As a result of living with the Thurms and socking away most of what he made, Irving was able to accumulate enough money to both expand his business and his lifestyle.

Intoxicating fragrances floated through Fannette's. These were a mixture of women's perfumes, wool garments, and various furs that were attached to those garments.

Each coat and suit carried its own smell, depending upon where its ingredients came from. For instance, a cashmere coat was soft to the touch yet had the faint odor of Chinese grasses where Kashmir goats grazed. A fox-trimmed coat smelled of the Alaskan tundra, clean and cold. On the other hand, a mink-trimmed suit mixed the odor of wool with a damp smell of the watery areas where minks could be found. Each fur had a different feel. A fox was puffy and soft. A mink was short and raspy. Yet a beaver's fur had a short but soft texture to it. Irving knew these furs well plus the difference between good quality and dreck. In addition, he utilized different fur textures to make a woman appear slimmer or more filled out than she actually was. One would never pile fox fur on a Rubenesque woman lest one ran the risk of making her look like a puffball.

To insure that he would always have adequate inventory for his store, Irving developed a buying regimen. In December and June, he would fly to New York and visit the buying office of Jack Bronstein. Irving's uncle Abe Thurm had started this relationship. Instead of having to visit ten different manufacturers, Irving was able to visit one office; and Jack Bronstein would do the negotiating for him. Irving, in turn, would haggle with Jack on prices he felt would be profitable to him. By virtue of his buying power, Irving was often able to obtain close outs that were still in style but which were able to carry a higher markup. He would stay at the Plaza Hotel, go to the buying office, and take in a show or two in the evening. By going to New York twice a year, Irving was able to obtain the newest styles, fresh from Europe for the next season. One thing about Irving Bartel, he was always fastidiously dressed. It could be ninety-five muggy degrees on a summer day in New York; and he would be wearing a white long-sleeved shirt, a black-and-red striped tie, and all this underneath a gray wool suit. He'd as soon have been naked as not fashionably attired.

In spring, Irving would trade the hustle and bustle of New York for the more laid-back atmosphere of Los Angeles. There, amid palm trees and burgeoning movie studios, were manufacturers of uniquely California fashions. These appealed to the younger woman who was the trendsetter on her block. Of course, most of these clothing manufacturers were Jewish; so though there was a camaraderie brought about by being a member of the same tribe, there was the usual give-and-take over price.

It was in Los Angeles that Irving developed a friendship with a man named Manny Hackel. They were introduced by one of Irving's clothing contacts. Manny was short, with a roundish face, darting brown eyes, and moppish brown hair. His eyes were like those of a lion; even at rest, they took in everything while recording images and numbers in his seemingly endless memory. Manny had accumulated some money doing a little of this and a bit of that. He then started buying real estate. He began with a little house then a duplex and, after that, a commercial piece. Irving found this to be fascinating. Here was a man who, it appeared, didn't have to work but had a consistent income coming in. He had no employees or labor unions to worry about. Perhaps there was something to be learned here. Manny was one of Irving's professors whose lessons were to be learned at the University Of The Streets.

CHAPTER 13
FAMILY—FIRST AND LAST

• • •

When relaxing at home in San Francisco, Irving would take his Aunt Fanny and his cousins Gerson, David, and Hilda driving to the zoo or Playland At The Beach, or ice-skating at historic Sutro Baths near the Cliff House. Hilda's curly hair would bounce up and down as she skated circles around her clumsier brothers. Her high-pitched laugh would mingle with the gleeful shouts of other children as their voices slid across the ice. Irving and Fanny tried their hand but did a lot of skating on their backsides. Sometimes, they would even go exploring down on the Peninsula. Prior to his passing, Abe Thurm invested in some lots that were once part of a country club in the small town of Belmont. This town was situated in the hills not far from the railroad. People would, on weekends or in the summer, take the train or drive from San Francisco to their country homes. A street with beautiful views of the city he so loved was named after Abe Thurm. At times, they would drive down Skyline Boulevard through the town of Woodside, where people kept horses. Irving would put the top down in the summer and let his cousins sit in the back seat with the warm wind blowing through their hair. He would then take them down curvy Woodside Road and into the exclusive town of Atherton. This was a part of the Peninsula where San Francisco high society had their summer homes. Some kept horses in Woodside. Others preferred the flat orchard land of Atherton.

All during this time, European influences still shaped Irving

Bartel. Though he had an American name, his family was still the Puderbeutels who dwelled in Poland. He kept weekly contact with his family. Though assimilated to San Francisco society, he spoke with a distinctive European accent. No one could put their finger on it. People would ask him where he came from because his particular accent contained so many ingredients. The answer was always Austria.

News from the old country was always of interest to Irving. It brought a moment of quiet contemplation to his mad hubbub of a world. Little Ethel was now a beautiful young woman in her teens. Her full hair hung down to her slender neck; and her brown, brooding eyes were so large they could see inside you. Ben was a stocky seven-year-old with an infectious grin. Abe, Gerson, and Jim were handsome young men ready to make their way in the world. But speaking of making their way in the world; despite Irving's success in America, his mother had sound words of advice.

My Dear Irving:

I hope this letter finds you in good health. How are our loving relatives the Thurms? May He, blessed be His name, always look after them. Gerson Thurm will be Bar Mitzvah age soon, no? How well does he know the Torah? What about Hilda, my lovely princess? She must have lots of friends. You tell Fanny to keep her daughter home for a while. A girl let out is like a cat let out. They jump the fence then are gone.

As for you, Son, I know you are working very hard. Your Father and I are most proud of all your accomplishments. Your father cannot help boasting about you at the Schul (Temple).

Far be it from me to interfere, but you can't live alone. You must find a mate! It's nature's way. Not only that, society frowns on men who stay single too long. Get yourself a nice Jewish girl who will be your helpmate. She'll keep you dressed properly, iron your clothes, keep the house clean, care for you when you're sick. Most important of all, she'll give you children that will be your legacy.

Another thing, Son; you must find yourself a place. The Thurms have taken you into their home and into their hearts. Do not wear out your welcome! It's time to have a place of your own. Let us hear from you more often!

LOVE,
MOTHER

As Leah carefully folded the letter and slipped it into its envelope, Gerson couldn't help asking her regarding Irving's most recent letter to them,

Mother? What's a convertible automobile? How can something go a mile a minute, yet you can put its top up and down? Wouldn't the people riding inside be picked up by the wind and be carried away?

Leah had other things on her mind; so she whisked her son away from her writing table with the admonishment that if he spent more time studying the Torah and less time asking frivolous questions, he possibly might obtain a sliver of knowledge before he died of old age.

CHAPTER 14

A WIFE FROM THE CITY OF ANGELS

• • •

One day in early March, Irving was on a buying trip to Los Angeles. As usual, he stayed at the plush Beverly Hills Hotel. Its white stucco exterior gleamed in the springtime sunshine. Cool winds whistled through the concrete canyons of Los Angeles as they were known to do in March. Irving drove to the various manufacturers, as he was wont to do, in search of hot sellers. At one of the suit manufacturers, the owner introduced Irving to a tall, clean-shaven man. He was thin but had a purposeful jaw. A full head of gray hair was neatly combed with not one out of place. The man's brown eyes quickly read the person he was introduced to.

Irv, I want you to meet Ike Barker. He has a sportswear store in Long Beach. Not only is he Jewish, but has two daughters as well.

Irving's attention level rose. Primarily on his mind was striking a price that would make him money back in San Francisco. Quickly, his thoughts had to change gears. All he could find to say initially was,

Oh really?

Before Irving had a chance to analyze his new acquaintance, this handsome man was, in turn, taking a measure of a potential groom

So, where are you from? inquired Barker.

San Francisco.

Oh? Beautiful town. One of my daughters goes to college up there. What type of business do you have?

The man looked successful enough for Irving to answer the question. Besides, with two daughters, this man might be worth knowing.

My business is women's coats and suits. What brings you here?

Irving would give if he got. A smidgen of information in exchange for a biography. As long as Irving got more than he gave, it was a worthwhile transaction either monetarily or socially.

As our mutual friend here told you, my name's Barker. Seems we're both in the Shmata business. In my business, the goods are cheaper and the turnover quicker. As good fortune would have it, my store has prospered in an affluent area. Yes, I have two beautiful daughters. It so happens that …

Irving's brain was reeling. He was trying to take it all in. His nostrils whiffed the smell of wool suits that surrounded him, an odor like the ink on US currency. Yet thoughts of his mother back in Poland, with her kind smile, went through his mind. He remembered her written words, *You don't want to be alone.* This man was successful, a person to be respected. In addition, he was handsome. Most likely, his daughters would be attractive. As Irving's parents said, *The apple doesn't often fall far from the tree.* Perhaps his mother's wishes and circumstance were destined to meet. It's strange how things had a way of coming to pass. All Irving came here for was to buy some suits for his store.

…Elian, my older daughter, is at Mills College in Oakland.

Jim Bartel (Irving's brother) provides some background.

Ike Barker adopted Elian and her younger sister, Ann, from his brother, a seaman, who couldn't support them.

Irving was thirty years old and Elian just twenty one. She was finishing her senior year at Mills College, a well-thought-of women's school located in Oakland, California. She was a thin, uncommonly beautiful young woman, who wore her reddish-brown hair in a bun. Her face was full and could change expressions on a dime. She was extremely well read but had a vivacious personality that drew people to her like a lodestone.

Ike took a liking to this young man who, he could tell, was on his way up in the world. He called his daughter with the familiar *I've got someone you should meet.*

Elian, for her part, had seen her share of uglies, dimwits, and assorted flotsam of Jewish mankind. She had even tried out some Christians with no better results; however, when it was her dad that recommended somebody, her ears were open though her intellectual mind still maintained a good portion of skepticism. Of course, the questions poured forth in a torrent.

So Dad, what does he look like? Is he handsome? Glasses? Dad, I'm not so sure about someone who wears glasses. Where did he get his degree? No degree? Dad, what are you bringing someone like this to me for? First of all, he's probably ugly. Secondly, he's got no education. What are we going to talk about, the magnification of his lenses? If we went out for a date and his glasses fell off, he probably wouldn't know which part of me to kiss. Yes. He is Jewish, that's true.

To say that Ike had an impetuous daughter would be an understatement. She was aware that she was known as a looker. In addition, this female could hold her own with anybody when discussing literature, history, art, or politics. As a result, Elian let her father know that the best mankind had to offer was none too good for her. But a surprise was in store.

When the phone call came, she was at first perplexed by being caught off guard. Her mental reflexes were to immediately shunt aside those who dared invade her privacy. But there was something about this voice that dismantled her defenses, a voice that echoed Europe's long cultural tradition. The tone was gentle yet persuasive, inquisitive but hinting at eons of knowledge. When the mention of her father Ike was made, Elian's attention was immediately aroused. Her preconceptions went out the window. On the phone was a man who, though not from the hallowed halls of academia, had a tone that resonated with confidence.

Elian ran into a force she could not resist. First came the endorsement of her father. Irving did the rest. He was a charmer. Though the girl came from a well-to-do family, Irving swept her off her feet. He would take her out to the finest restaurants. He knew the maître d' at all of them. He'd slip them a "sawbuck" (five dollar bill) and would be ushered to a choice table when others were waiting at the door. Elian couldn't, until years later, understand where this man was able to summon up the influence he did. They could sit at a table and talk for hours. True enough, he knew little of art and less about Hamlet. What he did know about was how her race evolved over thousands of years. He had a grasp of human psychology and could tell her story after story about this customer or that businessman and how someone else's success could relate to her life. She wasn't used to the real world, and it fascinated her. On his part, Irving wanted someone who was vivacious, who could converse on subjects he had no knowledge of. It was essential that she be Jewish and that she look good. Elian fit the bill on all counts. She would take Irving to art exhibits, where she was in her element, and he gazed in perplexed wonder. The wonder was: how could someone see beauty in some of these works? Irving could only see beauty in a coat or suit and how much profit it would produce.

Elian? How much did you say this painting sold for? You've got to be kidding. For that kind of money, it sure isn't very big.

Different perspectives, different points of view. He, the practical, the worldly. Her, cultured, book smart. Yet, strangely enough, the two of them hit it off. Each was looking for something. She wanted a provider—someone like her father. He was looking for a helpmate, a person that would take care of domestic responsibilities and could provide a social dimension he lacked. The eventual visit to her parents in Long Beach took place.

Though Irving hated to part with merchandise at less than what he perceived as a fair profit, he couldn't present himself to Elian's family as a cheapskate; thus, he took her to Fannette's and found her a coat she would be proud to wear. No, the coat she received was not the one she wanted. Elian wanted mink. Her husband-to-be gave her some mink but mostly wool. In other words, a fur-trimmed coat. Irving did not like to see high markup goods walk out the door for free. So came Elian's first experience with Irving's frugality.

Disappointment was soon forgotten, and Elian's beauty radiated from the new coat. Future groom was presented to future in-laws. Irving was out of his domain and not so self-assured anymore. He was now in the land of old Long Beach money. Ike Barker was already a formidable figure to deal with. Tall, self-assured, wealthy, and educated. His wife was a highly cultured woman, so much so that one might have thought she was carved out of marble. She loved anything that was not a haven for the masses. Her fancies were: art, opera, symphonies, garden shows, and book readings—in other words venues where she wouldn't have to mix and mingle with regular people. Out of this gilded environment stepped Elian. Into a world of privilege and knowledge walked a young man from Poland. Where he came from, roads weren't even paved. There was no electricity until about two years before he met Elian. Horses still moved people and goods.

One thing about Irving was that he never claimed to be something he was not. He didn't try to talk about literature he hadn't read or paintings he never saw or cared about. What he had was an intensity but also a disarming way of carrying on a conversation. He'd hold someone spellbound then convince them that he was right. In addition, there was something mysterious about him. What was that place like where he came from? What was his pedigree? Of course, he would always say he came from Austria. People pictured some quaint little alpine village, and Irving would let the subject rest.

Long Beach was a town whose white homes were inhabited by white people basking in the sun. Spots of light bounced off whitecaps and danced on the white walls of Mediterranean-styled homes.

Into this world walked Irving Bartel like a long vanished conquistador. He would overcome the natives, not with a sword, but with charm. His lean figure, tanned features, and black-framed sunglasses made him look like one of the many movie stars that graced the area, seeking seclusion from the bright lights of Hollywood. Irving could turn a conversation on a dime. If a lady was talking about art, he would tell her about the attributes of blue fox fur. She would suddenly develop amnesia concerning artists and paintings and, instead, would focus on herself. Irving's words would paint a picture of its own. Women would let his words take them to another place, a place where they were more glamorous. Oh yes, Irving was just as much an artist as Monet because he could paint word pictures in which people could envision themselves.

Both Ike and his wife could see qualities in this twenty-nine-year-old that would make him a good husband for their daughter. But prospective grooms, even in modern times, had to run a gauntlet similar to that of ancient Indian warriors. There was still Elian's opinionated younger sister Ann to consider. She gave him the who, where, when, why interview. When they were through, Ann took her sister into her room for a sisterly caucus.

What do you think, Ann?

I've got to tell you, Elian. You picked a looker.

No, I mean his manners. After all, I've got to be seen in public with him.

Frankly, Elian, he could charm your clothes off and probably did.

Stop it, Ann. You can pick out the grungy part of anything. What I'm asking you is, I mean, do you think I can do better?

Do you want the truth?

Your version of it, Ann? I'm not sure.

Look, you asked me. So do you want to hear it or not?

Ann, you know I respect your opinion even if you do look at the world through dark glasses. Nonetheless, you do have an uncanny way of picking boyfriends. Go ahead. Give me the straight goods.

Elian's facial features tightened. She asked for something she was not really sure she wanted. Her sister sought perfection in others to the same extent that she did. Both of them had been brought up by demanding parents, who were of the opinion that the world of manhood would be lucky to get their little princesses.

Ok, Elian, you asked for the truth. Take a look at what you brought home in the past. A queer.

Are you referring to Justin?

I sure am. Don't you think he was a little swishy?

The smile left Elian. She started toying with the ribbon on her hair, a sign that she was on the defensive.

By no means. He's sensitive.

Ann couldn't hold back her laughter.

Dothen he jift lithp a lot? Ha, ha, ha, ha.

Ellian's younger sister was laughing so hard she tottered on the edge of the bed ready to fall off. Needless to say, Elian found it necessary to put this jester in her place.

Speaking of boyfriends, you're a fine one to talk. How 'bout the one you dragged home and Dad sent packing out the back door 'cause he was a goy (Christian)? And remember the swell that invited you to dinner last week, and you had to pay the bill because he didn't have any money?

Elian's redness returned to a warm glow. She was no longer fumbling with her hair ribbon.

What the hell! It seems that some of your choices weren't exactly doozies. Let's call a temporary truce on boyfriends, okay? Now, what about Irving?

While the two sisters were discussing Irving's fate, he had nothing else to do but keep the parents company. Not a man to let his words fly, he allowed other people to talk. By doing so, they felt him to be a brilliant conversationalist. And so the subjects ranged from business to politics. Though Irving's politics were not yet formulated, he was still ready to discuss the attributes of The New Deal.

If Roosevelt can put people to work, then he's a good man.

When Elian's mother talked about opera, Irving thanked his lucky stars her daughter hauled him to *Carmen*. Yes, he balked at the price of tickets, never believing that he belonged there in the first place. But Elian convinced him that if he wanted to be part of high society, then he should be seen at the opera. As a result, he was slowly exposed to things Italian because most operas are sung in that language. Irving soon came to appreciate the splendor that was *The Barber of Seville, Aida,* and others; thus he was able to discuss the merits of certain opera arias with Elian's high-browed mother.

As to the field of business, Ike Barker found a kindred spirit in his prospective son-in-law. Irving could match him head-to-head when it came to the fine points of a real estate deal. In fact, Irving was negotiating, at that very time, to purchase his second retail building on Market Street. It would be next door to his Fannette's store. He would put another women's coat and suit business in it and call the store Juliette's.

While Irving was holding his own with Elian's parents, the prospective bride and her sister were discussing his finer and less fine points. Ann held up the scale of good and bad for her sister.

Elian, to tell the truth, he certainly is handsome. Even those thick glasses make him look studious. And his clothes ... This man knows how to dress. Like a mench. What's more, Sister, being that you asked, he does have money. Remember what Dad told us. It's just as easy to fall in love with a rich one as a poor one.

Elian interjected, *Maybe easier. Ha ha ha!*

That laugh of yours could kill a horse. But back to Irving. He's cultured, obviously from a good family, but not cultural, if you know what I mean. Let's put it this way. He's not the artistic type. And then there's that accent. Some might find it strange, but I think it's interesting. If you didn't know, you couldn't tell where he was from. On balance, Sister, I think you made a good pick.

Ann, that means a lot to me. Though I know my heart, I value your insights. Let's go rescue the poor man. He's been in the clutches of our parents far too long.

Irving felt relief at the approach of his beloved beauty but apprehension over whether he passed muster with her ever critical sister. He need have had no worry. Another family was about to take him in.

The scent of salt air hung in the warm Southern California air as it blew through their hair, a young couple on the brink of promise.

Irving had the top down on his Buick as he drove his fiancée back up the coast to the Bay Area. Wind ruffled their clothes as it caressed them. It carried away Irving's anxieties as every pore of his body became invigorated. He had uttered the fateful words, *would you?* Yes, uttered them in front of God, Elian's family, and—not least of all—her. Their cares floated above foamy waves. Yelling was necessary to be heard above the howling wind.

With Irving's arrival in San Francisco, his euphoria soon was replaced by practical cares. He needed to find a home of his own. Before focusing on real estate matters, he drafted a letter to his family back in Poland.

Dear Mother and Father:

Addressing your wishes, I have found a wife. She is, naturally, Jewish and of a fine family—merchants like you and I. The father, Ike Barker, is in the women's ready-to-wear business and lives in Southern California, about 300 miles south of San Francisco, on the Pacific Ocean. My future bride is named Elian and is graduating from a private women's college called Mills. It has an excellent reputation. She is well versed in art, history, and anything cultural. She can converse on subjects having to do with government or translate an opera from its Italian. She is beautiful to look at and, I believe, will be an asset to me. How are my brothers and sisters? I miss you all very much. We will come to Europe and visit. You, both, can be proud of her. Love, Irving.

The introductions were not complete, however. Irving may have introduced his wife to his family overseas, but the task now was to introduce Santa Barbara society in the form of Elian Barker to San Francisco society represented by his Aunt Fanny Thurm. Elian was duly introduced then mobbed by Gerson, David, and Hilda on the way up the steps to the Thurm home for what Irving thought would be a quiet dinner. Elian could now put herself in Irving's place when he made his trip to Santa Barbara and faced her family's version of the tribal council. Things were different in San Francisco. Society had been established longer in *the city*; thus questions asked were more oblique. Fanny would inquire with her warm smile,

Hmm, Barker? Doesn't sound Jewish. How did you say your family got that name?

In her charming manner, Elian would smile brightly and reply that it was a name taken for convenience, much as Irving's last name was. In addition, Fanny could be most assured that Elian was quite Jewish upon which she would quote the section of Exodus, where Moses encounters the burning bush. That may not have seemed so impressive, except for the fact that she quoted the passage in its original Hebrew.

After that, questions wandered from heredity to clothing. Since all the Thurm children, like Irving, were drafted into service at the clothing store, inquiries were addressed more specifically to what Elian wore. Hilda, who was in the flower of her girlhood, was the least sophisticated.

Aunt Elian, is that fur on your coat real?

That was Hilda, direct, embarrassingly to the point; then Gerson and David would chime in. Being almost Bar Mitzvah boys, they felt they were right on the verge of manhood and knew more than they really did.

Aunt Elian, is that coat made of cashmere or shearling lamb?

Before Irving had time to admonish his precocious cousins, Elian, in her own direct way, blunted their egos.

First of all, Hilda, the fur is indeed real. Here, feel it! Don't the hairs just slip off your fingers? Don't the hairs feel soft as morning dew?

Yes, Aunt Elian.

Then the fur is real. And furthermore, young lady, I'd suggest your mom lock you up in the vault with all those fur collars until they came alive again and told you they were real.

That was good for a few months' worth of nightmares for Hilda.

And as for you, Mr. David and Mr. Gerson (She would address someone as Mr. or Miss if she wanted to make a point that was not going to be pleasant.) … *your cousin Irving ought to have you spend the next ten years' worth of weekends in the store's basement so that you can differentiate between a cashmere and a shearling lamb. If the wool is soft as the breath of evening, it's cashmere, but if it is curly like your sister's hair, it's shearling. Okay? Now, David, how about …?*

Quick as a wink, she would turn the tables from answering questions to asking them. The Thurm children quickly came to the conclusion that this lady was way too smart for them. Their hands rested on their laps. Pretty soon, all that filled the air was food odors mixed with silence.

Irving filled the void by telling the Thurms about his purchase of the building next door to Fannette's and that he would call the store Juliette's. Next, he let the rich aroma of a black cup of coffee spiral its way to the ceiling; then he broke the news. Even Elian, his closest confidant, didn't know. There was a house he was negotiating to buy for his bride. It wasn't just any house.

CHAPTER 15

WHERE SWELLS DWELL

• • •

A trust officer at Hibernia Bank called on Irving at the store. He later related to the Thurms and his astounded fiancée that this well-dressed man had a proposition for him. The man was handsome with grayish hair, gray suit, black tie, and white shirt. Since the Hibernia Bank was a place where Irishmen who settled in San Francisco deposited their money, it was understandable that the man had a slight brogue.

Mr. Bartel, I've got a piece of property for ye that would be very special.

Irving replied,

What brings you to call on me? I'm just a small merchant.

We know times be tough. It's been said that you have money. There was a doctor owned the place. It seems he got too big for his britches and couldn't make the payments on his mortgage. The saints know we tried to help him keep the place but ... Well, we hada take it back. The house is in Presidio Terrace. Mr. Bartel, you know Presidio Terrace?

Not that well.

Actually, Irving knew more than he let on about the area. Presidio Terrace was only a short distance west of where the Thurms lived. It was known to be the most prestigious address in town. As Irving related to Fanny Thurm and Elian, it was all he could do to contain his excitement. He never dreamed of living in an area such as that.

Well, if ya cana excuse me for a asken, but where ye been living all these years?

Austria, for the most part.

Oh. Now I understand. So ye be an immigrant like our customers?

You could say.

Not to be lording over ye, but Presidio Terrace is the plum area of the city to live in. Now to the point. We took over the doctor's mortgage for $40,000, and we just want to get out from under it. In other words, we want the property off our books. What's ye think?

I'll give you $35,000 cash.

Mr. Bartel, we can't do that. We've got to at least get our investment.

Talk to your boss and let me know!

By that time, Elian had just about dropped from her chair in anticipation. This new husband of hers seemed like a chip from off her father's block though he was going to lose that home for sure. All of a sudden, dreams of movie queens passed through her mind. She, yes, Miss Elian Barker—soon-to-be Mrs. Bartel—would be queen of her own castle, a mistress of high society. But it was all slipping away because her husband's nerves were made of high tensile steel. Fanny Thurm added,

Irving, you did the right thing. Watch! He'll be back. Abe didn't teach you to be a schmuck.

Truth be told, Elian had her misgivings. She wasn't used to this man's style of negotiating. Usually when she wanted something, she just bought it and paid whatever was asked. Not Irving.

Sure enough, three days later, the Trust Officer paid Irving a return visit. In the meantime, Irving had time to take a walk by the property. He learned that it was right next door to another doctor—the well-respected Dr. Leon Goldman. Not only was this his late Uncle Abe's doctor, but he would father the future U.S. Senator Diane Feinstein. Irving discreetly wandered into the back yard and surveyed its highly manicured grounds. Yes, this was what he wanted; but he mustn't appear too eager.

So, Mr. Bartel, I happened to be in the area and thought to pay ye a visit. Have ye given my proposal some thought?

Thirty-five thousand and it's off your books.

We have a wee bit of a problem.

And what would that be?

It seems my branch manager was studying the ledgers. You know how it is, Mr. Bartel? We have shareholders to report to.

The Trust Officer's eyes were so sad-looking that it made one want to drench their handkerchief in tears.

Here's what he says to me. You tell Mr. Bartel he can have Presidio Terrace for $36,000 cash. You be a shrewd man, Mr. Bartel. What say you?

Though Irving hated to pay $1,000 over what he originally intended to, he thought about Elian's face and how it would look if he lost the place.

A deal. Meet me at Safeco Title Company, 39 Sutter Street, tomorrow. You'll call and let me know what time to meet you.

Mr. Bartel, it is a pleasure to be a doin' business with ye.

When Irving let Elian and the Thurms know that he had, indeed, acquired 28 Presidio Terrace, the excitement couldn't be contained. He and his new wife stood in front of the rolling front lawn and faced two sets of steps that led up from the street. In front of them stood a gray edifice that rose three stories high. It had two wings that branched off the main entrance. Each wing was two stories. In the center, like a cathedral tower, stood the master suite. As a backdrop loomed the huge dome of Temple Emmanuel. Surely, if ever there was a blessed home, this would be it. Little did they know.

Though the Depression's maw was chewing up souls and spitting them out, Irving began to build his estate. He already owned the store building at 771 Market Street, where Fannette's was situated; then, he acquired 775 Market Street, a three-story building where he opened Juliette's. Now he owned a home that was the address to be in San Francisco. Irving created slogans for his stores. Fannette's was *Famous For Coats*. Juliette's would be known for its *Fine Coats and Suits*.

Money has a strange odor. To some, it smells musty. To others, it has the odor of people's hands. Yet others find the smell of the paper and ink that make up money loathsome. When it came to money,

Irving found nothing objectionable about it. His parents raised him that way. To add to this, he had a wife who aspired to climb the ranks of high society. In order to support this growing mass of responsibility, Irving had to work hard. It was not unusual for him to spend seven days a week down at the store or on buying trips. Unfortunately for him, he had a wife who not only wanted him to be a pillar of society, but who also wanted his company now and then.

The amazing thing was that, for a while, Irving actually was able to juggle his life. A collage of photos showed him in sunglasses, with tan riding pants, wearing a suede riding jacket, on a brown quarter horse; or standing in front of a beautifully styled Mediterranean building dressed in white slacks, white shirt, white tie, white Panama hat, light blue double-breasted sport coat, and black-and-white saddle shoes. He could be found, at times, in his opera box. Elian was there also, her radiant beauty available for San Francisco's gentry to gaze upon. On Sundays, Elian would drag Irving to art galleries so as to satiate her cultural appetite or to nurseries enlisting his opinion on her new floral acquisitions. Actually, he would rather have been down at the store working to support it all.

When Irving went to New York, he'd room at the illustrious Hampshire House across from Central Park. He would visit his buyer Jack Bronstein and return with some profitable bargains. But now he had Elian in tow. So instead of making a quick return to San Francisco, he might have to take in some sights. His world turned from a me to an us.

CHAPTER 16

THE FIRSTBORN

• • •

On October 20, 1934, a warm autumn sun bathed San Francisco in its golden glow. Streetcars tumbled down Market Street. A cable car seeped out the smell of burning pine wood brakes as it slowly crept down Nob Hill. Bums on Skid Row asked, *Buddy, ya got a dime?* Dust was the only crop being farmed in the Midwest. Meanwhile, birth was taking place at Children's Hospital on California Street. A handsome little boy named Arthur Gabriel Bartel was being born to Irving and Elian. A nursery at the Presidio Terrace home was all decked out to accept him. And thus arrived the Puderbeutel's firstborn in America. Elian, of course, was the center of attention. She was the proud mother—and a beautiful one as well. Her room looked like a flower shop. Bouquets from everywhere. She was barely able to lift her head when the phone calls came in: her father, Ike; sister, Ann; even grandpa Simon (though she couldn't understand him). As for Irving, his appearance at the hospital was brief. It was thought that the mother had to do all the work and bear all the pain. The father was just a contributor.

Irving took himself to a venue that he was more familiar with and where things centered around him: the stores. A woman came to Fannette's to buy a coat. One of the older salesladies, Michal (who was 75), helped her. After spending an hour with this woman, Michal showed her a coat with a beaver collar. The woman asked, *Is this a male beaver?* Males have thicker fur. Naturally, she didn't want to pay much money. Michal said, *I wasn't there when it was circumcised.*

CHAPTER 17

DARKNESS ENVELOPES EUROPE

• • •

Back in Europe, the leaden cloud of Nazism and anti-Semitism began to cover the continent. European economies were sunk in a quagmire similar to that in America. Europe, however, had a group of people to blame this woeful situation on—a scapegoat that had been used for centuries. In Europe's case, there was a supposed international financial conspiracy. These bankers, according to the anti-Semites, were aided and abetted by liberal politicians worldwide with the help, of course, of their constituency.

The smell of Nazism began to rot the air of Germany in the early thirties. Poverty was the rule, not the exception, in Irving's hometown of Lizhensk, Poland. Though Poland obtained its independence at the end of World War I, its economy left much to be desired. By the time the thirties rolled around, Lizhensk was mostly non-electrified; and few households had a telephone. Horses were still the main means of conveyance. Men would stand on street corners begging for a dose of generosity from their Catholic brethren. Generosity was mostly found from educated Jews who had occupations or businesses. There were also poor Jews, but they were a minority. As a result, anti-Jewish sentiment easily rode the wind from Germany to Austria and over the border to Poland.

Sure, those merchants are still prospering. It's because of the international banking conspiracy. It's their filthy gelt (money).

Like a hoar frost from the north, it moved south. Governments started taking action to freeze Jews out of the general economy. In Germany, it was more overt. There, storm troopers would smash the windows of Jewish shops and beat Jews until the sidewalks were sprinkled red with blood. Poland's government was "humane." It set up a mechanism to segregate Jews economically then systematically excluded them from government service and from public education. Of course, Jewish people were still allowed to get themselves killed militarily.

Throughout the centuries, Jewish people have always taken care of their own and do so to this day. As a result, those Jewish merchants who weren't totally boycotted would hire Jews to work for them and, thus, kept much of their own employed.

Simon and Leah Puderbeutel could see a grim anti-Semitic future closing in on them. They still prospered due to the fact that their hardware business stocked necessities for both the Gentile population and for the government. Though both hated these merchants, business was still grudgingly done. Simon and Leah could see that there would be no place for their male children in Lizhensk. One after another would go to America. Irving was just the first. Others would follow.

In the meantime, the Puderbeutel daughters had blossomed into attractive young women. Jewish women were taught, at an early age, that their highest calling was wife and mother. After all, it was said in the Torah, *Be fruitful and multiply!* Sarah was husky, like her mother, but with a beautiful face. She radiated Leah's warm smile. By 1934, Sarah's daughter, who looked like a miniature twin, was eight and in the midst of young girlhood. Rose had married a handsome man from the local community, who met Simon and Leah's specifications as being from a good Jewish family. Good meant having money. He was clean-shaven with short black hair. His face was banker serious and full. He had a large Jewish nose and dressed impeccably in suit and tie. Sarah was the jewel of Lizhensk.

By 1934, little Ethel wasn't little anymore and had blossomed into a beautiful young woman of twenty-two. Her black hair hung down to her neck, and bangs almost covered her right eye creating a Polish Garbo look. Ethel's black eyes could pierce through the steel door of a bank vault. Her face was thin with a movie star's pouting lips. So if Sarah was the emerald of Lizhensk, Ethel was the diamond. It was time for her to find a husband. Through the auspices of the local matchmaker, a man was found who was deserving of this jewel. He was short, serious, and very intelligent. His name was Joseph Nagel. He lived in a neighboring village. Joe's hair was short and black as was his closely trimmed beard. A smile would be a foreign object on his face. Law was his profession. In those times, if anyone had a need for law, it was a Jew. For miles around, people would seek Joe out for one legal matter or another. It's not that Joe wasn't handsome. He was—in the way a marble statue, carved by a master, is—handsome. Every crevice of his face exuded strength of character. And so the beauty married the lawyer. Both settled in Lizhensk. It was a practical match. Strangely, arranged marriages have a glue holding them together that is invisible to the eye. These were two practical young people who were brought together. He was straightforward and lived in a black-and-white world of torts. She, though beautiful, was brought up to be a person of the world at a young age. To those Ethel knew, her smile was captivating; but to the outside world, she was a Sphinx.

Conveniently, the Puderbeutels had two spare rooms, seeing that both Rose and Sarah had been married off. Oftentimes in Jewish society, when a couple first got married, the parents would invite them to stay in the family home rather than depleting the couple's budget by renting from strangers. Such was the case here. Ethel and Joe, initially, took residence in Simon and Leah's house.

CHAPTER 18

GERSON ARRIVES IN AMERICA

• • •

Irving made preparations for the second Puderbeutel arrival from Lizhensk. Elian was consulted, if that could be the proper word. Actually, she was told they would be having a houseguest who would be staying for an undetermined period of time. This would be Irving's younger brother, Gerson. It must be said that Elian took it graciously due to the fact that her husband impressed upon her the fact that he paid for the house in Presidio Terrace and also paid for her much-better-than-average lifestyle. Her calling was one of the highest: mother and keeper of the home. There were plenty of extra rooms at 28 Presidio Terrace, and one was made ready for Gerson's arrival in 1935. All family members arriving in America took on the name Bartel. Gerson was thirty at the time. Like his brothers, he too was quite handsome. He wore thick-lensed glasses with heavy tortoise shell frames. His jaw was lantern shaped. Unlike his older brother, Irving, he had an infectious laugh. It would stretch itself out to a haaahahaha. Like his brother, Gerson possessed the family's black hair. Also, he chose to be clean shaven as his brothers were.

In San Francisco, Elian did her part in taking care of the home. She was in charge of the hiring and supervision of gardeners, house-keepers, and sundry repair people, who were needed to keep 28 Presidio Terrace in ship shape. Fortunately for her, she was raised with a silver spoon, so to speak, by Ike Barker and was trained in the art of handling household help. In addition, her beauty and vivacious personality lent themselves well to organizing social events. Now, it must be said that to maintain her vivaciousness, a drop or two of the old bottle was a necessary ingredient. Irving, of course, was too busy working to notice. To him, Elian was strictly a social drinker as was he. She did have a volcanic personality at times. Her high-strung behavior was attributed to her being a perfectionist and to the overwhelming responsibilities heaped upon such a young bride.

Gerson Bartel flew into San Francisco. He was warmly welcomed by his brother with a hug that would crush a bear. Gerson was stunned with Elian's beauty. Though he spoke very little English, Elian's kindness to a stranger showed through. The minute Gerson stepped into Irving's convertible, he was convinced that America was, indeed, the promised land where huddled masses were welcomed. As Gerson smelled the salt air and stared at San Francisco's white spires, he realized that one of the world's greatest cities was soon to be his home. He could hardly contain himself.

Ha, Irv. These car seats. They be expensive cows, yes? Ha ha. You able fit our whole town in this bay, yes? Those big white buildings ... That San Francisco? Irv, your wife, Elian, where she get beautiful clothes? Fannette's? Ha ha ha!

He sure has a sense of humor, Elian replied to Irving. Fog hugged the dappled hillsides and created a natural air conditioning system that cooled the interior of Irving's convertible. Gerson was lucky Elian was in a good mood, or she would have given him one of her cutting remarks that might have lowered his height a foot or two.

Irving said some things to his brother in Polish that got him laughing again. Elian understood that his brother did not have a fabulous command of English yet, but she would do her best to change that. They drove down Nineteenth Avenue on the way to California Street. Gerson was astounded at what his eyes were looking at.

Zeese cars that carry one hundred people. No horses need? Electricity run them? Called streetcars? Autos, autos everywhere. Where horses? Everyone here rich, yes?

Elian explained to him humorously that streetcars, indeed, ran on electricity. That quite a few Americans drove cars but that not everyone was rich. She also told him about the different climates in San Francisco and how it could be foggy on Nineteenth Avenue and, at the same time, sunny downtown. Finally, their car turned off California onto Masonic and, from there, onto the cul-de-sac that was Presidio Terrace. When Gerson saw his brother's home, his eyes just about bulged through the lenses of his glasses. Never had he seen such a residence. The scent of freshly cut grass filled his nostrils. Three stories tall? Royalty in Poland didn't live this well. Jews lived like this in America? Gerson couldn't believe it. The front lawns and shrubs were manicured like a European palace garden. Their family home in Lizhensk was one of the largest in town, yet it would fit in one wing of Irving's home. Not only that, but there were indoor bathrooms.

Gerson, like many immigrants, was a victim of sensory overload. America was too big and too technologically advanced to take in all at once. Irving even had a garage in which to park his car. Try as he might, Gerson was unable to find a stable or a horse anywhere. Truly, this was an amazing country. Elian, for her part, was not only glamorous and possessing a vivacious personality; but to top it off, she was a terrific cook. While she made sure her new guest's belongings were placed in his room, she began preparations on a scrumptious lunch.

Meanwhile, like his father, Irving brought his brother into the wood-paneled library for a talk. Since it was morning and too early in the day for alcoholic beverages, Irving got each of them a glass of seltzer water on ice. As Gerson raised the crystal glass to his lips, little bubbles bounced off his nose. As he leaned back in his chair, the leather warmed Gerson's back as though it were a woman's hand. Irving sounded so much like their father.

Welcome to America, my brother Gerson. I know you have had a long and tiring trip. My wife and I will provide a home for you while you get established. I am offering you a job in my store. You will learn the ready-to-wear business. As you may know, economic times are tough here though it may not seem so to you. We can provide a roof over your head. You will be well fed. Lastly, I can pay you fifty dollars a week to start. As you learn, so will you earn. What do you think?

Elian knew better than to disturb her husband, but to her, meals were an important matter as well; and her day could be ruined if a meal was ruined, so she took the chance of Irving's ire.

Lunch will be ready in half an hour.

Gerson quickly analyzed his situation. He couldn't speak the language well. He had little money. He had no marketable job skills. With Bartel practicality, he surmised that his prospects were better with his brother than anywhere else. He sat forward to address his brother.

Irv, you be most good to me. You take me your home. Your wife, she feed me. I live here like I be royalty. Jewish royalty. Ha ha ha! You generous brother. I try ready-to-wear business. I be good, you keep me. I not, I go.

And so it was that Gerson started at Juliette's. First, he was placed in thc basement to make boxes. He then advanced to opening merchandise and placing it on hangers. In the evenings, he would study English at Marina Junior High School on Fillmore Street. Pretty soon, like Irving, his suits would be covered with mink and fox fur. If he wore a black suit to work and handled too many white fox-trimmed coats, Gerson could be mistaken for an artic fox himself though a rather large one due to all the white fur that attached itself to his jacket.

It wasn't as though Irving lacked a sense of humor. He, in fact, had one. It just didn't surface very often because he was a serious man with heavy responsibilities on his shoulders. He did make people laugh when he told the story of his grandpa Shmul. As Irving would tell it, Shmul was so frugal that he and his wife would sit around the house naked so that they wouldn't wear out clothing.

In 1935, thousands of Okies fled the dust bowls of Oklahoma and, with all their possessions strapped to the tops of Model A Fords, settled in the boiling Central Valley of California. They traded their Midwestern dust for the fertile soil of Fresno, Visalia, and Bakersfield. Though the average summer temperature was in the nineties, bountiful crops were brought forth. Eventually, this area became America's breadbasket.

CHAPTER 19

A GIRL IS BORN

• • •

On April 1, 1936, Irving and Elian's second child was born at Children's Hospital. Her name was Glenda Louise Bartel. Whether Elian wanted a girl, it's hard to say. As later events were to prove, the jury would be out on that one. Elian, once again, would be the recipient of congratulations while Irving was content to sit on the sidelines as a facilitator. Ike Barker, her dad, phoned and sent her bouquets of flowers enough to start an arboretum. Ann, Elian's still single sister paid a visit to Children's Hospital and delivered enough sarcastic comments to put half of San Francisco in its place. When these two volatile sisters got together, the verbal barbs flew everywhere. Woe be to that innocent bystander, who had not their wits about them. Glenda was a promising-looking baby. She combined the attractiveness of her mother with the handsome looks of her father. Elian was numbed by the attention she was receiving and by the medicine she had been provided with.

Irving was quite proud of his brood. He was especially proud because they were pretty children, and he so wrote his parents.

Dear Mother and Father:

Elian gave birth today to a beautiful little girl. You would be most proud of her. She looks like her mother and I. As for my son, Arthur, he is two now and is growing up to be a handsome young boy. He looks like a Puderbeutel, which is probably why he is so handsome. As to whether he has the Puderbeutel brains, it is still too early to tell. Father, as you would say, a horse doesn't give birth to a donkey.

Mother, you could appreciate the fact that Elian loves her home and tends to it like a robin would to its nest. Our daughter was named Glenda. My wife left the walls in the baby's room white so she could paint them pink in case the baby was a girl. Enough about us over here. How are my sisters and their husbands? How fare my brothers? Abe? Jim? Ben? In your last letter, you mentioned that you and father were considering sending Jim to me next. What is your time schedule for that?

I have read what is going on in Europe. Though the two of you trust only to God, it doesn't look good. Far be it from me to render advice to those that know more than I. It may be a good idea to take shelter in America.

Tell all we send our love and best wishes.

Indeed, Simon and Leah Puderbeutel could read the writing on the wall. They knew it would become harder and harder for Jews to make a living in Europe due to the predominantly anti-Semitic attitude of many European governments. They, however, felt their business was secure because they sold what all governments needed—guns. On the other hand, they would spirit away as many children as they could to the prosperous shores of America.

Now Elian had more to tend to than just a mansion. She had two beautiful little children. Spring was in the air. It was that time of year when chill winter rains moved over and let dazzling sunshine warm the air and soul. Flowers splashed color in Golden Gate Park. White swans, with their long gleaming necks, came out of winter hiding and could be seen gliding across the Palace of Fine Arts lagoon down at the foot of Baker Street.

Irving was busy acquiring spring goods for his two thriving stores. Winter goods, to him, were like stale food. They had lost their taste. He would mercilessly mark them down until a point was reached where even the ugliest coat found its way into a Juliette's box that marched itself out the door in the hands of a bargain-seeking customer.

While Irving produced the bacon, so to speak, ghosts slipped through the windows of Presidio Terrace—wispy things that haunted Elian. It was uncertain whether she wanted a girl. Boys were so much easier to deal with. They weren't as intellectually astute and tended to not threaten her from a cultural point of view. In her circle, many of the men who frequented flower shows or art galleries were homosexuals (though this fact was kept hush hush). A little girl could grow up to be like her sister, Ann—intelligent, sarcastic, beautiful—or, worse yet, might end up being like Elian herself. As a result, an antipathy arose between Elian and her daughter. The mother liked to drink. It eased the pressure of a young woman with so many domestic responsibilities. More and more frequently, she would drink a bit too much. When this occurred, it was best to keep clear.

Finally, a third visitor among Elian's unholy triumvirate could best be described by Jim Bartel (Irving's brother).

Elian was a very nice person. She had one drawback. She liked women. Irving took her to a psychiatrist to cure her. When Irving heard what the psychiatrist's advice was, he took a gun and told him he would kill him.

Irving had a temper not to be trifled with. Both Elian and the psychiatrist believed that there was no form of violence Irving was not capable of. Despite a charming exterior, he had both the demeanor and physical strength to make his threats good. It was said that after this gun incident, the good mental doctor took up his practice in some town well away from San Francisco.

The time was ten in the morning. Irving was at the store working. The doorbell at Presidio Terrace rang. It was a stocky, well-dressed lady. Her face was somewhat manly. Even her black hair was trimmed short. She wore a fashionable black hat. *Was Elian in?* she asked the housekeeper, who was sworn to secrecy if she wanted to keep her job. *Ma'am, I'll see.* The lady was named Wolfson, and she was married to a jeweler in San Jose. While he was selling baubles and Irving was selling coats, Mrs. Wolfson was busy being Elian's girlfriend.

Irving, being a very private person, never told a soul about his wife's personality quirks. None would suspect. In public, Elian was as effervescent as a glass of champagne. She could entertain a group of the most diverse individuals by using her considerable intellect. Her laughter sprinkled around the room, instilling well-being as though it were a narcotic.

The year 1937 rolled around. In May, one of the twentieth century's greatest engineering marvels stretched its red span across San Francisco Bay—the Golden Gate Bridge. During its construction, eleven men were either crushed to death or fell into the bay's icy waters. It took four years and $35,000,000 to construct. Over a mile of steel linked Marin County to San Francisco. Fog would frequently cover the bridge's twin spires in its white cotton candy

CHAPTER 20

A VISIT TO THE OLD COUNTRY

• • •

Not only was Marin and San Francisco now connected, Irving felt this would be the time to reconnect with his family in Europe. As a belated honeymoon, he would take his wife to visit his home in Europe. There was an ulterior motive. Irving felt the trip would also serve to get Elian away from her lady friends; this might affect a cure for her lesbian tendencies.

Elian was thrilled with the idea since, cultured though she presumed to be, in actuality, her travels were confined mostly to California. Even if it was Poland, to her it was still Europe. They traveled aboard the Queen Mary, probably the most luxurious ship afloat at the time. Rich wood was everywhere. Crystal chandeliers graced the ballrooms. The British staff wore white livery. This was to be the honeymoon Elian waited five years for; nothing was too good for her. She would stay in a first class stateroom with an ocean view. Irving even did the unusual. Normally, he would prefer his wife wear clothes that he was able to acquire wholesale. He went out of his way, though it pained him inside, to buy her a mink coat even though he had to pay retail for it. Irving felt his investment would rekindle his marriage and would be an expenditure well made.

Everything looked good, at least on the outside. Elian, in her mink coat, could have easily been taken for a movie queen. She was only in her late twenties. Her young face radiated loveliness. If she was in the right mood, her personality would reel you in like a fish; however, if she was brooding, her rapier-like wit would cut you in two as though you were a piece of cheese on the carving board. Her reddish-brown hair blended so well with the mink coat that men would stare at her everywhere she went. This suited Irving fine. He took pride in everything he wore, including his wife.

During the time Irving and Elian were sailing to Europe, Irving's grandfather Shmuel Puderbeutel passed away in the town of Kanczuga, Poland. Because the man was stingy and severe, he was more feared than loved. Nonetheless, Simon, his son, provided for a headstone worthy of the family's name. Simon donned his tefillin and his tallis (prayer shawl). He shook as he sobbingly prayed for forgiveness of his father's soul. Rivka, Shmuel's wife, whose black hair had now turned gray, sold the family store as well as most of their possessions. She loaded what was portable onto a horse-drawn wagon and made the fifty-mile trip to her son's house in Lizhensk. He and his wife, Leah, welcomed her to their home and made a place of honor for her. Rivka would rarely smile because her life gave her little to smile about. Railroad tracks of time made their way across her broad forehead and bore evidence of the austere life she had led. Yet when she did smile, it was like the sun bursting out from behind a cloud and warming everything within its path. If one could get past Rivka's severe demeanor and her rigid lantern jaw, they would find inside a kind human being.

Thus, the Puderbeutel household, instead of being empty due to the exporting of two sons and the marriage of two daughters, was filled by an assortment of family members. Sarah was still home. Ethel and Joe lived there. And then there was the arrival of the family matriarch, Rivka.

When Irving and Elian arrived, a crowd gathered around the Puderbeutel house to view the Americans. These weren't just any Americans; this was a visit by American royalty. It was the prodigal son who made good. Irving and Elian sure looked the part. He was dressed in a navy-blue double-breasted suit with a red-and-blue striped tie. His tie was held in place by a gold tie clasp that had a two-and-a-half-dollar gold piece on it. His teal-blue long sleeve shirt sported French cuffs, each held shut by a gold nugget cuff link. Elian wore a stylish brown wool suit underneath her luxurious mink coat. The proud father, Simon, took it all in while his wife, Leah, basked in the glow of their newfound celebrity. People who normally just sneered when passing on the street would come up to Simon, slap him on the back, and say, *So this is your son Isaac? From America? And his wife. She is so glamorous.*

Silvia Bartel was a young girl at the time. She did not marry Jim until many years later. She recalls that she and some friends gathered around the living room window of the Puderbeutel house so they could view this American couple. Soon the towering figure of Leah confronted them and, with a baleful glare, sent them promptly scurrying in all directions.

Though treated like a queen, Elian had entered a cultural chasm. To start with, electricity had just entered the homes of Lizhensk. The bathroom was an outhouse fifty feet away from the home so that its odors could lace the air from a good distance. In addition, the main means of transportation was still by horse-drawn wagon, which threw up clouds of dust in every direction. And to top it off, the only one who spoke fluent English was Irving. Most of the conversation that went back and forth was in Yiddish. A funny German-like term would be mentioned, and howls of laughter would erupt. Elian was the only one not laughing. Though Jewish, she felt very un-Jewish. She had been brought up as a Reform Jew. Yiddish was not spoken around her house. The religious services she attended were partly in English. As to the Hebrew, that was relegated to the province of Rabbis and Cantors. Elian certainly felt the outsider in this Orthodox Jewish household.

Irving did his best to include his wife in the general joviality. He explained his parents' background, their family history as best as he could remember it. His memory only went back one generation. When the word *pipic* was brought up in one context or another, Irving would tell Elian that it was a part of the body that is not usually mentioned, which confirmed in Elian's mind that these Polish people were not only rustics, but that their humor belonged in the toilet. What was hidden to Elian were customs that dated back millennia and people of rock solid character beneath a language not understood. The Jewish people of Lizhensk, though lacking modern conveniences of the new world, had a richness of relationships that far exceeded the so-called trappings of high society exhibited by their American counterparts.

Elian was soon to learn that there was something deeper here that she was, at first, too shallow to understand. She observed a wife, Leah, who was able to help run a store, raise a family of eight, offer shelter for the mother of her husband, provide a home for her married daughter, and still be able to offer unlimited love to all who were in search of it. All this was without the aid of drugs or alcohol. Elian saw a father, Simon, who not only ran the most successful hardware business in the entire country, but was also a man the elders of the Jewish community would come to for wisdom and for Torah interpretation. She met Irving's brothers, who, like her husband, were full of ambition and in search of opportunity. Irving, though in his element, was actually not of it anymore because he had evolved into a place more advanced. He lived in California, a state that put its stock in that which was new, better. He lived in a land whose hallmark was freedom for all. Yes, Irving could speak five languages; but he found his Polish, Latin, and Yiddish fading a bit. He was slowly becoming Americanized.

Leah Puderbeutel knew how to make the disaffected feel like part of the family. She took Elian into the kitchen. Though knowing little English, she could make herself understood. She would show Elian how traditional Jewish dishes were made. Irving's sisters and brothers were able to practice their English on Elian. Everywhere she would go in town, she attracted celebrity-like attention. Her good looks and stylish clothes caused people to actually reach out and touch her mink coat in order to determine that it was, in fact, real. When they ascertained that it was, they would ask for her autograph.

Irving, for his part, always the dapper dresser, would stroll the streets of his hometown clad in an expensive glen plaid Hickey

Freeman suit yet was quite ambivalent about the attention he attracted. On the one hand, he simply wanted to enjoy the company of his beloved family. There was the other side of his personality that actually relished the attention. But Irving had more serious tasks in Lizhensk than simply showing the locals one of their own who made good though he wasn't above that. He loved visiting with his parents, his brothers, and his newly wedded sisters. It was nice to converse with them in the old language and to tell them that all the wonders they had read about America were true. He saw it and lived it. In addition, preparations were made for Jim's arrival in America. Jim was the second youngest brother. He, too, would work in the store. Gerson had learned enough to be able to run the stores while Irving was away in Europe.

You can go home again but can't stay. This was certainly true for Irving. Home was no longer horses tramping down dusty streets, nor was it groping through the freezing night air in order to relieve oneself. Irving, as could be expected, preferred his Buick convertible to a horse-drawn wagon. He knew the reasons he left Poland to be valid, and his visit just confirmed his conviction that he made the right decision. Now, with Jew haters coming to power all over Europe, he would do his utmost to secure a better life for the rest of his family, starting with Jim.

The trip was over, tears were shed. Yet try as he might, Irving was unable to convince most of his family that leaving Poland was a prudent thing to do. He would later drown himself in guilt over this inability to make his family see the dangers fast approaching.

Though Elian could never assimilate, she behaved like a true sport and, to her credit, tried. Everyone loved her for that. She was even sorry to leave these wise and loving people that constituted Irving's roots. She did, however, savor the prospect of returning to her comforts that awaited at Presidio Terrace. Irving's words were prophetic. *I'll see you all again in America.* The ship sailed away carrying with it a son who made good in the New World.

CHAPTER 21
A HOME IN THE COUNTRY

• • •

When Irving got back to San Francisco, waiting for him were the usual problems that await any business owner who dares go away on vacation: merchandise that didn't arrive, managers who failed to manage, salespeople who couldn't sell, and household help in rebellion. Irving proceeded to take care of all the things that went wrong in his absence. As to his brother's management skills, Irving decided they needed further honing. He was hard enough on Gerson but understood that his brother lacked experience at managing and was working on the English language as well; then there was the acquisition of a country home in Atherton.

The town of Atherton lay thirty miles south of San Francisco near Stanford University. It was a burg full of apricot orchards and "country" estates. Minimum lot size was an acre. Residents didn't usually know their neighbors; that's the way they liked it. Robert Frost, if he could have afforded to live there, would have felt very much at home. In Atherton, *good fences made good neighbors.* It was a very convenient place to get to from San Francisco because one could either take the steam train or go for a leisurely drive. Wealthy San Franciscans had "country" homes on the Peninsula—usually in Hillsborough, Atherton, or Woodside, where the acreage was larger.

Irving and Elian had, on weekends, explored Atherton on their drives through the area. On summer days, Irving would put the top down on the Buick. Elian would plop little Glenda on her lap while

Arthur giggled as the wind whipped through his hair. The route was the Old Bayshore Highway as it hugged the bay past Burlingame, San Mateo, Belmont, San Carlos; then Irving would cut through Redwood City's Main Street, and the El Camino Real would lead him to Atherton. He'd stop for gas at the Standard Oil station on Veterans and Main in Redwood City. Elian could stretch her well-shaped legs. Glenda would jump around while trying to say words that were new to her. At that age, all words were new to her. Arthur followed his dad like a lapdog. At that time, service station attendants filled your tank with gas, checked the oil and water, and cleaned the windshield. Arthur was full of observations.

Arthur inquired,

Dad? Can we leave Glenda home next time?

No! You should love your sister, admonished Irving

I do, Dad. But can we leave her home? Will the man who washes the windows wash the rest of the car?

The questions were good ones. The answers usually had one answer: *no.*

During their exploration of Atherton, the family came across a Coldwell Banker "For Sale" sign in front of a two-story, freshly painted house near the exclusive Circus Club. This was a club where men played polo, and access was limited to Gentiles. It was very expensive to join. Memberships were passed down from generation to generation. Irving's thoughts were far from wanting to join a Christian club. He did, however, relish the prospect of living near one. The house was being held open on a Sunday. Elian tugged on Irving's arm and pointed. He could take a hint. The kids were happy to get out of the car and romp around the spacious grounds. Stately oaks surrounded the property. It was located near vast open spaces better known as The Convent of the Sacred Heart. To the northwest lay the green lawns of The Circus Club. Irving, in his mind, knew that this house was in an area that would increase in value through the years.

While Arthur was exploring native animal life consisting of squirrels and birds, Elian followed Irving as he carried Glenda on his shoulders (much to her delight). They strolled through, acting very noncommittal. If there was anything Elian learned from Irving, it was never to show desire when contemplating a purchase. In those days, conversation was addressed to the man because it was presumed he was the decision maker. The agent, dressed in a navy-blue suit with matching hat, was in her mid-thirties. Her somewhat attractive thin face was framed by long, brown hair that ended in a bun on the nape of her neck, as was the style. Irving, actually, was more interested in selling her a new suit than in buying another house; but there was the matter of his wife. Though his face was made of steel, his wife and children found it well neigh impossible to hide their excitement.

Sir, I can tell by the glow on your wife's face that she loves this house. How old is your little girl? Two? Think of her growing up and romping around these beautiful grounds. And the schools. Very highly rated. Your little boy, so handsome. He looks about ready to start first grade. Las Lamitas is just a hop, skip, and jump from here—very well rated.

She glanced at Elian and smiled as though her remarks were addressed to the wife as well. Of course, Elian was intoxicated with the house and, though used to commanding respect due to her intelligence, let it all pass over her head with just a slight sneer and a

They'll go to school in the city. This is just a country home.

Irving, who the saleslady was really interested in hearing from, thoughtfully put his hand to his chin and said,

It's nice and might work, but I've got to give it some thought.

The saleslady's reply was that it may not last.

Irving knew that there was still a depression going on, certainly not a time where country houses in luxurious areas were being snapped up. Despite moistened eyes of his wife and imploring looks of his children, he trundled them back into the Buick and told the agent,

Livie, I'll be back to you.

She had heard that one a hundred times before. Odds were that it was the last she would see of them. But she didn't know this shrewd man from Poland. Irving was aware that his ride back to the city was going to be a miserable one; however, he stood his ground. Fortunately for Irving, the convertible's top was down so the wind drowned out Arthur's whines and Glenda's cries. But he could catch bits and pieces of Elian's biting commentary, something to the effect of,

Cheap son of a bitch. Can't you tell a good value when you see one? What are we holding off for? You to die of old age? Or me perhaps? Of all the husbands, I have to have the cheap one. Others give their wives jewels and furs. Me? I've got to put a coat on layaway and pay for it on installments out of my house allowance. Does he get me a car? Hell no. He says, "take the bus!" Cheap son of a bitch. Culture? Irving, your idea of reading is perusing the columns of a ledger. My father was right. You know the value of a buck, all right. Irv, you could squeeze a quarter and make Washington tell a lie.

Irving just drove, knowing the conversation about him was not complimentary. The wind carried Elian's words away and drowned them in San Francisco Bay. Irving knew what he was about and what he was going to do. Despite several days of Elian's frosty disposition and some half-cooked dinners, Irving noted a change for the better in her personality.

After two weeks went by, Livie the real estate agent picked up the phone and, to her surprise, who was on the other end of the line but Irving?

That home on Emily. Is it still available?

Livie answered in the affirmative. These types of homes weren't flying off the shelves like loaves of bread.

Good. My wife and children liked the home. I've got a check for you in the amount of $20,000. See what you can do!

Mr. Bartel, do you realize that the home sits on a full acre? That the grounds are meticulously landscaped? That the house has been fully updated and has 4,500 square feet? And not least, Mr. Bartel, not least is the fact that the sellers have reduced the price to a very reasonable $30,000.

Livie, are you buying the house or am I? I will pay $20,000. You can check me out at the Bank of America. Mr. Giannini knows me. The check is waiting for your sellers' acceptance. If you're successful, Livie,

I have a brown cashmere coat with mink trim on it that would look terrific on you. Call me!

Irving, after leaving his phone number, clicked the black cone-shaped receiver back on its base.

Sure enough, two days later, he answered the phone; and it was Livie, the real estate agent.

Congratulations, Mr. Bartel! I'll take you up on that cashmere coat. The sellers accepted your offer with just a slight modification. The price to be $25,000. They met you halfway. Surely you can do the same. A deal?

Irving hated to see $5,000 go out the window instead of into some well-priced coats for his store. Nonetheless, there was the matter of a marriage that was stretched to its limits. Besides, the kids would love it. The property was well located and a good buy. Not just that, the stock market, which he knew nothing at all about and never would, was going nowhere. He gave his reluctant reply.

Livie, I don't know. The price is higher than I wanted. Against my better judgment, I'll do it. The check will be at your office tomorrow morning—9 a.m. There, we'll sign the appropriate papers. When it closes, you come to my store on Market Street, and I'll fix you up in a coat that will make you the talk of the town.

Irving made the phone call to his still moping wife. Her shrieks of joy almost broke his eardrum. He could picture her thin lips go from somber to a crescent-shaped smile. To Irving, it was just money. It was about rising another notch on the social scale. Elian, too, now had a house in the country. Not just anywhere on The Peninsula, but in Atherton, where only the upper crust lived. As usual, Irving didn't believe in debt or in paying interest. His parents told him to *pay cash*. That's what he did with merchandise, his car, and his homes. Now that his spouse had a country home, Irving surmised she would be spending less time with her lesbian friends, whom he deplored.

CHAPTER 22

A THIRD SON LEAVES POLAND

• • •

The next project was getting brother Jim over to the United States. Irving made the necessary arrangements with the Immigration Department. By now, brother Gerson had moved out of the Presidio Terrace home and into an apartment in the Marina that he shared with mutual friend Arthur Grey. This friend, though his name was Christianized, was actually Jewish. Wherever a good time was to be had, there in the midst of things was Arthur Grey. As to what he did, that was sort of hazy. When asked, he was in the retail trade. In actuality, he was such a charmer that he seemed to have a never ending string of rich girlfriends.

With an empty room in their home, Elian made it ready for its next guest, Irving's brother Jim. In 1938, Jim arrived in San Francisco speaking as little English as his brother before him. Elian seemed to have a way of communicating with people she could not understand. She read feelings, wants, and desires. When his brother showed him to the car, Jim was perplexed by a car whose top could go down. Irving explained.

Jim. Here many people have a car. Those who can afford it have a car like mine where you can keep the top up or put it down when it's warm.

Jim asked, *Why it cool and cloudy here in the summertime?*

Irving answered, *The fog. We have fog that comes in everyday and cools things off. It clears up by midmorning. Isn't my wife beautiful today?*

He was attempting to buoy a marriage that was headed toward rocky shoals. In fact, though she was wearing pants and a scarf, Elian was still strikingly attractive. But because of her close friend, Mr. Bottle, her mood swings took place more often. Fortunately for Jim, she hadn't had a drink in a couple of days and showed to him her A personality.

Jim was still taken aback by his surroundings and by this American goddess he had first seen in Lizhensk, Poland.

She be beautiful, all right.

How very nice of you to say that, Jim, cheerfully replied Elian. *I'm afraid you're not seeing me at my best. We dashed out the door, and all I had time for was to throw a few rags on. The scarf is because my hair is not fit for public display. I think Marie Antoinette said something to a similar effect as she walked out of the Palace of Versailles for the last time. If she didn't say it, she should have.*

Elian's humor was well over Jim's head. It was even beyond Irving's grasp. They both laughed all the same. And so it went. Another brother moved in replacing the one who moved out. This one was a skinny twenty-eight-year-old with the typical Bartel features: black, curly hair and thick glasses. His accent was similar, but he talked slower than Irving or Gerson. Like the other brothers who set foot on the shores of America, Jim ended up in the women's ready-to-wear business or the schmata business as Jews called it. As Jim related,

I had a room bigger than the house I lived in (in Poland) and a bathroom. I never had a bathroom in my life. They (my parents) had no electricity. Nothing. You can picture what I looked like when I came over. One hundred twenty pounds. When I was going to Lowell High School (to learn English), *I was going there full time. After school, I went directly to the store.*

Arthur, Irving's son was going around Presidio Terrace looking for cigarette butts. He was only four or five at the time. Gerson Thurm, his cousin, got ahold of him. He said, "You want to smoke?" He lit a cigar and said, "Smoke!" Arthur started choking.

One thing about Irving, when he took you out to dinner, money was no object. No restaurant was too good. You could eat whatever you wanted to eat. You had dinner. You had dessert. But don't leave anything on your plate.

In the store, when you had to wrap a package and you had to tie it with a string, you had to measure out the string, not to have too much left. He would kill if he would see waste.

About this time, a heavy burden was starting to lift off the shoulders of America, the Depression. Slowly, President Roosevelt's New Deal was beginning to take effect. The economy was groaning to life again. Sallow-cheeked masses of unemployed were going back to work.

CHAPTER 23

THE NAZI STEAMROLLER

• • •

The year was 1939. In Europe, a steamroller was beginning to slowly make its way across the continent. Eventually, it would crush everything in its path. This war machine, called Nazi Germany, would bring with it the rumble of Panzer tanks and shrieks of Stuka dive bombers. Whatever lay in its way was flattened. The lucky ones perished quickly. Others were selected for a far worse fate, hideous slow death in concentration camps. At last, death would inhabit their skeleton bodies and God would call them home.

This steamroller didn't start with a roar. Its movement began with the high pitched jabbering of a little Austrian corporal with fuzzy mustache and an inferiority complex. He wore a light brown military uniform with an armband that had as its emblem a twisted cross, fitting symbol as it turned out. Both he and his adopted country, Germany, had feelings of inferiority following World War I. The Germans thought they should have won. As a result of not winning, their economy was in shambles. Losing the war wasn't their fault. They were undermined. Germany's ills had to be laid at the feet of somebody other than themselves. As is usually the case when we have broken our mirrors, there is always a scapegoat to be found. In Germany's case, it started with the perennially disaffected of society. Jews, gypsies, homosexuals, mentally ill, the crippled. After that, Germany's enemies included England and her allies. Following that, anyone who didn't subscribe to Nazi doctrine was to be marked for extinction.

Soon squares were packed with rank upon rank of precision placed men wearing brown uniforms and carrying Mauser rifles. The German people need not blame their lot on themselves because there were enemies within and without the country. They were a superior race and once they had rid the world of those inferior to them, they would be able to establish a new world order that would live forever—a litany that whispered from the smoking ashes of many a previous civilization. Since starting with England was impractical, due to her military might, a good place to begin was with the Jewish population. This would be easy because there were sympathetic governments in other parts of Europe. These governments were well practiced at blaming their ills on minorities.

First, minority rights were restricted; then came the ban from governmental jobs. After that, anti-minority laws forced the disaffected to move to selected parts of the country, usually those parts that were least desirable. These communities were called ghettos, named after the walled areas that Jews were forced to live in during the Middle Ages. Once this was accomplished, overt terror began. In Germany, it started with a night called *Kristalnacht* or the *Night of Broken Glass.* Nazis stormed through Germany breaking windows of Jewish shops, burning Synagogues, and beating bloody any Jew they found.

The public bought into this. After all, it wasn't them. Their leader was right. After World War I, their economy was ruined by a group of international bankers. The German people even hopped on to the superior race train. So, it was with general acquiescence that inferior people were put away in order to cleanse society of them. In the case of mentally ill individuals, they were gathered up by Nazi Germany's hatchet men, the Gestapo, and placed in "hospitals." Of course the government never told its people or the world that nobody ever returned alive from these "hospitals." In the case of the crippled, they too, were sent to "hospitals" to be "cured." It would not have been prudent to have told the public that the "cure" for these people was death.

Jews, gypsies, and other inferior citizens such as dissidents were sent to "camps" in out of the way places, behind walls where no eyes could peer. There the apparatus was put into motion for the extinction of millions, all this with the help of Europe's citizenry. Those who participated kept their mouths shut. As for others who didn't much care for those targeted, it was okay to put these people somewhere safely away from general society. What happened to them there? Don't ask! We don't want the details. What was the smell floating over the walls of little, out of the way, towns in Germany, Poland, Russia? Don't ask! Where were those trains, loaded with miserable looking people, headed? Keep your mouth shut! The Nazi propaganda machine told the citizens that these poor wretches, on the trains, were going to be resettled. Resettled where? Better not to ask.

Your neighbors are being hauled away. You don't want to know the details. It's not you. Besides, you get their house, their belongings. They're inferior, why worry? Now your neighbor is blonde and Nordic. Their leader was right. Europe was on its way to a perfect society, a Reich that would last a thousand years. First there were certain details that had to be taken care of, like overrunning all of Europe. Throughout history, great empires started by conquering their neighbors first then expanding from that base.

On March 15, 1939 German forces entered Prague, Czechoslovakia. With this country in its talons, Germany gave aid to General Franco's Fascist forces which, after a bitter civil war with the Communists, took over Spain. For years the world had turned a blind eye to Germany. Now it was surprised at the powerful military machine Germany had created; then it happened.

CHAPTER 24

POLAND FALLS

• • •

On September 1, 1939 Germany's Panzer tanks rumbled into Poland quickly followed by the Luftwaffe's screaming dive bombers. Germany called this type of attack the *blitzkrieg*. It was sudden and effective due to its use of overwhelming force. Belgium remained neutral. Britain and France pledged assistance. Once in the grasp of the German eagle, however, a country was pierced through its skin and left to bleed its sovereignty away. The Nazis moved so swiftly that soon the entire country was blasted from above. On the ground, there were rumblings in the distance.

In Lizhensk, Poland it was a warm, fall day. All was quiet. Yes, there had been frantic news about the Germans crossing the border. Simon Puderbeutel didn't feel there was anything to worry about. After all, he told Leah, the Polish army would take care of them. Leah, with a woman's sixth sense, wasn't so sure.

Abe! Get Ben. Bring him into the house! Ethel! Go find your sisters. Get Rose and Sarah. Make sure they bring their husbands. Simon, while we have time you should bury the money and some guns in the back yard. They will be safe and won't be found. We'll lock the store and trust in HIM.

Leah didn't know much about Nazis, but had heard stories. She knew enough about her own government and its treatment of Jews to be doubly wary of the Germans. Simon took his wife's advice and with sweat dripping off his forehead and forming little droplets on his beard, he used his well-muscled shoulders to bury, in different holes, jars of paper money and coins. In other holes lay some Mausers for future use.

On the German war map, Lizhensk was listed as a regional manufacturing center, in other words, a prime target. It was a warm, autumn Sunday, the day after the Sabbath. Rumors spread, on foot, that Nisko and Rzeszow were bombed. The weather was perfect for German bombers. Skies were warm and bright. Out of the blue they came, raining death and hate.

On Monday, the dreaded bombers showed up in the skies of Lizhensk. Initial results were only a baby injured. The normally quiet town was pierced by high pitched whines of bomber engines; then there would be several explosions. Train cars flew in the air, raining a shower of shard on whatever was in the way. Nazi planes were like angry wasps stinging the life out of gigantic caterpillar trains.

It became horrifyingly clear that the Polish army had not held. Germans marched into the town of Lizhensk with no resistance. Fear hung in the air like a shroud. People started leaving, piling all their belongings on horse drawn carts. As they walked beside their worldly possessions, they'd kick up puffs of dust. Waves of refugees from the west clogged the roads. Pretty soon Lizhensk became a ghost town. The Puderbeutels, however, stayed. It was decided by Simon to await the outcome of events then make a decision.

As it turned out, a bridge over the San River was bombed out. A temporary bridge had been built by local citizens. In addition, the river was low at that time of year and was passable by wading across. This was a significant fact because the north side of the San River was Russian held territory. The Nazis had a nonaggression pact with Russia at that time.

On the eve of Rosh Hashanah (Jewish New Year), the sun rose to greet the goose stepping cadence of German soldiers. Nazis had finally set foot in Lizhensk. On the second day of Rosh Hashanah, prayers floated out of the synagogues in thanks for a good year. The door of one house of prayer burst open. German soldiers, in their brown uniforms, stomped up to the alter while prayer was still being conducted. They demanded volunteers for a work detail. After the exit of worshippers, gurgling cans of kerosene were poured over neighboring synagogues. Flames and smoke scorched the sky. God's words soared up to him in the form of prayer book ashes.

A hasty letter was secreted out of the country via its postal system.

Irving, our loving son:

German planes have bombed your beloved home town. Soldiers entered Lizhensk this morning. So far, we are safe. Ethel and Joe are here with us. Sarah and Rose, along with their families are staying here for the time being. We are not sure where we go. Do not worry for us. God will watch over.

The family sends our love to you and to Gerson and to Jim. This will probably be our last letter for awhile. We hope it gets through.

Love always, Mother and Father

No sooner had the letter been spirited away than a Nazi soldier knocked on the Puderbeutel door. He was in his early twenties with some brass on his shoulders, an officer. He had short cropped blonde hair, blue eyes, and a well fed, handsome face. On his hip was a Luger pistol. Simon opened the door. In the background could be heard the sobbing of women: Ethel, Sarah, Rose. Leah came forward and looked at him stoically.

Juden! Pack your belongings! You have three hours to leave. Though I have my orders, you look like a good family. Take my advice! Cross over to the north side of the San River! There the Russians will take you. Stay here and … Dat is all.

He made an about face, in military fashion, and walked out the door. Imagine, you have three hours to pack your most precious possessions into something you can carry with you, say a suitcase or pillowcase. The home you had lived in for a lifetime was to be turned over to the Nazis along with every prized possession in it. In addition, the business that took years to build was to be confiscated. The crime? Their faith.

There wasn't much time. Decisions had to be made. Despite tears and hasty gathering of prized possessions, who would stay and who would go was something that needed to be decided. What's more, there were little children's lives which fate would decide. Ethel had a one month old son—Michael. Sarah had a twelve-year-old daughter with a cherubic face.

Outside, the noise was nightmarish—shouts in guttural German, doors being rudely hammered on with rifle butts, women's cries, children's sobs. As a backdrop to it all was the sound of soldiers' crunching boots making their deadly imprints in the dust of Lizhensk's streets. As Simon looked out his front window, he saw his lifelong friends either with family and prized possessions packed on horse drawn wagons or lugging suitcases down the streets of Lizhensk.

In the Puderbeutel house, it was as though a morbid poker game was being played. Each drew a hand that would ultimately determine whether they lived or died. Simon, Leah, Abe, Ben, Ethel and Joe and Rose's husband, a handsome and well-dressed young man, decided to cross the San River thus taking their chances with the Russians. Sarah, husband, daughter, and Rose opted to remain in Lizhensk. After all, they thought, all those stories about the Nazis couldn't be true.

As Ethel Nagel (Irving's sister) tells it,

The San River was near the town. When the Nazis came, if you were on the north side of the river, you were exported to Siberia, in Russia. But if you were on the south side of the river, then you were captured by the Nazis. The San River was the dividing line. The Nazis found all the food, took all the food. Two thousand Jews that lived in Lizhensk, they gave no notice. Michael was one month old. The Nazis came in and told everyone to go to the Russians. Sarah and Rose stayed. Rose's husband left with me. Sarah's husband stayed. Everyone who stayed went to the concentration camps with their children.

Jim Bartel (Irving's brother) relates,

I'm going to tell you the story she (Sylvia Bartel) *told me. I wasn't there. Before they crossed the river, before they left the town, the Germans were examining the people that were leaving. They looked in their mouths. They looked them all over for valuables. If they saw gold in their teeth, they pulled the teeth out. So after all this, they left and there was a bridge across the river. The bridge was destroyed so they formed a bridge made out of little boats. Then they crossed.*

Ethel Nagel (Irving's sister) adds,

The Russians took them but didn't say where they were taking them. At that time, they were sent to Russian work camps in Siberia. I went to Siberia but my sisters and one husband stayed on. Instead of keeping them there, they put them in railroad cars and day and night they came to the camps. They stayed because there was no place to go. They didn't go over to the Russians because there was chaos. Nobody knows where to go, what to do. And we were lucky. After they (Nazis) *displaced me and my family, we went to the San. One night there was knocking. We opened the door and there was the Gestapo. In this place there were Polish people that were clients of my dad and they took us in overnight. The following day, my sister Sarah found out where we were. So, she came and took us together and we went to her place. People from all over came. There was no room to stay so Joe and I left her and we went to walk and we met a man. I don't remember the name. They were wonderful people. And one night, the Gestapo knocked on the door and they said, "Juden ocht" Jews out. So I went with the baby and Joe. We went out to the train and for eleven days we were going in this train. We didn't know where we were going. We were starving. Once every day, every so often, they opened the doors and put in some food. We went from Minsk to Siberia. From the train we went to the barracks. And around us, trees, No houses. From then on, that was it. They put Joe to work. He cut the trees for wood because they needed to build some other place. I had the baby. I couldn't go any place. Other women, everybody, had to work. A woman was walking around and said "why don't you go to work?" I kept on saying because, "I have a baby and I cannot leave the baby." They told me to "kapofnish." This is a Polish word that means "drop dead." And I hated that.*

Sylvia Bartel fills in,

From there (across the San River) *they went to a town called Volk. We went from village to village. They would not accept us as Jews. So my grandfather was a merchant and he knew the head of the village. He* (the head of the village) *let us stay in the barn only for two days. The second night he took a horse and buggy and took us to the next village. And so we went from village to village till we came to a bigger town, Volk where my father's brother lived. And they were supposedly already very comfortable and had a few extra rooms and five of us; one room for five people. And one day, we didn't know about it, the Germans and the Russians decided; we should take some Jews and you should take some Jews. And they put us aboard a train to Siberia. That was all they gave us---water and salt. The baker was stealing the flour. How we survived? Many, many people were dying.*

CHAPTER 25

SIBERIA

• • •

It was 1940. Those members of the Puderbeutel family not captured by the Nazis were settled in Siberia. At night, through the freezing cold, stars would twinkle in the clear northern sky. Sometimes colorful lights would roll through black space and create an artic tapestry. Winds whistled through cracks in the barrack walls. The air was so cold it was as though the wind was saying, "If I touch you, your life will leave." All able bodied Jews were put to work hauling lumber for the Russians. They used horse drawn wagons for this task.

One day Rose's husband, who by this time was weak and tired, was not paying attention to where he was standing. A group of Jews, along with their Russian overseers, were lugging heavy beams to a wagon. A Russian whipped the horse so that the wagon would be closer to the spot where the wood beams lay. Rose's husband didn't see the wagon rolling forward to where he was standing. There was a scream then a gurgling rush of air out his windpipe as the wagon wheel crushed his chest. Other Jews shouted for the wagon to stop. After the wagon rolled off his chest, all that was left of Rose's husband was a large red patch of blood on the snow and his broken rag doll body which the Jews buried in the forest.

According to Sylvia Bartel, the barracks in Siberia were built out of logs just before the Jews were shipped there. The buildings looked like large log cabins except that they were built quite poorly. In the winter, dirty rags were used to plug cracks between the logs. Frigid air wrapped itself like a freezing towel around these structures while their skeleton inhabitants coughed and wheezed. The healthy ones, if they could be called that, would shuffle around in their rags bringing a bowl of hot water with a bone in it that the Russians called soup, to those that were wandering between this life and the next. On the floor was a little sink and a small stove to cook on. Sometimes the hoarfrost came in from the north at fifty degrees below zero. A sharp smell of pine would permeate the frozen landscape. As far as the eye could see, it was white tundra pricked by groups of trees here and there. Jews shivered in their coats until their teeth couldn't stop chattering. Indoors, it wasn't much better. The heater was a big barrel. It was supposed to warm an entire barrack building. As a result, Jews had to stay wrapped in whatever warm clothing they had because it was always cold. Bathing was sporadic and a shocking experience as the air was forever frigid. Since most were cold and sick much of the time, they shook so much that it was a chore just cleaning themselves. Each barrack had about thirty people including crying children. The smells of unwashed bodies added an unwelcome aroma.

In Siberia, the Jews were safe from the Nazis at least; if you could call their condition safe. Sylvia Bartel heard scratching sounds outside the barracks at night; then there would be a baleful howl. It was the sound of wolf packs searching for food. A sick or injured person who went outside to relieve his misery might never come back. His bones would be found scattered willy-nilly throughout the forest. People would be afraid to go to the bathroom and rightfully so.

Ethel Nagel guarded her small children, literally, with her life. When weak from hunger and exhaustion, she shuffled off to her duties. Simon and Leah Puderbeutel would take turns caring for little Michael. Though the lad was deathly sick for a time, he survived.

Rabbi Yoel Moshe conducted prayers in his hut. His children stood guard so that the N.K. V.D. (Russian Secret Police) and other non-Jewish informers would not pay attention to those wishing to worship. The Puderbeutels and Nagels spent World War II being transported by train throughout Russia's vast countryside. Ironically, they were slaves that helped a Communist form of slavery fight off a Fascist form of slavery.

Sylvia Bartel's words,

So my sister and me would go out and get a couple of trees and bring them back to the barrack. The fire was going all day and all night. We were getting food if you worked. I was forced to go to work and my younger sister too. I was eighteen and my younger sister was sixteen. After work, we were forced to go to Russian school and we learned to speak Russian. They told us, "You'll be here in Siberia till you die."

CHAPTER 26

A MARRIAGE UNRAVELING

• • •

Back in San Francisco, California events were unfolding for Irving Bartel as well. He could escape San Francisco's fog by spending time at his country house, in Atherton. What he couldn't escape was his life. As to his family in Europe, he felt helpless. He'd lost all touch with them. After their last, desperate letter, his parents, brothers, and sisters vanished. As if that wasn't enough, Irving's marriage with Elian was unraveling. He would walk in the door at 28 Presidio Terrace after a long day at the store only to find his wife either entertaining her "girl friends" or woozy and abusive.

So, finally you waltz in. It's about time. Of course I'm getting a post graduate education sitting around alone waiting for you to come home. Let's see, today I read Sartre and Fitzgerald both. Poor Ruth, the cook, probably burned all the food because it was supposed to be ready an hour ago. Yes I know. A damned coat is more important than your wife. Irving, I've had it.

Mentally, he was beside himself. His temper thermometer was rising.

Late? You've got a nerve. Who do you think pays the bills around here? Why if it were for you, you'd be out in the gutter with your "girl friends," not living in the lap of luxury with two homes. I work my ass off for this? For you to play around with women when I'm at work? And

I'm putting you on notice that your women friends are unacceptable to me. Do you think I'm supporting you so you greet me, reeling drunk, when I come home?

Oh, you're a fine one, Irving, for bringing up the negative qualities of others. If you were half a husband and spent some time with your wife, I wouldn't need girl friends.

Irving's eyes were magnified behind his thick glasses. They were blood red. All he could see was pulses of red light, though there was an attractive drunk woman standing in front of him. He raised his hand. She screamed. The black cook came running out of the kitchen her eyes wide in terror. What was the commotion about? If Irving had his way, he would have knocked his wife through the living room window and all the way into San Francisco Bay. Suddenly his hand stopped midair. He looked at it as though it were some disembodied thing. At the end of a suit sleeve was this hand that stopped in mid-flight and sort of hovered, quivering in the air. Irving then smashed an end table sending its bric-a-brac skidding across the entry hall. He didn't say another word, but turned on his heels and drove, recklessly, down to Jack's Restaurant where his favorite table and a scotch on the rocks was waiting. The two women stood there, stunned. It seemed like many minutes went by before either of them moved.

The next day, Irving was at Juliette's. He had two offices. One was upstairs on the third floor. It had a large semicircular birch desk. It also had other features: a bed with white fur bedspread. There was a hidden panel in the wooden wall which concealed a swinging door. On the back side of this door was a full bar. Behind this secret door was a bedroom with bathroom containing a full shower. On the store's main floor was a small office cubicle where Irving could write things and observe all that took place on the sales floor. He was in his office, on the sales floor, when a man wearing a police uniform slowly shuffled his way toward Irving's office. The man was tall with a pot belly and thinning brown hair beneath his peaked cap. In fact, he was a deputy sheriff not a cop. To Irving, both meant about the same thing—trouble. Irving got up from his seat.

Is Mr. Irving Bartel here?

It was obvious that the man he was looking for was right in front of him. Who else, but the store's owner, would be dressed in a business suit sporting an expensive looking tie and a gold Boliva watch?

I am he. What brings you to see me? Are there any laws I have broken?

No, sir. If you are Irving Bartel. I have these papers for you. Would you please sign for them?

Papers? What are these for? Divorce papers? From my wife? It must be someone else. You've got the wrong person.

I can understand how you feel, sir. It says Irving Bartel on 'em. Just sign right here. I'm sorry.

The deputy, with the pot belly, took his proof of service and slowly shuffled off into the clatter that was Market Street. His tired eyes squinted in the sunlight. He was used to this. As an older deputy, this man's job was delivering bad news in the form of summons.

Irving's hands shook. How could she do this to him? He didn't want a divorce. He, despite her faults, still was in love. Actually, he was in love with the concept of somebody taking care of details at home so he could be left free to make money, but that was not how he viewed it. He provided Elian with fine clothes, two prestigious addresses, social position in the community and this was his reward? Those divorce papers might as well have jumped out of Irving's hand and slapped him in the face. In numb silence, he sat in his upstairs office and read the summons where nobody could see him. It was hard to read due to the fact that he had to continually use a white handkerchief to either wipe his glasses or wipe the tears from his cheeks. All she wanted was the children and the house in Atherton.

During this same time period, Irving had acquired a hundred acre dairy ranch in Ukiah, a farming town about a hundred and twenty miles north of San Francisco. On this ranch: cows, chickens, dogs, cats, and buzzards were raised. The ranch was used for a tax deduction. The milk, butter, and eggs created an income and expense stream that was tax exempt. Furthermore, Irving's brothers, Gerson and Jim, served as ranch hands and were exempt from military service because the ranch's production went toward the war effort. In 1942, Gerson joined the army as he wanted to directly serve his newly adopted country. Jim, the skinny one, remained as a part time ranch hand until the end of the war. Though Jim looked like an unlikely ranch hand, with his string bean physique and his wire timed glasses, he bailed hay and hooked the cows up to milking machines with the best of them. Jim didn't wear a cowboy hat. His preference was a white tee shirt, jeans, and the sun blasting down on his curly black hair.

On the day he received his court summons from his soon to be ex-wife, Irving wandered around in a stupor. Finally he pulled into the garage at 28 Presidio Terrace. The afternoon fog lay over the city like a lead gray piece of cotton candy. The droplets would cool off everything but Irving's heart. His mood was somber as he walked in the front door. There was an eerie quiet about the place. Gone was Elian's drunken bluster. Instead Ruth, the housekeeper, clop-clopped into the entryway to greet her employer.

Mr. Bartel She done gone. Just left. Took most everything of her clothes. Said if you want to talk to her about anything, talk to her lawyer. Ain't that a fine thing to do? After all you done? My, my. Ize just can't thinks what gets into these women sometimes. I'll takes care of you, Mr. B. You just sit yourself down and rest you feets. Hm, umm. Can you smell it from here? Ize gots your favorite tonight—lamb stew with extra onions, just the way you like it.

Irving straightened himself so that he was almost standing at attention. It was all he could do to keep from bursting out in tears. Here he was, alone in a 5,000 square foot house. No wife, but at least a loyal housekeeper. Yes, savory smells wafted through the air from the kitchen. His taste buds yearned for this favorite meal. A Chivas Regal on the rocks, that would do a world of good. Talk to her attorney. Hell would freeze first. She'd be back. What Irving didn't understand was that he didn't understand.

Irving, like many other successful people, seemed to thrive on turmoil. His life may have been a cauldron of despair, but his business was just the opposite. While his wife was suing for divorce, Irving found the presence of mind to open his third store. He located it on the best part of Market Street just one block west of Fannette's and Juliette's. The address was 812 Market Street, across from San Francisco's renown department store, The Emporium. Irving named his new store Bartel's. He entrusted management duties to his brother, Gerson. Later, when his brother joined the army, a thin blonde by the name of Miss Francis managed the store. She wore her hair in the fashionable bun that was so popular during World War II. Her face was young, but her eyes, instead of being a delicate blue, were more like hardened cobalt. Toughness was a necessary trait in the clothing business or the customer would steal you blind and have you asking if you could throw in a suit as well. Whenever a customer walked out of Bartel's, they would carry a distinctive red and white striped box that read, "Bartel's House of Coats."

Irving would sometimes take Gerson on buying trips with him, to New York. One time, one of Irving's manufacturers addressed Gerson, who had similar handsome features as Irving but with a fuller face. Since Jewish people hate to see anybody single, the manufacturer just assumed Gerson was unmarried.

Hey Gerson. I got someone you should meet. You shouldn't be alone. You are single?

It sounded like echoes of Gerson's mother, Leah. She couldn't take for anyone to be single either. He was used to being introduced to young women. Used to and skeptical of. He tried to put on his best positive attitude but his mind betrayed him. Was she fat? Was she ugly? Did she have that Jewish whine so prevalent in New York? What about a big nose? Big lips? On and on he thought about all the negative attributes that he had been surprised by in the past. However, this manufacturer was a friend of his brother, a friend who provided the stores with good selling merchandise. With optimism in his voice that he may not have actually felt inside, Gerson replied, *Yes, I'm single. Not only that, I'd love to meet her."*

Ah, A mench. Such a brother you have, Irv. This is a man after your own heart. A prince. Gerson, you won't be disappointed. The young lady I want to introduce you to; her name is Helene. If she is not the most beautiful woman you have laid eyes on, I'll give your brother this order of coats free. And you know me by now. I don't like the word free.

Gerson's eyes turned appealingly to his brother. All Irving could do was shrug his shoulders. He had never met or seen Helene. As it came to pass, Gerson was not disappointed. This young lady accompanied the manufacturer, Irving, and Gerson to dinner at the Waldorf. Helene was mesmerizing. Long brown rivulets of hair cascaded over her bare shoulders. She possessed pouty lips—the type that were made to kiss. Her complexion was flawless. Though she stood only five feet five inches, she seemed to engulf Gerson in her warmth. Here was Jewish girl who didn't put on airs but just radiated goodness. Though Gerson was at a loss for words due to the fact that this young woman was so gorgeous and he was still working on his English; he didn't know a lot of words in the first place. What Gerson lacked in vocabulary, he made up for in the form of effervescent personality. In addition, he had what many Helene went out with lacked, sincerity. In other words, he wasn't just after her tail.

They saw more of each other. One thing led to another. Her parents liked him—very important in Jewish families. When you marry the daughter, you marry her parents as well. They wed before Gerson's army unit shipped out to the islands. Of course, Irving was best man. He was dressed in a black tuxedo, the one he used for the opera. He looked so dapper that he could have been mistaken for the groom. Gerson's ushers included his brother, Jim, his cousins: Gerson and David Thurm, and his friend Arthur Gray.

CHAPTER 27

A KNOCK ON THE DOOR

• • •

It took place soon after the Puderbeutels were put aboard a train and shipped to Siberia. Those Jews who remained in Lizhensk were rounded up by the Nazis. Scared, cowering human beings were huddled like cattle and marched to the market square. A warm rain was falling. Those carrying their pitiful possessions in bundles were weighted down by their damp burden. The ones not arriving at the square voluntarily were dragged there by the Gestapo. The cowering crowd was ordered to walk. Whoever was slow got a sharp pain in their back courtesy of a rifle butt. If a person had valuables, they were relieved of them by the Germans. This was the lucky group for they were sent across the San River to join the Russians.

Soon the *Aktions* (elimination of Jews) began in Lizhensk. Inside the old Puderbeutel house were Sarah, her daughter, Rose, and Sarah's husband. On the street in front could be heard the sound of polished jack boots. The rap rap rap became louder; then there was pounding on the front door as though two small battering rams were trying to break down this last vestige of safety. Sarah and Rose started shaking. Sarah's daughter hugged her mother's waist while her mother's tears dripped on her daughter's silky brown hair. Sarah's husband crammed his gold watch and wedding ring into his pants pocket then stood stout heartedly facing the front door.

Gestapo!

That horrid word that meant death came from outside the front door. Gestapo officers shouted to those inside while their pistol butts pounded on the front door. The ones inside knew that if they did not open the door, the Nazis would either break it down or set the house afire from outside. Sarah's husband slowly undid the latch while the rest stood shaking in a corner of the living room.

In strode two Aryan looking young men in brown uniforms. Each had two things in common, a Lugar nine millimeter pistol in his hand and a hard look across his face. These were two mother's sons who were forged by the Nazi government to be unfeeling killer dogs. Not a trace of emotion could be seen. Their eyes held no sentiment- almost rolling back in the head shark-like. Yet because of their Gestapo uniform, these clean shaven young men welded enormous power over their victim's lives. Any resistance meant instant death in the form of a nine millimeter bullet. Implored a quivering voice,

What are you going to do with us?

Relocate you. Swine we take to the sties. But first ...

Prior to being shuffled out the door single file, Sarah's husband went over and planted a kiss on his wife's tear streaked cheek; then, he gently kissed his daughter. There was no time to think, just to do. When outside the door, the Gestapo agents threw the young family up against the outside wall. Sarah's husband hit his head and stood there, stunned. Before he could regain his senses, one of the Gestapo reached his hands into the pants pockets and pulled out the gold watch and wedding ring. The other Gestapo trained his Luger on the group. When the husband tried to resist, a pistol barrel cracked into the side of his head. Down he went with a red line on his hair. As he slowly stumbled to his feet, drops of red ooze dripped down his face. Sarah screamed. Rose cried. Sarah's daughter tried to go to her father's aide but Sarah held her arm in a vice like grip.

Thieves you are. Like gypsies . See here. Look what we have. Our people have nothing and look at the gold these vermin horde. Our Fuhrer was right. They are a plague upon the earth. The rest of the world starves while these fine folks feast on gold dishes. Now for the women. Let's see what dainties we have here.

Sarah, Rose, and the daughter stopped shaking. They became resolute to face whatever was in store. A tear or two rolled down Sarah's face. Not for herself, but for what was to be her future-her daughter. As one Gestapo smilingly waved his pistol barrel in front of the women's faces, the other proceeded to paw his hand inside blouses and up skirts looking for valuables. He ripped off a necklace leaving Rose's neck with a red welt. The man seemed to relish his search up and down the daughter's legs. He grabbed all purses and left the group with nothing but each other and their destiny.

Sarah's husband stood against the wall with a glazed look in his eyes. His handsome face was pale. Two parallel rivers of blood flowed down his left temple only to turn into a mottled puddle of crimson on his short beard. Sarah turned her kindly face to her husband and was about to walk over to snuggle his bloody head on her shoulder. She never got the chance. A rough young hand pushed her forward. *March!* came the order to the group. Rose hesitated for a minute. A gun barrel jabbed her in her back causing her to stumble forward. One of the Gestapo officers led the way in front while the other picked up the rear ready to shoot any who straggled or tried to escape. The women and the husband were marched down their dusty street and over to a cobblestone wall that surrounded the canal. This wall had been there for centuries. Though it was September and warm, moss formed green and brown splotches on the wall. The group arrived almost in a trance. What was happening was so unreal. They came from a good family, now this. An officer pointed his finger, it was in a direction behind the stone wall. The sisters looked at each other than at the daughter. Sarah's husband was still in a daze, so he needed prodding by gun barrel. Words from the Gestapo officers were few.

Strip!

Sarah looked at Rose in disbelief. Her large brown eyes turned even larger. Take off their clothes? In front of these beasts? Accompanied by tears and low moans, an officer proceeded to rip the dress off the shoulder of Sarah's daughter. Her white skin gleamed in the sunlight. Rose's beautiful face, tear-streaked and dirty, turned toward her sister.

A numbness set in. They had a strong inkling of what their fate was to be. Staring at each other, the women took their clothes off. Sarah's husband removed his jacket and his pants almost folding them for the next person who was to use them. This family soaked up images of each other much as a blotter soaks up ink from meaningful words.

Put your clothes in a pile over there!

The young Nazi with a mean mouth motioned with his pistol. The other one was having fun. He smiled.

Look at the breasts on that one. Lots of milk I bet. Ha ha ha! . Hey, Gunther. They got big ones ya? A spank might be good for you where you fraus are going.

The laughing one stepped over to spank Sarah and her daughter on their butts. All these women could do was stand stoically and let their tear ducts moisten the earth; then the stern-faced officer spoke.

Against the wall! All of you. Against the wall!

If a poet was there that day, he would have described the sun casting its warmth on bare skin. He would bring to life the sounds: water gurgling through the canal, insects buzzing, birds singing their melodious tunes. Yes, if a poet was there he could have described how blue the sky was or how wind whispers through trees on a warm autumn evening. He would be able to paint, in words, light as it dances across moving water. True enough, if a poet was present, he could provide the right words to describe what it means for a man to love a woman and for both of them to love a child. Maybe this poet would even be able to come up with words enough to adequately explain the ties that bind families together: father to mother, brother to brother, sister to sister, and brother to sister.

There was no poet at that wall, only two Gestapo officers *doing their duty.* First one Luger went off. It made a loud pop. Someone screamed. There was a dot of red on Rose's left breast. She slumped to the ground. A second pop was heard and Sarah's daughter grabbed a red hole in her leg. As she spun around, another bullet made its red mark visible on her back and she lay still. Sarah and her husband clutching each other's hands were hit at about the same time. He first clutched his face then reached for his stomach as his lifeless form rolled over on its side. The word *shama* was on the edge of Sarah's tongue; then she cried out. A nine-millimeter bullet broke her left wrist. She grabbed her blood spattered arm.

Vat kind a marksman you are? Can't hit her tits?

Two more pistol pops. It sounded like a couple of firecrackers. Sarah sighed as her soft body thumped to the earth.

CHAPTER 28
ROMANCE ON A WINTER'S DAY

• • •

A little after Gerson and Helene settled down in San Francisco, Irving was dressing a mannequin in the window of Bartel's. As was his custom, he was in shirt sleeves with his tie swinging like a clock pendulum. Oblivious to passersby, he was arranging a coat so that its folds were so seductive, the garment could literally drag people off the sidewalk and into the store. While Irving was engaged in work of couture art, a young man with a full head of red hair pointed his finger in Irving's direction. This young man was a friend of Gerson's named Ellis Glassman. He was twenty nine years old with a full face and laughing mouth. He was handsome yet trim. He, too, was raised in the women's ready to wear business. His family came from the Salt Lake City, Utah area. They migrated to Los Angeles then to San Francisco, where they settled in a large house on Fulton Street, near the Golden Gate Park panhandle.

It was a blustery January day. As was typical for this time of year, the rain came down in cold, dreary drops. A wind blew in from the Pacific Ocean and drove these drops like stinging bees, against the face. Irving paid no heed to the shivering humanity who slogged by his store window. His eyes only focused on the coats and suits he was trying to arrange. The smell of wool, warmed by the store lights, was like a narcotic; then, something caused him to look outside. There was a girl standing next to Ellis. A well-dressed girl, wearing a chic-looking brown raincoat with a fur-trimmed hood. A patterned green scarf covered her neck length red hair. She didn't look to be much over eighteen and a trim five foot five. Rain drops dampened the back of her hair where it hung outside of the scarf and formed little rivers down her cheeks, framing a beguiling smile. There was something about it. She didn't actually smile as laugh.

After just finishing up with Elian, the last thing Irving needed was another romantic entanglement. Or so he thought.

Though he was anxious to get his window display finished and escape the hot lamps, Irving didn't have the heart to let this friend of his brother and the girl just stand out there in the freezing rain so he beckoned them inside. As they dripped into the front door, Irving's white shirt sleeves emerged to greet them. He sported a healthy looking tan in the middle of winter. The couple carried pre-packed smiles. Ellis radiated friendliness. You wanted to like the guy. He stuck out his arm. The warmth of the store brought out the odor of damp fabric.

Hello, Irving. I'm Ellis Glassman, a friend of your brother Gerson. This is my sister, Peggy.

She shook her red hair and sent a spray of little droplets showering onto her shoulders. She had a happy smile, like her brother's except for the fact that while his was inviting, hers was mesmerizing. Irving didn't want to shake her hand. He waited to see if she would welcome him into her world.

Peggy, this is Irving Bartel. He owns this store and two on the other side of Market Street. Irving, we were just passing by when we looked in the window and decided to come in and say hello.

So far, Ellis' shy-looking sister didn't say a word. She didn't have to. Her face spoke for her. Finally, without taking off her coat or scarf, she managed,

Irving, it's so very nice to meet you. Thank you for taking the time to say hello. Ellie and I will be on our way. Maybe I'll be back for a new coat.

Irving didn't quite know how to respond to this girl. Her English was immaculate. Her manners, exquisite. Her eyes, hypnotic. Peggy's words were music to his ears—new coat. But, after one romance that was left on the litter pile of alcohol and lesbianism, Irving was leery of female entanglements. Leery yet lonely was his condition. He had everything, yet his house was empty. Irving's first foray into matrimony ended not as he had planned it. His mother's words repeated their unrelenting echo in his mind, *you need a mate.* Oh well, back to work. He probably would never see this girl again. She was just another young woman looking for a new coat. Besides, she was too young.

Was he in for a surprise!

CHAPTER 29

ANITA IS BORN IN SIBERIA

• • •

Meanwhile, back in Siberia, Ethel's second child was born—a girl. Ethel named her Anita or Little Anna. It was a desperate life. Ethel now had two small children and little to eat. Michael was now two and there was the baby.

Treacherous minds think alike. Stalin knew Hitler couldn't be trusted, yet he forged an alliance with him in order to buy time so that he could shore up his country's defenses. It was only a matter of time before Hitler would cross the border and attempt a takeover of Russia. Whatever time Stalin had prior to Hitler breaking their agreement could be utilized for building munitions. It was on a sunny morning in June of 1941 that Hitler launched Operation Barbarossa. When his Wehrmacht (army) crossed into Russia, insects could be heard buzzing among the shoots of wheat in the fields; then came tramping boots and clanking tank treads as had been heard so many times throughout Europe.

This was why the Russians had wanted Jews. They could be used for building railroads and structures. The Russians didn't feed Jews much, but at least they didn't murder them in wholesale fashion like the Nazis did.

As the Wehrmacht overran parts of Russia such as Estonia, Latvia, Lithuania, and western Byelorussia, it turned over these areas to German civil administration. A Reichskommissar would oversee these areas and implement the eradication of all Jews.

Case in point. Gebiestskommissar Hingst realized that he had not reduced the Jewish population of Vilnius (in Lithuania) sufficiently. His ghettos were still too crowded. He needed to deal with 30,000 people. Thousands of Jews were marched to Lukiszki like pigs led to slaughter. In the dark of night, they were beaten with rubber truncheons. Old men and women stumbled, fell, and expired under the blows. All their relations could do was wail. Cries rose in the night air to an unhearing God. Children lost their parents. Germans and Lithuanians opened the prison gates and at the same time, beat the children and parents while shouting curses at them. These humanitarians promised the poor wretches death as their ultimate fate.

Once at Lukiszki, the prisoners were kept outside for two days before being crammed into cells. One mild September night, the prison square was lit up by searchlights. There the prisoners were separated. Previously the SS men confiscated money and valuables by filling pails provided. The men were separated into groups of those with valuable skills and those that were expendable; then, those crammed into the thick air of the prison square were loaded onto trucks (fifty to a truck) and driven to the slaughter area. A hillock dotted with pine trees greeted those Jewish animals crammed into the trucks. Diamond stars poked out through a cover of velvet night. A pop, pop, pop could be heard in the distance.

After being dumped on the ground, the prisoners were arranged into rows of ten with their arms on the shoulders of the one in front of them. Behind, they were prodded forward with rifle butts. Women sobbed to their sentries offering them rings, watches, and more. Some dropped to their knees kissing the dusty boots of their captors. Other women tore their hair and their clothes. All to no avail. A strange smell was in the air. It was a mixture of gunpowder and quicklime. There was a large pit surrounded by armed SS men and Lithuanians. Jewish men, women, and children were made to strip. After all; why should good clothing be wasted? In groups of ten, like naked sausages, they were made to stand their last minutes on the edge of this pit, quivering and crying; then, the bullets tore into these bodies. Light and shadow played with each other beneath the searchlights. It was a hideous sight. Grimacing faces, flapping limbs, splattering blood, and a dull thud of dead humanity tumbling into a pit. When all was silent, except a moan here and there followed by rifle shots, quicklime was poured over what were once living, loving human beings. The quicklime was used to cover the smell. It could never cover the smell of those that perpetrated these deeds. That smell lingers to this day.

The Nazis were very efficient. They would keep records that included the date, place, victims, and total murdered (though they didn't call it that). The following is a partial account:

> Date—9/17/41 Placc—Vilnius (Lithuania)
>
> Victims—(993 Jews), (1,670 Jewesses), (771 Jewish children) Total—3,334

As Ethel Nagel (Irving's sister) relates,

We stayed in Siberia about a year and a half. All of a sudden, they told us to pick up and go. They took us to the train. They took us away from Siberia. They figured that the German army was coming soon and they didn't want us to be there.

It was very cold. Joe had typhoid and the two children. I don't know how we survived. There was no food. We worked every day and it was so terrible.

CHAPTER 30
DAWN

• • •

It was a warm afternoon in San Francisco. The sun bathed Market Street in warm splotches of orange. As was his custom, Irving Bartel was up in his third story office, stretched out on his white, fur covered bed taking an afternoon nap. His dreams were those of the financially comfortable, quiet and warm. Suddenly he started awake. He felt a sharp burning pain in his chest much like that felt by his sisters when the bullets ripped into them. His eyes were so wide open, the eyeballs were in danger of dropping to the floor. Yet he had been to the doctor recently. He was a young man, late thirties, the picture of health. Maybe it was something he ate for lunch. Couldn't be. He had his usual bland lunch at the Palace Hotel. He'd heard about heart attacks, but those happened to other people. Irving breathed deeply. No shortness of breath, a good sign. It was unexplainable. Thoughts turned to his parents, sister, and brothers in who knew where? Then, there were his other sisters. What were their fates? He was afraid he knew. It was all very unnerving. He attempted to find out through State Department channels, useless. All that could be done was wait. Eventually a Jewish organization would have some word, a valuable nugget of information. In the meantime there was only mental anguish. Best not to think too much about it. Better to lose oneself in work.

Two days later, Irving was up in this same office paying bills. He looked at the manufacturer's invoice, scribbled the ten percent discount he would get by paying the bill within ten days of receipt then wrote a check for the invoice total less his ten per cent discount. That's how he did business. That was why Irving Bartel lived in Presidio Terrace. A voice came over the wood loudspeaker on his desk. It was Tillie, the store manager.

Irving's family was no easier to find than a ship wrapped in San Francisco Bay's murky fog. They would stay, lost in Europe's Holocaust smoke until winds of change finally blew it away. Meanwhile Irving, in order to stay a functioning human being, compartmentalized the dark side of his existence and placed it in a part of his mind that said, "Do Not Enter." Once again, Tillie on the loudspeaker.

Mr. B? Did you hear me? A young lady is here to see you. She says you know her.

To Irving, young and lady were two words that, together, meant the opposite of loneliness. Know her? Who could she be? Certainly someone with chutzpa. Possibly this one could be worth his time.

I'll be right down.

No need, Mr. B. She says she'll come up to see you. Her name is Peggy. Says you've met before.

Irving had an excellent memory. He could tell you the color, size, and price of every coat in his stores. Not just that, but where to find them. What he couldn't recall, however, was Peggy. He searched his memory to recall any Peggy he had met, but no luck. Well, she was young and assertive.

Send her up, Tillie.

Those were the low sonorous words that crackled out of the loudspeaker on the main floor.

Irving was at his desk, pen in hand, ready for the next invoice. In the background was a humming sound. It was the hydraulic elevator slowly making its way to the store's third floor. The door to Irving's office was open. Her sharp footsteps echoed down the hallway. These were steps with purpose. Irving, pen in hand, looked up. Standing in his doorway was the most beautiful woman he had ever laid eyes on. Irving's memory immediately took a right turn to that cold rainy January day when Ellis Glassman brought his rain drenched sister in and introduced her. Only this time, her full head of red hair hung about her shoulders. She had a pug nose and soft brown eyes that could harden in an instant. Her freckle dappled cheeks made her look even more alluring. She looked eighteen but was really twenty one. Her high heel shoes made her almost as tall as Irving himself. Her suit, if not a Dior original, was a good knock off.

Hello, Irving. Remember me? I'm that wet mop of a girl you met with my brother, Ellis. You were in the window of your other store. It was raining cats and dogs. You so kindly invited us in.

Irving's memory was trying to catch up. In his life, lots of things took place. A particular incident could easily hide in his brain cells and not emerge until it was ferreted out. This was a young woman, though not formally educated, who possessed wiles passed down through eons of women. She was canny and as a result, did not give Irving time to roam through his memory or even gather his thoughts.

Of course, you're busy. I don't mean to usurp your time. I did tell you that I needed a new coat. Do you think you could help me?

There she stood, a wide smile on her freckled face and her doe eyes looking at him, imploringly.

She had that way about her. Whatever psychological burglar alarm Irving had was defused and the door to his emotions was left hanging open. He thought to himself and the answer was rather apparent; would he rather pay bills or sell this lovely creature a coat? Guess which option won? Though Peggy was barely over twenty and Irving was almost twice her age, she seemed to have a sophistication far in excess of her years. He had traveled half way around the world and she, barely cross town, yet her reading supplemented her deficiencies. She was able to converse with anyone about almost any subject. Not just that, she kept them enraptured because the subject of the conversation was usually themselves. In Irving's case, Peggy knew that the key to his heart was the sale of a coat. Her sales skills would come into play later. It would be a much bigger ticket item- marriage. Naturally, Irving took charge, as she anticipated he would.

I have just the coat for you.

My. Aren't you even going to ask my size?

You're a six. I don't have to ask. That is the correct size isn't it?

Why yes. But how did you know?

I'm paid to know. Now, let's go downstairs and we'll find a coat that will turn heads whenever you wear it to the Fairmont Hotel.

He knew she was young and wanted something sophisticated. Irving also knew that a young woman like this would want to be taken to the finest places. He was also aware that she looked about five years younger than she really was thus leaving any mention of age out of his conversation. Although Abe Glassman's wife said, *All she had to do was wiggle her behind* to attract attention, Peggy was coy.

The Fairmont Hotel? Why Irv. I hardly ever go out. Nobody takes me to the Fairmont Hotel.

Far be it from me to critique your social life, Peg, but if they aren't taking you there, they should. And if what you say is true, then this coat will have them taking you to the Fairmont. Not just the Fairmont, but the Top Of The Mark too.

Oh Irv. You're a true gentleman.

Without hesitation, over to the size sixes he went and pulled out a camel hair coat trimmed with red fox. Not just the collar was red fox, the sleeve ends were as well.

Go take a look in the mirror here. See?

Needless to say, she looked absolutely stunning in this coat. The light brown of the camel hair along with the fox trim highlighted her hair's sparkling red sheen.

Hmm. I've got to admit, you sure have the ability to make a girl look swell. The coat is absolutely ravishing. But you know, Irv; I'm a girl of modest means. I could never afford something like this.

Peg, I can certainly understand your thinking. I don't want you to walk out of here with something that would be a burden to your budget. Instead of wearing this coat with pleasure, you would be wearing its cost. Let me tell you what I'll do. Over here I have a snappy green wool coat from Lilli Ann. Are you familiar with Lilli Ann?

Well. No, not really.

Though Peggy put on a sophisticated front, practically speaking, she was inexperienced and not versed in the ways of the world.

Adolph Schuman, my very good friend, owns Lilli Ann. He travels to France twice a year to see what the houses of Dior and Channel have. He then buys their hottest styles and has copies manufactured right here in San Francisco. . What you are now wearing is the latest that France has to offer. What's more, the green goes excellently with your hair color and will compliment many of your wardrobes. The bottom line is that the price is $50 less than that fox trim I showed you.

Problem was, Peggy may have been a young woman of modest means, but she dressed like a society matron. Her heart yearned for fox while Irving's logic and her wallet called for the Lilli Ann.

I can see that you're a smart young lady and picked the Lilli Ann. You won't be disappointed. You'll get compliments everywhere you go. I'm so confident of it that if you find what I say is not true, you bring the coat back. Here's what I'll do to make the purchase even easier on your budget, Peg. We'll put it in layaway. It will be your coat and you can pay for it over three months at no extra charge. Shall I put your name on it?

What was she to say? Peggy got a little taste of her own persuasive medicine. Here this handsome and successful store owner was making her a proposal that was impossible to refuse. She could, however, sense that Irving was reticent about entangling himself romantically. She was sure time was on her side so she pushed the coy button.

You've been ever so kind. I had been down the street, at Ransohoff's, shopping for a coat and the chap wouldn't lend me the time of day. I'm sure I'll just love what you picked. It would look charming at the opera.

Then, she left off talking. How she knew that Irving had a passion for opera, only he who created us can say. Women have a sixth sense that gives them insights that no one can explain. A glow welled up in Irving's breast that had to be squelched with considerable effort. Peggy then left with considerable effort.

I've taken up enough of your time. You should be getting back to your bills. I'll be back to pay for the coat. We'll see each other again.

Yes, Peg. We will.

That's all she needed to hear. As her high heels tapped toward the door, Irving walked with her out to where the din of Market Street enfolded them. She turned toward him, gave a coquettish wave of her hand and left him gazing at a smile warm enough to melt the South Pole.

It was true. She would see him again. A month later, Peggy brought her brother Ellis with her to Juliette's. She would make the first payment on the coat that was being reserved for her. As it happened, Irving had just finished checking in some new garments down in the basement. He navigated the stairway to the first floor. It was time to check the daily receipts which lay in the cash drawer, waiting to bring their glad tidings. There was that soft voice again. Not only that, but a voice accompanied by an exotic perfume that could only have had its origins on the Champs Elysees. Only a sorceress from days of old could have assembled a more effective potion. The scent floated in the air, got caught in Irving's nostrils and then filtered to the brain where it disengaged his powers of common sense.

Oh, Irv. What a coincidence. I just brought Ellis, you remember him, to see that ravishing coat you picked for me. Would it be too much trouble to show it to him?

Too much trouble indeed. This time, Peggy had on a snappy red suit with a dress that hugged her waist like a long lost lover. This was a young woman used to attracting attention. What's more, Peggy didn't care whether Irving showed the coat to her brother, she wanted him to be close to her again. Since men weren't used to these pretexts, he willingly obliged. Down to the vault he went. Up the stairs he scampered, with the coat. When Irving arrived back on the first floor, breathing a little harder than when he left, Ellis inquired off handedly,

*Say Irv. Jackie (*his steady girlfriend from New York) *and I are going to the Venetian Room next Saturday. There's this new singer that everyone's been talking about, a guy named Frank Sinatra. Would you like to take Peg and join us? By the way, you picked a swell coat for my sister. It'll match the French Poodle she just got—green after she fed it its first meal. Ha, ha, ha.*

Irving was caught quite off guard. This he wasn't prepared for. If he were just showing somebody a coat, that was one thing. He wasn't used to people that told jokes nor was he prepared for romance. But, who is?

Why, thank you for endorsing my taste. I can only hope that the coat looks better on Peggy than the poodle's coat looks on it. The Venetian Room? I've heard of Frank Sinatra. I'm sure the girls would love to see him. Maybe we better get Peggy's opinion. Peg, what do you think?

The Venetian Room in the Fairmont Hotel? That's so generous of you to ask. I'd love to go if you'd have me along. There's only one thing.

And that is?

I don't have a thing to wear. Would it be possible to wear that new coat to The Fairmont? It sure would look fetching. I did put a third down on it. Please?

Irving never let a coat out of the store without full payment. It just was not good business. Yet this young woman didn't ask for the coat in normal fashion; she purred. All his judgment and good sense melted away.

It's against what I ordinarily would do, but I'm setting a precedent only for you. Be sure to have the coat back to the store on Monday.

I knew you were a sport. Of course I'll have it right back to you. When it's fully paid for, I'll pick it up for good. Oh Ellie, we'll have a splendid time. Do you think Harry and Jack want to go?

Irving would soon learn that when he got one, he actually acquired the entire family. It was commonplace in Peggy's family for one to be invited then include all the others. What Irving thought to be an intimate get-together actually was a prologue for things to come. Peggy felt if she was going to have fun, why not triple the fun by including her single brothers Harry and Jack? Once Irving was wrapped up and sealed, like one of his coats, Ellis brought up a hitch to the plan.

Irv. I've heard this Sinatra kid is quite popular. Suppose we can't get tickets?

Your point is well taken. I know Ben Swig. He owns the Fairmont Hotel. Don't worry. Through connections, I'll see that we have tickets.

A warm autumn day. The top down. Irving and Peggy were driving down Skyline Boulevard to *visit the horse* (in Irving's words). A balmy wind rubbed the neck and caressed the shoulders. The musty smell of ancient redwoods filled every pore. The air was at once warm and cool—ever changing between the shadow and light of tall trees that serve as sentinels beside the two lane road. Woodside Road wound its way through more tall redwoods until the road opened up and revealed pastures where horses grazed. The skin that had been pleasantly chilled by shade gladly accepted the warmth that now shined down on it. So began Peggy's introduction to the Peninsula.

As it is said, one thing leads to another. Irving and Peggy were married in 1942. Peggy moved from her family's more modest abode on Fulton Street to Irving's mansion at 28 Presidio Terrace—now vacated by Elian Bartel. The huge three story home welcomed its new occupant with open doors. The pretty girl from Utah was, at the age of twenty one, asked to run a large household. Though she could convince an Eskimo he was in Palm Springs instead of Alaska, when it came time to produce the goods, she was found wanting in experience. Her education ended somewhere in high school. So, into the lion's den she was thrown. What Peggy did have, in spades, was good looks and street smarts. Both would, ultimately, take her far.

On June 23, 1943, I was born at Children's Hospital on California Street in San Francisco. Though babies aren't generally attributed with large amounts of intelligence, I could swear that my brother Arthur and my sister Glenda were standing by my crib when I was brought home. There was this cute baby, some said, wrapped in a diaper. Arthur was nine and Glenda was seven. They were discussing this addition to the family in the addition's presence. Here is what they said because what could a baby know, right?

Boy oh boy. Now I have someone to beat up on. I can't pick on you Glenda because you always run to Dad and I get in trouble.

Glenda's response,

If you think that's nifty I now have somebody that I know more than. I can't bring up anything I read to Mom because she's already read everything. Whatever I know, she always seems to know more. You're right, Art. It sure will be nice to have somebody smaller to beat up on. I'm tired of being the weakest one.

This was a sneak preview to my life. Unfortunately for Glenda, she was a very attractive little girl. Now, she wasn't unfortunate because she was attractive, but because neither her mother nor her father knew how to shower her with love. As a result, she grew up to be a resentful, jealous little girl. This posed a problem when she was in the vicinity of Peggy. She too was a very young woman barely out of girlhood. Glenda resented the attention her father lavished on Peggy because of the drought in his attentions toward her. Thus a hatred developed toward the new wife.

All this time, Jim Bartel (Irving's brother) still occupied a room at 28 Presidio Terrace. As he recounts,

Peggy was very, very nice. When Irving married Peggy, she was a young, young woman. And I'll never forget; she didn't know the value of a dollar. So, one day we were in the store and she comes in with a beautiful new fur coat from Livingston Bros. She bought herself a fur coat.

In answer to the question "What did Irving do? Jim replied,

I don't have to tell you. I think you can guess.

In this case, though not on the scene at the time due to having been recently born, I can surmise what took place. Knowing my father as I did, the fur probably did fly. When angered, his kindly cheeks would develop creases. He had brown eyes that would turn black. His physical strength was enormous. It was developed from carrying heavy loads all his life and he often matched his body against those of various horses. Most of the time he won. My mother also had a temper that was equal to that of my father's. After all, redheads are famed for their flaming dispositions. She was, however, no match for her husband's animal quickness. Knowing him, he would have, within a split second, bounded over, unbuttoned the coat, and physically snatched it off her body. Before she could have uttered a surprised word to the amused bystanders, the coat would have been on its way, double time, down the sidewalk. It might have been draped over my father's arm with wisps of fur being blown hither and yon upon the winds that blew down Market Street. The coat's rapid destination? Livingston Bros. I can picture a surprised Carl Livingston, the store's owner, when he spotted a handsome gentleman dressed in a gray and blue glen plaid suit, wearing black thick rimmed glasses. My father would have marched up to the front counter, threw the coat and whatever fur was left on it, down and demanded his money back immediately. He would have then explained that he had a wife who, though charming, was young and hadn't developed the appreciation for a dollar that a life of hard work brought. I am also sure that Carl Livingston was glad to return the money to his fellow merchant. He was also probably glad the coat had any fur left on it, knowing Irving's feisty reputation around town.

As for Peggy, she grew wiser as time went on and learned how to acquire things by more circuitous means.

In 1944, Irving sold the ranch in Ukiah. It broke his heart because he loved to hear the cows bellow and hawks scream. He was able to go out riding in the secluded hills of his acreage. The brown grass would whisper and trees would shake their leaves in a language he could understand. Irving would even take his wife riding though she had never been on a horse in her life. But this was California. The way it had once been … open spaces. Sadly, it all became a burden to oversee. Gerson was in the army. The ranch and three stores were too much. As a result the ranch had to go. Irving got a price that he always felt was too low.

CHAPTER 31
ATHERTON

• • •

The mansion in Presidio Terrace was also becoming unwieldy. Irving liked the warm sunshine the Peninsula offered. Besides, he could be near his horses. So, with Peggy in tow, he went on a house hunting expedition in the place Irving liked to live—Atherton. He already had one wife, Elian, ensconced there. She, Arthur, and Glenda lived on Emily and McBain. Irving didn't mind being in the same town, he just didn't want to be in shouting distance so to speak.

First they stopped off at the stable on Canada Road in Woodside. Irving had to visit his beloved horse first. There was something of the aphrodisiac in the smell of horse sweat mixed with the pungent odor of manure. He always brought some apples and carrots to Rowdy the horse. It would snort then bare its teeth. Irving held his hand flat so that the teeth would take the apple but not any fingers. Though Peggy rode some up at the ranch, she was not enamored with stables, dust, and manure. She was fashionably dressed in a pant suit and exhibited her usual aloofness to those around the stable in anticipation of what she was really interested in doing, previewing houses in Atherton. She literally tugged Irving to the car despite his farewells to Rowdy and his pals, the stable hands.

They drove past historic Roberts Market, an edifice that had been in the same spot for seventy five years. After that, on their right, was the Pioneer Hotel, a place Wells Fargo stage coaches stopped at on their way to the Port of Redwood City back in the late 1870s. Down

San Carlos Street they drove. This was working class Redwood City. Between groups of empty lots stood little two bedroom one bath houses that looked like they belonged on a Monopoly board; then, they turned onto Selby Lane and what a difference a block made. This was Atherton. Lots had mature landscaping on them. Parcels were either one acre at the smallest or perhaps even two acres. There were empty lots where horses grazed on very expensive Atherton hay. It was by pure chance. The convertible Buick seemed to turn by itself and made a left on to Stockbridge Avenue. Irving was familiar with the feeling he had. His horse, when hungry, would guide itself back to the stables while Irving would let the reins go slack around the saddle horn.

The street was speckled with apricot and plum orchards. In between these orchards stood comfortable looking ranch styled homes. Each was at least 4,000 square feet. A quarter mile east of Selby Lane, on the north side of the street, stood a white wooden fence held up by brick pillars. Behind this fence lay a field that was painted with pink and white blossoms. Spring had her pallet out and was coloring the fruit trees in her finest hues. Immediately ahead, on the left, was a huge old oak tree. Its base was painted white along with the brick border that surrounded it. An open house sign stood in front. It read—*Grubb & Ellis*. Beyond stretched a circular driveway.

Turn in here, Irv. I think this is it.

Irving knew to trust his wife's judgment. Though she was young and unsophisticated in many ways, she had an intelligence about her that defied explanation.

The mailbox read 126. Beyond the driveway lay a sprawling carpet of green. Next to the lawn was another huge oak. Just behind this oak lay the house's entrance. The house was a brick and stucco rancher built in 1942. It had four large bedrooms and four baths mostly on one level but with two of the bedrooms on a second story. Two acres made up the grounds which also included a rumpus room with maid's quarters. This rumpus room was about 1,500 square feet with a built in barbeque, a wet bar complete with brass spittoon, and wild animals, stuffed of course. Light green deep pile carpets covered the floors of the main house, which provided plenty of room for Irving's growing brood. Though Peggy wasn't as fond of *the country* as Irving would call it, she didn't object to becoming an Atherton dowager at the tender age of twenty one.

They walked up the brick steps leading to the front door. Irving's walk was deliberate, Peggy's almost a skip. After the fashionably clad real estate agent greeted them, she was thrilled to take them through all 5,500 square feet of the house and walk them throughout all two acres of the grounds. After all, this was the middle of World War II and people weren't lining up and taking numbers to buy luxury estates at that time. Despite Peggy's young looks, the agent felt, what the hell; these could be her only prospects for months. The agent told them about the home's brief two year history. She told Peggy more than the latter ever wanted to know about the sellers and their family. It was easy to determine that Irving held the purse strings. What's more, Peggy was still in a learning state. Irving was the decision maker.

This was a savvy agent. After walking the soles off her shoes, she invited Irving to have a seat in the living room. She allowed the couple to absorb the home's atmosphere. A smell of winter fires past floated from the fireplace. This may have been a Jewish couple, but Peggy was brought up in a decidedly liberal household where the family had Christmas trees in their living room. Here was a place she could call her own. Of course, Irving was not so quick to pull the trigger, though it broke his new wife's heart.

So? What do they want for this place?

Because the owners have taken such scrupulous care of this home and because they wished to price it in a way that would encourage the new buyers to treasure the property as they have, they are only asking $40,000 for it. Pardon my amnesia, sir, but what did you say your name was?

Actually, you weren't being forgetful at all. I never did say what my name was. I just let you show us the house figuring that sooner or later you would ask. Being that you did, it's Bartel. Irving and my wife, Peggy.

It's so good to make your acquaintance, Mr. and Mrs. Bartel. I could tell the minute you walked in that you were a discerning couple.

Peggy was a more to the point kind of person. Pleasantries were not a part of her personality. She succinctly added,

I'm not too sure how discerning we are, but we are looking for a house. This does have some features to recommend it. I don't know about those wild animals in the rumpus room, but I'm sure they would appeal to some chaps. As for the price, you'll have to discuss that with my husband.

Irving added as an aside,

We were just driving by when we spotted your real estate sign. Grubb & Ellis? They've been around for a while haven't they? I know Mr. Banker of Coldwell Banker. They got their start in San Francisco where I live. Back to the price. Yes I realize the owner is a famous hunter, but I wasn't looking for a hunting lodge. True, the place has some appeal. I don't know about the price though. Peg and I will talk about it and get back to you. I pay cash. No loans. May I have your card? By the way, your suit is elegant, but I've got one that, if you were seen in it, your real estate production would double.

You don't say.

I'm at Juliette's on Market Street, in the city. Ready, Peg?

Out the front door they strolled, leaving this well clad real estate agent wondering if they were for real or not. If they were, she would be about to trade in her Chevrolet for a Chrysler. Before the week was out, she called Irving. For one, maybe she could sell an expensive home and for two, maybe he was right about the suit. If it could help her sell more houses …

Irving picked up the phone. One never knew whether it brought joy or sadness, profit or loss. A telephone handset was made out of a black plastic that was warm to the touch if the message was warm. Somehow this same substance was able to bite the hand depending on the conversation. It was the Grubb & Ellis agent calling to discuss Stockbridge Avenue. Irving put her at ease,

It's so kind of you to remember me. I'm sure you saw many others.

So, you called me about the home we saw. My wife likes it. I suppose I could live there.

Actually, Irving fell in love with the garden. There was an orchard with figs, plums, peaches, and an area to grow corn. An added bonus was the myriad of flowering trees. Dotting the grounds were reds, pinks, and yellows. A plus, to Irving, was the chicken coop where he could raise chickens and have fresh eggs fried sunny side up.

Then the agent spoke to the heart of the matter.

Mr. Bartel. I have been selling real estate for a long time and can tell that you and your wife would be a perfect couple for Stockbridge Avenue. I so told the owners and you know what they did?

What?

They told me I could give you $1,000 off the price.

You know that is very thoughtful of them. Because they thought so much of us as to make that generous gesture, I'll tell you what we'll do. I never do anything without consulting my wife and she said, offer them $30,000 cash and we'll take the place. Guess what? I'll throw in a new suit with a mink collar for you as well. It'll double your sales. See what they think.

Mr. Bartel, I can't take that to my sellers. Why, they'd fire me. Surely you are a reasonable man.

Present our proposal!

I don't feel too good about this one, but you're the boss, so I'll do what you requested.

Irving no sooner walked into the hallway at his Presidio Terrace home when Peggy greeted him with a hug and big kiss. Being the optimist she was, Peggy had been making preparations for the sale of Presidio Terrace. She sashayed over to the bar then brought a scotch on the rocks. After that, she proceeded to sensually unloosen his tie. She snuggled next to him while purring like a contented cat.

Dear? Did you get any word on the house?

The agent called. I'm working on the price. So far, they're only dropping it a thousand. I think we can do better. What about you, Peg?

I think we should offer thirty.

Really? For a woman of your few years, you're astute and pretty as well. That's exactly what I did.

What if they don't take it? Then?

I've already got something in mind. What we'll do is offer something in-between; presuming they don't just throw us out in the street with our offer.

You know best. As for me, it seems like a good value, from what we've seen—if we get it anywhere near the price.

Irving was in his store when the inevitable phone call came. Yes, the real estate agent had a counterproposal. It seemed that the sellers really had a good feeling about Irving and Peggy. As a result, they were ready to make concessions they wouldn't make to anyone else. What they were proposing was that the price be $37,000 and the owners take the rumpus room's wild animals with them.

Irving liked the wild animals. There were elements about them that mirrored himself: the foxes with teeth bared, the eagles and their outstretched wings soaring above the mundane, and a leopard with its amber glass eyes blazing. In order to succeed among denizens of others, it was necessary to utilize some of these animal qualities that became part of us millions of years ago.

He told the agent to get to work because a suit with mink collar was waiting for her, if she succeeded. He would pay no more than $35,000 cash for Stockbridge. In addition, the wild animals would stay. It was three weeks and no word from Grubb & Ellis. Irving was not used to failure but in this case, perhaps he pushed his hand too far. Though far from homeless, he was homeless as far as Atherton was concerned.

To console himself, he took Peggy to see *The Barber of Seville.* The San Francisco Chronicle described it as "an ebullient, thumbs-up production." Irving could sink himself into the music, get the wrinkles out of his black tuxedo, and show off his attractive young wife. Though Peggy no more understood Italian than she did Hebrew, she loved to go out on the town. It enabled her to wear the Lilli Ann coat of which Irving gave her credit terms above and beyond the ordinary.

Furthermore, she managed to cajole him out of a new suit that went with the coat. Her husband wouldn't admit that he had failed to acquire the Atherton home and that, perhaps, their thinking was flawed. The opera would take their attention away from more pressing matters, at least temporarily.

A month went by. Finally, when Irving least expected he would hear about Stockbridge Avenue, the phone call came. He was down in the basement of Juliette's, checking in some leather jackets. Their tanned odor brought the outdoors in. Irving could picture each coat leaving his store in a colorful box at $25 more than he paid. This thought made the leather smell even better. Just as he was multiplying $25 times the number of coats hanging on the steel rack in front of him, a familiar "Mr. Bartel" barked out of the loudspeaker.

Yes?

It's a lady from Grubb & Ellis. She says it's important. Do you wish to take the call?

Have her hold. I'll take the call.

Mr. Bartel. I know it's been awhile since we last talked. Maybe you've even forgotten who I am. If so, I'm the real estate saleslady who wants a suit with the mink collar. But, first I have to get you that home I know both you and your wife want—on Stockbridge Avenue.

You're such a good salesperson that you probably have that owner living in the street with the house waiting for us.

Not exactly. Here's what we have. The owner will leave the animals. He's moving back East and, really, what would he do with a bald eagle back there? Besides, it's attached to a branch and the branch is attached to the wall. Not only that, but the leopard can't walk to the car with him because it is flat and also attached to the wall. Ha, ha, ha. He won't sell the place for $35,000 but will take $37,000. You better act before someone else does. What do you think, Mr. Bartel? Oh yes. Don't you think I still deserve the suit with the mink collar?

Be up here in an hour! Though it's more than I wanted to pay, I'll have a check for you. Bring a deposit receipt with you! My wife and I will sign it, and we want the owner's signature on it as well, the corpus delicti. Escrow will close in thirty days. Upon closing, you may come up and get your suit, with one proviso. You tell everyone who admires it that you got it from Bartel, in San Francisco.

Yes, sir. We have ourselves a deal. It's an honor doing business with you.

And that was that. It didn't take long to sell the house at Presidio Terrace, the home I spent my first year in. The Bartels moved to 126 Stockbridge Avenue, Atherton—lock, stock, and relatives. There was a room for everyone. My older brother Arthur and my sister Glenda lived with Elian at the Emily and McBain house, in Atherton. There was a room set aside for each when they visited us. Arthur occupied the dark wood paneled room downstairs also used as a library. Glenda's room was more of a pastel color befitting a young girl. It was right next to the master bedroom. Initially, as a toddler, I also resided in that room where I was able to develop all my fears of what lay outside the window that had tree branches scraping against it when the wind blew. And upstairs, in the blue room, resided Jim Bartel (Irving's brother). Since his arrival in America, my uncle had resided in every house Irving owned from Presidio Terrace to Emily and McBain and now, Stockbridge Avenue.

When the weather was warm, Peggy would invite her family down to spend Sundays in "the country " The whole bunch would show up. Annie (my grandmother), Jack and Lucille Glassman, Ellis Glassman and Jackie (his girlfriend), Harry Glassman, and even Jack Seaman along with Esther Seaman (Peggy's personable sister). Irving would prepare a barbecue on the patio outside the rumpus room. He'd make mint juleps or Moscow mules at the bar. Laughs would float on the warm spring air carrying themselves over the green carpet of lawn. The mint julep glasses would actually sweat as dew drops of moisture hid their refreshing contents.

CHAPTER 31

GETTING THEM OUT

• • •

In Russia, it wasn't so warm. The year was 1944 as howling winds swept in from the north covering the steppes in chill that was bone deep. As Sylvia Bartel relates,

Our hearts broken, forced labor. It was like a prison, like a concentration camp. Not allowed to leave that fence. Five thousand of us. Many of those in their fifties lost the will to live. It was the younger ones, like Ethel, with two little children, that were survivors.

Finally, in 1945, the war was over, but not for those of the Bartel family still in Russia.

Ethel Nagel (Irving's sister),

We were in Kurdistan; the war was over and they let us go anywhere we wanted. So, I decided to go back to Poland, actually to Austria because Poland was under Russian control at that time. Simon, Leah, and Abe met us. Ben was with them as well. All I remember is that we were staying in the trains. Abe and Ben eventually went to Israel.

When Irving heard that the war was over, he contacted influential people that he knew. They, in turn, put him in touch with the proper organizations that could help track down those of his family that still remained alive. He would spend hours in his upstairs office talking on the phone with different individuals who could be of help in finding his lost family. He then cut through red tape at the State Department in order to arrange the necessary papers to get those still alive into the United States. It wasn't going to be easy. Fates were unknown. Irving could not have foreseen that one quarter of his siblings lay buried in Poland's ashes. The rest, including his parents, were scattered half way around the world.

It was at this desperate time that Irving made the acquaintance of Admiral Worrell. This man had served with MacArthur in the Pacific Theater. He was not terribly tall, maybe 5'7." He had a youngish face with prematurely gray hair. His body was lean and muscular. Though not tall in stature, he would stand ramrod straight which made him appear larger than he actually was. He was a fascinating conversationalist because there was many a tale to tell—most cloaked in enigma. All one could discern about him was that his wartime position in the Navy was important enough to exclude idle chatter. At war's end, the Admiral and his wife were stationed at Treasure Island, a Navy base out on San Francisco Bay—midway between San Francisco and Oakland. All he would say about his job was that he served the State Department.

Irving's friend, Adolph Schuman was a large donor to the Democratic Party which happened to be that of the current administration. By contacting influential people, Schuman had put Irving in touch with the Admiral.

Ethel Nagel (Irving's sister) narrates,

All I remember is that we were staying in the trains. From there we went to the DP camp in Germany. It was a Displaced Person camp. There, Irving started working on the visas and all of that. Dad, mother, and all of us.

No possibility was left unexplored. Finding the Puderbeutels became a priority in the higher up reaches of the State Department. The "right" people were contacted. Slowly, rusty wheels of government turned.

Meanwhile Simon, Leah, Ethel, Joe, Michael, and Anita waited in a barracks, when they were lucky. All around them the smoldering embers of what was once a Reich that was going to last a thousand years sent its stench up to heaven. Deluxe accommodations were barracks because they better kept out rain and snow. Sometimes, however, there were so many refugees in Displaced Person camps that some residents had to live in tents. Of course, these were a luxury compared to freezing on the tundra of Siberia or residing outside in Nazi death camps. Even in tents, the Puderbeutels had their faith and the warmth of each other's company.

It was the winter of 1947. The United Nations was finalizing its preparations that led to the realization of a dream. Finally—2,000 years after the destruction of the second temple in Jerusalem and the scattering of its remnants throughout every crevice the earth had to offer, a homeland for the Jews was about to come into being. Its name—Israel.

Israel was where part of the Puderbeutel family headed. Irving's older brother, Abe and his youngest brother, Ben packed themselves on board a ship crowded with stories it would take five hundred years to hear and more tears than an ocean could hold. *In Jerusalem,* they said as they bid farewell to their parents and to their one surviving sister. In Jerusalem is where all of scattered Jews throughout the ages will meet someday. Abe and Ben, like Irving, would take on the name, Bartel.

Somewhere among the rubble of Berlin lay a skeleton clothed in a tattered brown army uniform. In its forehead was a hole about the size of a dime with jagged lines radiating out. On its waist was an SS officer's dagger. The weapon was still in good condition. Its black handle bore the SS eagle and death's head emblem. On the nickel plated blade were etched these words *Meine Ehre heist Treue* (My Honor is Faithful).

An army captain, in his green fatigues and field jacket with twin bars on the shoulders, walked smartly up to the barracks front door. He knocked. The door opened.

Mr. Bartel and Mr. Nagel?

Yes. I would be Mr. Nagel.

I have tickets to San Francisco and passports.

Joe Nagel was not a man to cry. In fact, he was a man of few emotions. He had been through too much to have any left. He turned his back to the American officer, ran over, and with tears streaming down his face, hugged his wife; then he rushed over to Simon and Leah, hugging them as well. The children, Michael and Anita, were jumping up and down with a joy that had been stifled for many years of their youth.

We're free. Irving is bringing us to America. Thank God, thank God.

He didn't abandon us. Even in Siberia, God was always with us. At long last, we are going home, but home is in America.

On a blustery winter day, gray clouds hung over San Francisco Airport like cotton drapes. Staccato drops of rain dented the many puddles that lay on the tarmac's shiny surface. A white airliner slowly lumbered up to the terminal. Its insignia was red, white, and blue. The insignia read, *Pan American.* Four propellers droned then coughed quiet, one by one. A stairway was rolled up to the front and rear doors. On each stairway stood a stewardess, dressed in a navy blue uniform with a military style dress cap. The stewardesses were young and were there to smile and greet each passenger upon departure.

After about half the passengers disembarked, a short man with a mustache stepped out onto the departure ramp. He wore wire-rimmed glasses and was in his sixties. His gray suit bespoke breeding. He wore a broad grin and said, without saying a word, *I am home.* Behind him was a woman, also in her sixties. She was almost six feet tall and was wearing a black wool suit with a silver fox collar. She had a full but kindly face that bore a full smile. Behind them was a handsome couple. First came the woman, short, pretty yet with a face that bore the marks of determination. The man was almost as short as she was. His handsome face had a rugged jaw that was covered by a black beard. Not a hint of laughter crossed his lips. Occasionally his tongue would catch a stray tear. Following them hopped a five-year-old boy with a round cherub face. He held the hand of his little sister. She had a beautiful, full face framed by silky brown hair. If anyone doubted the concept of reincarnation, here was proof positive of its existence. This little girl was her slain aunt reborn.

There was a sudden movement. Bounding toward the departure stairs came a thin young man in his early forties. He was wearing a black and white pin-striped suit, and white shirt. His tie was vivid red. His hair, ink black and curly. He wore black thick-rimmed glasses, but his eyes were hard to see because the lenses were fogged up. The rain that fell was a rain of redemption. As he ran, the arms of Irving Bartel were stretched wide open.

Epilogue

On October 25, 2003, Susan Berman (Anita Nagel Berman's daughter) was married to Robert Mumford at the Congregation Sherith Israel in San Francisco. The reception was held at the Ritz-Carlton Hotel on Stockton Street. Across the table from your author sat a handsomely dressed short woman in her nineties. Her face flowed with well-deserved pride. This woman was Ethel Nagel.

1943 Peggy and Irving Bartel
Ukiah, CA

1943 Peggy and John Bartel Ukiah, CA

1943 Presidio Terrace home San Francisco, CA

1944 Peggy and Irving Bartel

1944 Jim Bartel

1947 John Bartel
126 Stockbridge Ave.
Atherton, CA

1944 Jim Bartel
Ukiah, CA

1947
126 Stockbridge Ave.
Atherton, CA

1947 Anita Nagel, Irving Bartel, Ethel Nagel, Simon Bartel, Michael Nagel, Leah Bartel, Joseph Nagel

Bibliography

Jewish Wisdom
Rabbi Joseph Telushkin

The World Book of Bartels
Halberts Family Heritage

The Holy Scriptures
The Menorah Press

Pictorial History of the Jewish People

Memorial Book of the Martyrs of Lezajsk Who Perished in the Holocaust

Masters of Death
Richard Rhodes

Encyclopedia of World History
Patrick O'Brien

Chronicle of America

Transcribed Conversation with Ethel Nagel (February, 2002)

Transcribed Conversation with Jim and Sylvia Bartel (February, 2002)

Jew Summary

Jew is a compelling historical fiction novel that traces the history of the author's family, from biblical times to the end of World War II. The tale places readers in environments they hope never to find themselves. Readers will cry in despair as they visit Nazi concentration camps. Their teeth will click with cold as icy winds blow across Siberia's tundra. Interviews with living characters are provided in order to bring a sense of authenticity to the story. As if in a movie, the reader will vicariously experience the desert with biblical patriarchs, medieval life with fictional ancestors, Holocaust Europe with the author's relatives, and redemption in America with the author's father.

Jew teaches its readers many lessons on tolerance while escorting young and old on a marvelous journey and adventure. Since the content of this novel is mostly factual, real documents and historic photos are provided in order to bring the past to life.

John Bartel Biography

The greatest day of the author's life was when he was born in Children's Hospital, San Francisco, California. The year was 1943. Things then deteriorated from there, as they do for many.

No street urchin stories have been penned by this author since his father was an extremely successful clothing merchant, leading to a rather affluent childhood.

Unfortunately, the father's business acumen found its way to the son in what could best be described as a light dosage.

Nonetheless, the author did graduate from San Jose State University with an English degree and achieved his first successes in the writing field by penning articles for the college newspaper and by contributing both short stories and articles to the university feature magazine *Lyke*. Further, despite the fact that he wrote entries in his checking account register in red ink, he miraculously earned an MBA degree in accounting.

Armed with theory enough to carry even the most stalwart to starvation, the author actually established successful real estate and financial consulting practices.

Today, he resides in Placer County, a picturesque location that has spawned stories from some other writers of note.

Printed in the United States
By Bookmasters